THE DEATH COLLECTOR

JUSTIN RICHARDS

ff

The Death Collector

Justin Richards is the author of over twenty novels, as well as non-fiction books. He has also written audio scripts, a television and a stage play, edited anthologies of short stories, been a technical writer, and founded and edited a media journal.

He is best known for his series of children's books *The Invisible Detective*, and as Creative Director of BBC's highly successful range of *Doctor Who* books.

Praise for *The Death Collector*:

'A very exciting novel, reminiscent in some ways of Philip Pullman's Victorian novels . . . a real page-turner – and the ending is quite spectacular.' *Books for Keeps*

'[A] lively dose of child-friendly Victorian intrigue . . . rip-roaring stuff.' *SFX Magazine*

'A thoroughly enjoyable romp full of chases, high drama and a hint of romance in great old-fashioned style. Simply smashing.' *Kirkus Reviews*

'This thoroughly absorbing page-turner is a terrific blend of horror and mystery with three teen protagonists. It is a quick read packed with twists, turns, and just enough gore to keep things interesting. A great choice for horror fans.' *School Library Journal*

'This is a real page turner. The book starts with a dead man walking back into his kitchen and then dragging his terrified dog out for a walk! . . . Once you've finished it, you'll want to find another book just as exciting.' *CBBC Newsround*

by the same author
THE CHAOS CODE

The Death Collector

Justin Richards

ff

faber and faber

First published in 2006
by Faber and Faber Limited
3 Queen Square London WC1N 3AU
This paperback edition published in 2007

Typeset by Faber and Faber Limited
Printed in England by Mackays of Chatham plc,
Chatham, Kent

A CIP record for this book
is available from the British Library

ISBN 978-0-571-22991-8

2 4 6 8 10 9 7 5 3 1

For Alison, Julian and Christian – with love

The Death Collector

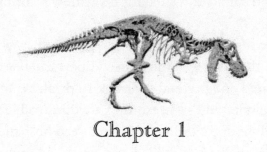

Chapter 1

Four days after his own funeral, Albert Wilkes came home for tea.

Even the dog knew there was something wrong. He was a mongrel called Pup, although it was many years since he had last been mistaken for a puppy. Stretched out in front of the fire in the living room, Pup raised his tired head. His ears were slicked back and his mouth curled away from yellowed teeth. Paws skittering on the wooden floor, the dog pushed itself backwards panting heavily. It never took its watery eyes off the figure in the doorway.

Even the ear-splitting shriek from Nora Wilkes when she turned to see what Pup was afraid of did not break the dog's stare at its late master. Woman and dog mirrored each other, transfixed, backing away from the nightmare that walked into the room.

Albert Wilkes, oblivious to the reaction he had provoked, sat down at the small round table. Just as he had every evening for the last thirty years. He sat, silent and still, and waited for his widow to bring him his tea.

When he had been alive, it was Mrs Wilkes who did most of the talking in the house. Albert had been content to nod and pretend to listen, to drink his tea and eat his dinner and sit in front of the fire reading until the small hours. Nora watched her dead husband, saying nothing. Yet he nodded and muttered and stared back at her through blank, dry eyes just as he always did when she was speaking.

Without thinking, Nora Wilkes had put the kettle on. Her mind and body settled back into the familiar routine to prevent it from having to accept what she was seeing. But her heart was thumping in her chest and she could feel the blood rushing in her ears. Her hands were shaking as she stroked Pup, comforting him.

Then another pair of hands reached out for the dog, reached out to cradle its whiskery head in an age-old routine. The dog yelped and backed away. Nora shrieked in fright. The spell broken at last, she ran from the room.

Hands so cold and pale they were almost blue took Pup's lead from a hook by the door. The dog cringed away as the lead was fastened to its collar. A croaky, rasping cough echoed round the room, sounding as if it should have come from the crackling fire rather than the throat of the man dragging the reluctant dog towards the door.

Nora Wilkes sat on the floor of the small back room, her head in her hands, rocking gently to and fro as she cried almost without making a sound. The front door slammed shut, and she looked up.

When all had been silent for a while, she slowly pulled herself to her feet. She edged back into the front room and looked round. The light had dimmed in the last few minutes but even so it was obvious that the room was empty. She would have liked to have dismissed the last hour as a delusion or dream – a nightmare. Except that the hook by the door was empty, and Pup was gone.

She felt hollow inside, like her heart had been scooped out and thrown away. It was worse than when she had found him dead in the bed beside her – his mouth open as if caught in mid-snore. For years he had annoyed her with the sound of his snoring, and that morning it had been the lack of the sound that had made her suddenly cold with fear. She reached for a log to put on the dying fire.

The fire threw up sparks and crackled as it accepted the wood. But before Nora could enjoy the benefit, there was a sudden loud hammering at the door behind her. Normally it would have made her jump. Now, she walked slowly to the door and opened it, not daring to think what she might find on the other side.

The figure was tall but stooping, wrapped in a dark cloak. The firelight flickered across his wrinkled features. Nora crossed herself, realising that Death himself had come back for her Albert. But then the old man smiled thinly. 'May we come in?' and his voice was quiet and kind.

The 'we' worried her. But his companion was a young woman, about eighteen years old. She was wearing a long, shapeless coat though her face was lively and pretty. The fire danced in her eyes and her blonde hair shone as they stepped into the room.

The man was talking again, his voice cracked with age. 'Horace Oldfield. The rector asked me to stop by if I had a moment. You know he is away this week?'

Nora nodded quickly, though she had not known. In the better light she could see his clerical collar, and noted how frail and bent the old man was. The girl was holding his arm to help him stay upright.

'I used to be the vicar of St Bartholomew's, not far from here. Until I was forced to retire.' He seemed to realise that the girl was holding him and struggled without success to tug his arm free. 'My daughter, Elizabeth,' he explained, as if to excuse her.

Nora found her voice at last. 'I'm sorry. Please sit down.' She was surprised how calm she sounded. 'Can I get you a cup of tea? The kettle's on. My husband has just . . .' She stopped, pulled up abruptly as she realised what she had been about to say. How natural it would have sounded. How ordinary to say that Albert had taken the dog out.

'We know,' Oldfield said sympathetically, sitting down where Albert Wilkes had sat for his tea year after year. 'He passed away last week, I understand. Very tragic.' He shook his head sadly. 'You have our sympathy, doesn't she, Elizabeth?'

The girl said nothing, holding her father's hand across the small table as she sat opposite him. But her emerald eyes were full of pity and feeling as she looked at Nora.

And then, only then, did Nora collapse to the floor, sobbing and crying for her dead Albert. Desperate for him to come home again, no matter how he stank of the earth and reeked of decay.

It was early evening and the light was fading. The sun was giving up its last attempts to break through the smog that shrouded London, and everything was washed in a grubby haze. Eddie Hopkins leaned against a wall, feeling the cold roughness of the crumbling brickwork through his shirt. He watched the people on Clearview Street, assessing them with a young but professional eye.

It was not a good area for him to be looking for work – too quiet by half. He worked better, and safer, in the rush and bustle of more crowded streets. He preferred his 'clients' to be ostentatious and wear their wealth on their sleeve – or rather, in easily accessible pockets. A dilapidated carriage went by, the horses looking old and tired. A group of children ran past, laughing and joking. One of them stuck his tongue out at Eddie. Eddie ignored him. Just a kid. Eddie himself was nearly fifteen. Or almost nearly.

Then he saw the old man with the dog. He watched the figure shuffling awkwardly along the pavement – head down, jacket caked in dirt, hands twisted into claws and every movement an effort. An easy target, Eddie thought as the man went slowly on his ponderous way. The dog wouldn't be a problem.

But as he passed, Eddie caught a whiff of him. The air was heavy with coal smoke and smuts from Augustus Lorimore's nearby foundries. It had an acid tinge to it. But even so, Eddie could almost taste the smell that was coming off the old man. A cloying, slightly sweet smell that spoke of decay and neglect. A graveyard stench.

As he walked, the old man kept his head down. It swayed gently from side to side with each heavy step. What Eddie could see of his face was lined and saggy. The face was angled so that Eddie could not see the man's eyes, just the shadowy outlines of the sockets. Like the blank eyes of a skull.

The dog was straining at its lead, as if trying to escape. It struggled and pulled and yelped, but the old man refused to quicken his pace.

Eddie turned away. As he turned, he saw that he was not the only person interested in the old man. Though they were on the other side of the street, two men were following him. They were walking too slowly to be as casual and at ease as they tried to appear. And their eyes were fixed on the old man. Even through the gathering gloom, Eddie could tell that they meant the man no good.

Of course, Eddie would have been happy to relieve the old man of his money. But the methods the two men opposite might employ would be far less gentle than Eddie's quick dip and away. Their hands were already clenched into meaty fists. Their eyes were dark and narrowed and focused with violent intent. As they began to cross the road, Eddie could see that the larger of the two men had a pale scar running down the length of one side of his face. It started above his eye and disappeared under his chin. None of what Eddie saw boded well for the fragile old man, and although it was none of his business, Eddie was annoyed.

The man with the scar was speaking quietly to the other as they crossed the road. They both ignored Eddie as they walked past him. But he caught a few words, spoken by the scar-faced man to his sidekick in a surprisingly cultured voice: '. . . went the wrong way. It isn't working, and we need to . . .'

Eddie stepped back into the shadows to let the two of them pass by, then followed. He pulled his cap down low over his eyes, hiding his face. He straightened up and made a show of staggering drunkenly along the pavement, weaving back and forth. Catching up with them, he stumbled into the smaller of the men from behind, knocking him sideways.

Sidekick pushed Eddie roughly away as he hurried past, but Eddie caught his sleeve. Anything to slow him down.

'Sorry, guv,' he said, his accent thick and his words slurred. 'Didn't see you dawdling there, and that's the truth, sir.'

'All right, all right.' Sidekick pulled away.

Eddie made to grab his sleeve again and continue with his apology. Scarface's index finger jabbed into Eddie's chest before he could move.

'Enough,' the man said, his scarred face suddenly close to Eddie's. Then it was gone, and the two men were hurrying away after their prey.

Eddie crossed the street, and ran after them on the other side of the road. He could have overtaken them easily, but he kept a short distance behind, watching. The indistinct shape of the man and his dog appeared out of the evening. But Scarface and Sidekick made no attempt to catch him up. They turned into a wider road, with houses on one side set back from the street behind iron gates and long driveways. The other side of the road was a high, solid, unbroken wall. Behind the wall, Eddie thought, would be a small area of parkland – countryside surviving in the heart of London as part of some private estate belonging to someone rich. Some way ahead he thought he could see a set of enormous gates, a pale gravel driveway snaking beyond. But the mist was closing in and it was difficult to be sure.

Eddie returned his attention to Scarface and Side-kick. They were almost level with the gates as they followed close behind the old man and his dog.

When they made their move it was sudden and swift. Eddie darted across the road, but he knew he would be too late. The dog was gone – lost in the foggy night with a volley of barks and yaps as it fled down the road, its lead trailing behind. As before, the old man seemed totally oblivious. His stooped shadow merged with the silhouettes of the men as they took his arms, turned him sideways, dragged him away.

He seemed to put up no fight at all – not even a plaintive cry for help. Running as fast as he could, Eddie saw why they had chosen this moment. They were outside the high, imposing wrought-iron gates. In the middle of each, what looked to Eddie like a lizard's head was fashioned out of the ironwork. The design echoed the creatures that stood guard on the stone gateposts – a large statue of a lizard rearing up on each side of the entrance. Eddie could imagine a long forked tongue ready to lick out at anyone who tried to enter without permission.

One of the gates was open, and the men dragged the old fellow through it, kicking it shut behind them. The gate squealed on its hinge, then clanged into its fellow. The stone lizards ignored the intruders.

Eddie was angry with himself. He should have realised what was happening. He should have helped earlier. He could have shouted a warning to the old man, or got the two thugs to chase him instead. Without planning what he would do, without wondering if it was a good idea, without thinking of the possible consequences, Eddie shoved the gate open again and squeezed through into the grounds of the house beyond.

Ahead of him, he could hear low voices, the scrunch and drag of feet on gravel. What sounded like heavy breathing, but must be just the wind in the trees. The drive was unlit, and curled away through a small wooded area. Somewhere at the end of it would be the house – huge and imposing, belonging to someone very rich. There would be servants and lights. The thugs would want to finish with the old man out of sight from the main road, but before they were within view of the house. If he cut through the trees, Eddie thought . . .

A layer of thin fog wreathed the trees, making it even darker. Skeletal branches whipped at Eddie as he pushed past them. The damp coldness clung to his skin and bit through his clothes. It seemed as though the trees were breathing, whispering, turning to follow his every move. Then, suddenly, Eddie emerged on to open grass. In the hazy dark distance he could see smeared patches of light – windows of the house.

The sound of breathing was still there. Louder now, it seemed to come from all around him. And something else – a clanking, metallic noise – huge, oily and industrial. Eddie could smell the tang of machine oil, the warm smog of steam. He could see almost nothing now as the mist rose over his eyes, the smog of the city was closing in, the clouds thickening the night around him. A ball of fog blew across Eddie's face like smoke. He coughed and waved at it. Realised that it was not cold as it should be. It was warm – like a hot breath.

Moonlight struggled through the thinning cloud. The fog evaporated. The metallic clanking echoed through the night close beside Eddie, and he spun round. It sounded like chains rattling down at the docks. It sent a shiver of fear through his whole body, but it did not even begin to prepare him for what he saw.

A massive head roared out of the darkness high above him, steam blowing through the enormous mouth – like a dragon. The clanking was the snapping of its jaws and warm liquid dripped off the sharpened points of the teeth, raining down on Eddie. The beast's dripping saliva stained his clothing and burned his terrified face. The nightmare creature roared like a train hurtling into a tunnel and clouds of hot breath erupted into the air around Eddie.

He saw it only for a moment before it was lost in the swirling steam and the blackness of the night. But that was more than enough. He was already running, the old man forgotten. Eddie pushed through the clutching trees, smearing the viscous liquid across his face as he choked back tears of fright. Running for his life.

Chapter 2

The British Museum was closed, and the early evening was to George's mind the most productive part of the day. It was a quiet time when he could get things done before he got too tired or hungry.

Most people liked to get off home. But there were a few, like George, who continued working into the evening. Albert and Percy down in documents had always favoured the end of the day rather than an early start. Sir William Protheroe, the elderly man who had paused to watch George at work, seemed to be the same. George had noticed him several times – had even exchanged the odd word or two out of politeness. He had assumed that Sir William had no idea who he was, so when the man greeted him by name, George was taken aback.

'Working late again, Mr Archer?' Despite his lined face and white hair, Sir William's voice was strong and confident. His eyes were bright with intelligence behind the round lenses of his spectacles. He whipped them off, polished them on a grubby handkerchief, then replaced them. 'It sounds to me, young man, as if one of that clock's cogwheels is stripped,' he said. Before George could answer, Sir William went on: 'Actually, I've been meaning to have a word. Tell me, has Mr Mansfield spoken to you yet?'

Jasper Mansfield was the curator George worked for. He had not spoken to him for over a week. So George shook his head, wondering what the man was talking about.

Sir William sighed. 'Typical. Head in the sand, I suppose. I shall have to ask him again, no doubt.'

'Ask him? About what?' He said it before he could stop himself, so George quickly added: 'Sorry, sir. I hope that isn't an impertinent question.'

'Of course not,' Sir William told him with a smile. 'After all, it's your career.'

'I – what?'

'I have asked Mr Mansfield if he will allow you to come and work for me.'

This was news to George. He stared at Sir William. 'For you?'

'In my Department. I need someone you see. Too much work, too few people. You'll like it, I'm sure.'

'I'm sorry, Sir William . . .' He seemed to be apologising all the time, George thought vaguely. But then he had not realised that Sir William was a Curator. Important, yes – but George thought he knew who the

Curators were for all of the Museum's Departments. 'Er, what is your Department?'

'Ah, well, we shall have to see what Mansfield says before I can tell you that.'

George frowned – what could he mean? But Sir William had already turned and marched off into the depths of the Museum.

George watched him disappear, then returned his attention to the clock. Horology was his business – cataloguing and maintaining the clocks in the department. It had been his life for several years now – since he had left school and finished his brief apprenticeship at Chandler's Engineering. He was sitting at a table in amongst the displays. There were rooms where he could work away from the exhibits, providing useful solitude during the day when the Museum was open. But when it was all but deserted, whenever possible, George preferred to be with the clocks.

He loved to hear the familiar, comforting sound as they beat out the seconds around him. Every tock, every tick wore away at the mechanisms and brought them closer to needing repair, just as every beat of George's own heart brought him closer to his own maker. There was something regular, dependable, pro dictable about clocks which George preferred to the eccentricities and randomness of people.

The clock he was working on today had not yet been catalogued. It had only just been bequeathed to the Museum by an old woman whose late husband had run a watchmaker's and repairer's somewhere near the City. She had brought several clocks to the Museum. But this one was the most interesting – and the one that needed the most work.

During the day his time was taken up with servicing and tending the main exhibits. There was precious little left after that and the incessant cataloguing. George had spent three evenings working on the clock in his own time. But only tonight had he got to the actual mechanism. At first glance the clock was a model ship. It was about a foot long, exquisitely crafted from metal and wood. The dial of the clock itself was set into the side of the ship's hull. The ship's wheel clicked round with every second. A miniature captain stood watching it move. Other sailors went about their duties on deck – scrubbing the planks, opening hatches, even scaling the rigging. Each and every one clicked forward as the second hand on the dial moved: brushing back and forth; lifting and closing; hand over hand. There was even a tiny monkey that appeared at the windows of a cabin to stare out at the real world beyond the ship.

And every hour, on the hour, a varying number of hatches above the dial in the side of the boat snapped open, and a varying number of cannon emerged to fire however many shots the hour called for – one cannon for each hour past noon or midnight. Every percussion was a hollow click of a lever hitting a drum deep within the hull where the mechanism was housed. If you peered into the dark interior, behind the cannon, it was just possible to make out the diminutive figures of the sailors touching their tapers to the cannon to fire them. Every detail was true to life, apart from the size and the need to reload between shots.

It had taken George many hours to rebuild the model. He had repaired, replaced, cleaned and polished. Now he turned his attention to the clockwork itself. At the moment, the clock was hesitant. The second hand moved erratically. The sailors jerked and spasmed. The cannon in the hull only worked occasionally. From inside came the constant grinding of gears and crunching of cogs when a mechanism as delicate and precise as this should be all but silent.

As he carefully unscrewed the deck and lifted it clear of the hull to expose the workings within, it occurred to George that a cog with its teeth worn away from over-use was exactly the sort of problem that might cause this erratic behaviour and he wondered again what Sir William's role at the Museum was. But he was soon lost in his work, the words of Sir William Protheroe forgotten.

At eight o'clock, George was shaken from his concentration by the striking of the hour. Almost simultaneously and all around him, hundreds of mechanisms clicked into place – bells were struck, chimes rang, even a cuckoo appeared. And to George Archer's immense pride and satisfaction, eight small hatches sprang open to allow eight tiny cannon to emerge and fire eight staccato shots.

He sat back, folding his arms and watching the little figures go through their clockwork motions. George found himself wishing Sir William would return, so he could show him the clock. So he could tell him what he had done to get it working again, and how the teeth had indeed been stripped from one of the cogs by years of measuring time. But the Museum was silent, save for the constant ticking from all the clocks. George carefully picked up the ship and took it through to one of the store rooms.

There was a dusty mirror propped against the wall of the little store room. It was fifteenth-century French, the plaster frame chipped and discoloured. The silvering of the mirror was tarnished and worn so that looking into it was like seeing your reflection in a pool of muddy water on a bright day. George paused to straighten his tie and smooth down his tangle of brown hair. He looked tired, he thought – with his curly hair more under control, his long face seemed all the longer. Or maybe it was the angle of the mirror. He grinned at himself, and his boyish expression made him look even younger than his nineteen years.

Walking swiftly through the exhibition rooms

towards the way out, George realised he was hungry. He could not remember if he had bothered with lunch. He would have to get his own dinner when he got home. Only a year ago, his father would have had it waiting – would have complained at George's lateness. Only a year ago, they would have eaten together in the tiny dining room of father's little town house and then talked into the evening until father fell asleep in front of the dying fire, his mouth open and his snores making George smile. Only a year ago. He sighed softly to think of it, smiled slightly at the memories of good times gone by.

Memories of his dead father made George think of old Percy Smythe. He might still be working in Documents, on the way to the Museum exit. He could look in on his way out of the building, and George would delight in telling Percy about the clock. No doubt Percy would have a tale of his own to recount – a manuscript preserved, a code deciphered, a book found to be wrongly catalogued . . . Now that his colleague Albert was gone, Percy would welcome the company. George would welcome the company too. He had seen no one since Sir William. Now the Museum seemed gloomy and deserted – the corridors echoed to George's footsteps, and the galleries and viewing rooms were shadowy and empty. Or rather, they were not empty. They were crammed with exhibits – statues, relics, machines, manuscripts

. . . All standing silent and still in the gloom of the evening.

At first George thought that Percy Smythe had already left. The room where he worked, where they stored the uncatalogued manuscripts and volumes seemed to be in darkness. But when his eyes adjusted, George realised there was a faint glow from the back of the room, and as he approached, he could see that it came from a single oil lamp on a desk piled high with books. The light was almost lost behind the stacks, and he had to pick his way carefully through the gloom.

Once he was close to the desk, George could see Percy Smythe. Or rather, he could see his head. It was completely bald, the top reflecting the yellow glow of the lamp like an old blank page as Percy peered down at his work. George watched him making meticulous notes in a ledger. He held a small notebook in his left hand, angling it so he could read the text. Close by was a small pile of identical notebooks, leather bound and dog-eared. George pulled the door shut behind him and cleared his throat. There was no reaction.

'It's past three in the morning,' he announced loudly, 'and your wife is here to collect you.'

This did get a response. But Percy replied without looking up. 'I doubt if it has gone nine,' he said. 'And I am happy to report that I am no more married today than I was last time you claimed my wife was waiting for me, Albert. Whenever that might have been.'

The pen scratched a few more words, then Percy set it down. He carefully replaced the notebook on its pile and rubbed his eyes. 'I am sorry, George,' he said, looking up.

'No,' George assured him. '*I* am sorry. It was a silly thing to say. I shouldn't have reminded you of . . .' He sighed, shaking his head at his own thoughtlessness.

'It wasn't silly of me *because* when Albert used to say it.' The lamp gleamed in Percy's moist eyes. 'Though it did become a little wearing, I have to admit.'

'It was silly because Albert used to say it,' George confessed. 'I thought it might amuse you. Instead . . .' He shook his head, annoyed at himself.

'I'm sure poor Albert would not mind you stealing his joke.'

'That isn't what I meant.' George moved a book from a chair on his side of the desk and sat down.

'I know,' Percy said. He pointed to the pile of notebooks. 'Albert had started on these, so I suppose he was in my thoughts anyway. Don't worry yourself. It is better to remember him fondly, to recall his jokes . . .'

They sat in silence for several moments, each remembering their friend and colleague. The oil lamp flickered and Percy turned up the wick.

'So what are they?' George asked, pointing to the notebooks.

'Diaries. They were bequeathed to the Museum recently and unexpectedly. Found when Sir Henry

Glick's house was finally cleared out. There are over a dozen and I am not yet half way through them.'

George shook his head. 'Glick – never heard of him. Was he famous?'

'I suppose not,' Percy admitted, raising an eyebrow at George's ignorance. 'He was a scientist. A geologist mainly, but with a keen interest in fossils and the origins of life.'

'And he kept a diary.'

'Indeed. Very useful too. He describes his theories, keeps sketches and diagrams. Even pressed flowers.'

'Albert would have loved that.'

'I'm sure he did.' Percy nodded slowly. 'Yes, I think he was enjoying his work. Except . . .'

George waited. But when Percy said nothing more, he prompted him: 'Except what?'

'Oh nothing. Just some nonsense he was telling me that last morning. Another of his jokes, perhaps.'

'Oh?'

Percy ran a hand over his smooth scalp. 'He said that someone had approached him with an offer. For the diaries.'

George frowned. 'What sort of an offer?'

'Money, I assume. I didn't really pay much attention. He said someone wanted to get hold of the diaries. I suggested he tell them to wait until they were catalogued and on display or lodged in the Library. Then they could see them. But he implied they wanted to keep them, and that there was some urgency. Even the trustees cannot sell off items from the Museum, Albert knew that. And this knave, whoever he was, must have known that was the case too.

'Joking, perhaps,' George agreed.

'Albert or the person who approached him?' Percy shook his head. 'Anyway, it doesn't matter. And we can't ask him now, can we?' Percy got to his feet and took his jacket off the back of the chair. 'You're right, it is time I was getting home,' he decided.

'I can wait if you like. If you want company while you finish.'

Percy smiled. 'Thank you, but I have done enough for today. We can walk together.'

They made their way carefully through the semi-darkness of the office. There was a noise coming from outside, from the corridor that led to the main entrance. A bang, like a door being shoved open, and then running feet.

'What's going on?' George wondered.

'Goodness only knows,' Percy said without apparent interest. They were almost at the door when he turned back towards the desk at the far end of the room. 'I forgot to extinguish the lamp.'

'I'll get it,' George volunteered, already picking his way back through the stacks of books and papers.

Which was why he was not standing with Percy at the door when it crashed open.

The first man through the door and into the office was enormous – his frame almost blotting out the light from the corridor beyond. The man who followed him was only slightly smaller. The door caught Percy on the shoulder and sent him reeling backwards. He gave a cry of pain and surprise, trying to catch his balance. But before he could manage, the large man stepped forward and smashed his fist into Percy's face – sending him spinning backwards. Percy's feet collided with a stack of books and he fell heavily. Even from across the room, George could hear the crack as Percy's head smashed into the edge of a low table.

George had no time to react. Already both the intruders were striding across the room towards him. He backed away, knocking over a stack of papers. He was not afraid to put up a fight, but he doubted he could take on both the men. And he was worried about Percy – now lying still amongst the manuscripts and books at the other end of the room.

'Where is it?' the big man hissed. His face was glowing in the lamplight as he leaned across the desk. A pale white scar cut like a shadow down the whole of one side of his face, pausing only to let his bloodshot eye stare out at George.

'What?' George replied, his voice hesitant and taut with nerves. 'I don't know what you mean.'

'Could be anywhere,' the other man answered. He kicked at a pile of books, sending them sliding across the floor. One volume flapped open, its pages bent and torn. 'Look at all this stuff.'

'We don't have time to go through this lot,' the big man decided. Unlike his comrade he sounded educated and refined, almost deferential. But then he lunged suddenly across the desk, arms out, reaching for George.

George stepped back again, feeling his feet tangle with books and papers. The man's stubby fingers closed just in front of this throat.

'Where is it?' the man demanded again. His face was twisted into a snarl of rage, and with a single savage movement, he swept the desk clear. The various piles of books toppled, papers sliced through the air. The oil lamp crashed to the floor, spilling a pool of fire across the bare wooden boards. 'Where is Glick's diary?'

George swallowed, staring into the flames as they raced through the pool of liquid and attacked the nearest papers. In seconds, books were burning too – the volumes from the desk curling and blackening as the flames set to work.

'Right now,' George said slowly, his throat dry and scratchy as the smoke clawed at it, 'Glick's diary is on fire.'

For a single second the two intruders stood absolutely still, staring into the gathering flames. Then they both hurled themselves at the fire, reaching in for the burning books, cursing as the fire bit and spat at them. George left them to it, watching them reach in and pull out the volumes one by one as he himself edged quickly round the other side of the desk and ran to where Percy was lying.

'It's the last volume we want,' the larger man was saying. He tossed several of the notebooks aside. 'The one that he never finished.' He kicked papers and books out of the way of the flames in an effort to stop it spreading.

The other man was riffling through another volume. He dropped it when he saw there were no blank pages at the end.

George spared them little more than a glance. He knelt down beside Percy, shuddering at the sight of the gash across his head. He almost cried with relief as Percy moved, and a groan of pain emerged feebly from his lips.

'They want Glick's diary,' George said quietly. 'Are you all right?'

Percy's eyelids flickered in response. His whole body seemed to be shivering in the firelight. From somewhere in the distance came the sound of a whistle.

'Peelers!' One of the men shouted urgently. They both dropped the books they were holding, and ran for the door.

'Hold on,' George said. 'Help's coming.' He cradled Percy's head in his lap, not knowing what else to do. Percy was staring up at him, his eyes wide but unfocused. George felt he should try to keep him talking until someone came to help. Keep him conscious. 'Why do they want the diary?' he said. 'Why the last volume? Do you know?'

Percy swallowed, his whole body shifting slightly with the effort. His lips quivered. 'Lori . . .' he gasped.

'What?'

'Lorimore,' Percy managed to say. 'They – help . . . Or . . .'

'Or? Or what?'

But that was not what Percy was trying to say. He shook his head slightly as he forced out the words: 'Augustus Lorimore.'

His whole body arched in a sudden spasm. Then he slumped down heavily, and was still. George slowly took his hands from under Percy's head. To his surprise he saw that they were dark and wet.

Someone else was crouched down beside George and Percy. 'I'm afraid he's gone.' George wondered how long Sir William Protheroe had been there with him, holding Percy's hand – or rather, George now saw, his wrist.

'There's no pulse,' Sir William said. 'I am so sorry.' He straightened up. 'I found the guard at the entrance unconscious, so I blew his whistle. The policemen from D Division who are supposed to patrol the Museum have now given chase, but I rather doubt they will catch the miscreants.' He looked down at Percy's staring, sightless eyes, as if realising how inadequate the word was. 'The murderers,' he corrected himself.

Gently, George lay his friend's head on the floor and stood up. Even in the glow of the dying fire, he could see that he was himself coated with blood. He felt empty and numb and cold. 'We should put the fire out,' he said, and his voice was calm, emotionless, dead.

The flames had died down to a flicker now the oil had burned away. The fire struggled to reach more paper or books, but was unable to jump that far. George stared down at the embers – at the charred, curling remains of the books. One of them was almost intact, he saw. So before he stamped out the remaining flames, he picked it gingerly out of the ashes. The leather cover was hot, but not too hot to hold. The book was one of the volumes of the diary, and without thinking, George opened it. The pages were dry and brittle and yellowed with the heat. The surviving cover was the back of the book, and he saw that the pages were blank. The final volume. The book the men had been searching for.

Not that it would have done them any good, he realised. All the remaining pages were blank. The front of the book had burned completely away. A single charred fragment of paper detached itself from the spine and fluttered down towards the flames. As it fell, George could see that there was writing on it. He dropped the book, and grabbed at the piece of brittle paper, catching it just before it fell back into the dying fire.

It was barely a quarter of a page from the notebook. Neatly written across the remains, a fragment of handwriting. A line and a half of words that emerged from the torn edge and disappeared into a charred blackness:

*'. . . now know which came first, and I can prove it.
The answer lies in the Crystal . . .'*

'Sir Henry Glick's diary.' The words cut through George's reverie, and he saw that Sir William was carefully picking up the surviving notebooks.

'The last volume got burned, I'm afraid,' George said.

The elderly man clicked his tongue. 'A shame. But his first work, his greatest discoveries will be detailed in the earlier volumes. At least we still have them.' He picked up several surviving volumes and stacked them on the desk before looking round, shaking his head sadly. 'Such a waste. Even without the loss of life, it would be unforgivable. As it is . . .' He spread his hands out as if trying to show how great a crime he considered it to be. 'What could possibly be worth this?'

'What indeed?' George agreed. As he spoke, he took out his wallet and tucked the fragment of paper inside. That must be what Percy had been trying to tell him he realised – that if anyone could help George discover the truth and avenge his friend's death, then it was Augustus Lorimore.

Chapter 3

George hardly slept at all. After describing his evening's experiences to the police and answering their questions, he did not get home until well after midnight. Lying in bed in the dark, all he could think of was Percy Smythe's face; all he could feel was Percy's sticky, heavy head cradled in his hands. And even when he eventually managed to banish his memories of that, he could see Sir William Protheroe looking intently at him. Sir William had told George that he was Curator of the Department of Unclassified Artefacts.

George had worked at the Museum long enough to know all the Departments. 'I'm sorry,' he said slowly, 'I have never heard of it.'

'Ah,' said Protheroe sympathetically. 'Well, that would be because it does not officially exist. Also,' Sir William admitted, 'my Department is unique in that while it is funded and administered by the Museum, I was actually appointed by, and answer to, a small committee of the Royal Society. A secret committee, just as my Department is secret.'

'Secret?' George had echoed. He remembered how Sir William had smiled in reply. And what he had said:

'No one apart from myself knows about my Department, other than the inner committee of the Royal Society, my immediate superiors at the British Museum and the senior trustees, and my assistant Mr Berry. Except for you.

'Which is rather ironic I always think, given that it is called The Department of Unclassified artefacts. But it is an apt title, despite the fact that the work we do and the items in the collection itself, are kept secret – not only from the public but also from the majority of the scientific world. Put simply, it is to my Department that artefacts are sent which do not fit in other Departments.

'At first, it was a catch-all – a home for finds that were genuinely unclassified. But over time its function has changed. Now, the Department is home to those relics and finds which not only fail to fit into other Departments at the Museum, but which do not fit into established archaeology or history or science. Some are items which contradict current thinking. But others are artefacts the existence of which would be simply too frightening for public awareness. Things that should not exist, but do.

'Most of our artefacts seem innocent enough on

first inspection. It is only when scientific and historical examination throws up contradictions and paradoxes that they come to us. A tooth might seem normal enough, unless it is the tooth of a vampire. The pelt of an animal of the canine family is unremarkable, unless it was taken from a werewolf. A stone tablet engraved in the Queen's English is unlikely to cause controversy, unless it was unearthed from a site which is several thousand years old and might be the lost city of Atlantis.

'Now, I'm not saying that we have any of these items in our collection. They are merely examples of how the apparently commonplace may be remarkable. And of course there are also items which are instantly recognisable as out of the ordinary. Inexplicable. Perhaps impossible, except that they do indeed exist in our vaults.

'It is the job of the Department, of myself, to acquire and research such artefacts, to discover what they really signify – while knowing that my work may never be made public.

'So why am I telling you this? For two reasons. First, believe it or not, the work of our small Department is on the increase. Now more than ever science seems to throw up things it cannot – will not – understand. As a result I find myself in need of a second assistant to help Mr Berry. It strikes me from what I know of your work, Mr Archer, and from what I have been told by others, that you would be ideally suited for the position. If you are interested. If not, then so be it. I have told you of my secret Department and its work, but no matter. Even if you wanted to make my work public, which I doubt, who could you tell who would believe you? But I think you would find the work rewarding – financially and intellectually.

'The second reason I am telling you this relates to Sir Henry Glick's diary. It seems that tonight someone has gone to great lengths to acquire the final volume of the diary. It may turn out to be nothing to do with my Department at all, but since I have been in some small way involved, I should like to know why.'

Sir William was looking at George carefully, his expression grave. 'And I think,' he finished, 'that you would like that same question answered, would you not?'

Again and again George went over the conversation in his head. Again and again he replayed Sir William's words. The notion of the Department of Unclassified Artefacts was at once both intriguing and a little frightening. And to be offered a job there . . . George eventually dropped into a fitful and restless sleep as the first hint of dawn was washing across the sky outside.

By eight o'clock, George was awake again, and he felt as though he had not slept at all. The events of the previous night and Sir William's words all seemed a blurred dream, and it was only when he opened his wallet and carefully drew out the ragged slip of paper from inside that he really believed that those things had actually happened.

Lorimore – he knew the name, he was sure. All the way to the British Museum, he tried to recall where he had come across the name. It worried him on the walk to the underground station. It rankled as he stood on the crowded, smoky platform waiting for the train. It was at the forefront of his mind as he sat inside one of the tiny carriages and hurtled through the dark tunnels. But by the time he arrived at the Museum, he had remembered, and he wondered how it had taken him so long. Augustus Lorimore – the industrialist. He owned a string of factories and workshops, financed experimental development work, supplied the latest technology to Her Majesty's government, and was quoted as an expert almost daily in the papers and engineering journals.

It was not difficult to discover the address of Lorimore's offices. For one thing it was stamped on the frame of the Museum's goods lift which George had not realised was a Lorimore product. As soon as he took a break, George wrote Lorimore a short letter. Probably he would never hear back, but he owed it to Percy to try to contact the man. He gave his address as care of the British Museum, thinking this at least might impress and lend authenticity to his story.

Briefly, George explained that the Museum had

suffered a break-in that was being investigated by the police. He mentioned Percy's death, in case Lorimore and Percy had somehow known each other. He wrote of how the thieves had been after Sir Henry Glick's diaries, but had fled empty-handed after the volume they wanted had been burned. He asked Lorimore if he could help in any way, unsure really what it was that he expected of the man. As an afterthought, George wrote that he had the last surviving fragment of the final volume of Glick's diary in his possession.

'It is not much,' he admitted. 'Little more than a few words. But it may furnish some clue as to what the ruffians were after. If it can be of any help, I am more than happy to show it to you in return for your assistance in this matter.'

George sent his letter by the next post, expecting to hear nothing for several days and then probably a simple acknowledgement from one of Lorimore's staff.

The reply arrived at the Museum that afternoon by return of post. It was handwritten on paper headed with Lorimore's home address, and George read it three times.

Dear Mr Archer

Thank you for your letter pertaining to the unfortunate events of last night at the British Museum. Please accept my sincere condolences on the loss of your colleague.

I appreciate your writing to me so promptly, and would indeed be grateful for sight of the page fragment you mention at your earliest opportunity. I am at home today, and look forward to receiving you and arranging whatever 'assistance' seems appropriate.

I am sure that we shall both benefit from this meeting which I know you will treat with the strictest confidence.

Yours sincerely

Augustus Lorimore

Doctor Archibald Defoe was a small man with a loud voice and an enormous beard. When he spoke, the sound seemed to be amplified by the mass of red hair round his mouth, and made more intimidating by his broad Scottish accent. His head was almost level with Sir William Protheroe's, but that was only because Protheroe was sitting at his desk.

In the corner of the room, Garfield Berry – young and lank, his dark hair slicked back – stood with ill-concealed fear and watched as Defoe leaned across Protheroe's desk to unleash his wrath.

By contrast, Protheroe seemed unimpressed. He was leaning back in his chair, turning gently to and fro as he waited for his superior to finish. The fact that he was polishing his spectacles on a large white hand-kerchief made it even more apparent that he was not paying full attention.

'And not only can I see no reason for you needing a second assistant, I cannot even begin to think where the funding would come from. Do you think I'm made of money, man?'

'Evidently not,' Protheroe said quietly, putting his glasses back on.

'In fact, I'm not entirely sure that you need Berry here, let alone another assistant. What are you doing that can possibly warrant such extravagance?'

Protheroe leaned forward, his hands clasped on the desk in front of him. 'If I may make two points,' he said. Defoe made a sort of snorting sound which Protheroe took to be permission to continue. 'First, I believe my Department is the least expensive of any in the Museum.'

'That's because you don't *do* anything!' Defoe roared, standing upright and folding his arms.

'And second,' Protheroe continued without reaction, 'what we do, and why we do it, is none of your business.' He paused just long enough for the parts of Defoe's face that were visible behind his beard to become the same colour as that beard. 'I mean that in the politest way of course.'

'A law unto yourself,' Defoe spluttered.

'Not so. Just because you do not hold sway over my

Department's activities does not mean that no one does. As you well know, I answer to an inner committee of the Royal Society for what I do. Unfortunately, and I mean that in administrative terms, I rely on you and the Museum for funding to carry out that work. Funding that is generously given, but a less than generous amount. I now need to increase that amount to enable me to employ a second assistant to help Mr Berry.'

'As if I have nothing else to do with the money,' Defoe said. But his voice was quieter now, and Protheroe sensed that he was making some headway at last. 'It will take a while to find and allocate funding,' Defoe went on after a pause. 'If it is possible at all.'

'You're very kind,' Protheroe said smoothly.

'But then I suppose it will take you a while to find a suitable candidate for the job. Whatever the job entails.'

'Oh I don't think so,' Protheroe said. 'In fact I have someone in mind. Since he already works here at the British Museum, it would be simply a matter of transferring him across to me. Together, I assume with his salary, though naturally we would want to increase that in line with his new duties. Whatever they may be.'

Defoe spluttered at this, and from the few words that escaped the beard Protheroe got the impression that he was far from happy with the idea of his approaching members of the Museum's staff and offering them alternative employment, even under the same roof.

But before the splutters and exclamations could be resolved into a coherent argument, Protheroe stood up. His mass of white hair quivered as he leaned across his desk. 'I have approached the gentleman's superior and I may well ask you to expedite matters shortly if I don't get a favourable and timely response. Now if you will excuse me,' he said sternly to Defoe, 'there is a matter that demands my attention.'

On the desk in front of Sir William was a pile of books. Although they were neatly arranged, several of the books were badly burned. Sir William did not wait for Defoe to leave before picking up one of the diaries and starting to read.

Jasper Mansfield, the curator who organised George's time and directed his work, seemed surprised that George had turned up for work at all after the events of the previous night. He made no objection to George leaving early and made it clear that if he needed a few days to recover from his experiences, that would also be no problem.

Mansfield was a portly man who wheezed when he had to move, which was infrequently. 'You are quite happy with our Department?' he asked George, a bead of sweat running down from his hairline. It was the first time he had ever seemed concerned for George's feelings. 'I would hate to think you might be considering moving on, my boy.' He wiped distractedly at his cheek with a red, meaty hand.

Significantly, Mansfield still made no mention of any job offer from another Department, or of Sir William Protheroe. So George assured Mansfield that he had been given no reason to consider moving on just at the moment – which was strictly speaking true. His superior smiled broadly and continued quickly: 'I know you work hard, my boy,' he said. He always called George 'my boy' even though he could not be much more than ten years older than George himself. 'And your efforts are always of the most diligent and highest quality. You're not a skiver like some I could mention. Take as long as you need, my boy. Within reason of course.'

George thanked him, glad not to have to explain why and where he was going. He did not understand Lorimore's reasons for wanting to keep the meeting secret, but he respected them nonetheless. Perhaps all would become clear when they met.

Lorimore's house was not far from Gloucester Road station, so George returned to the underground to make his journey. Coming out of the station, he paused for a minute to get his bearings. It was not a part of London that he knew, and as he stood on the pavement looking round for street names, someone bumped into him, making him take several steps backwards.

It was a lad of about fourteen, dressed rather scruffily.

His coat was scuffed and torn and his grubby cap was pulled down so low over his eyes that George was not surprised he could not see where he was going. The boy's trousers seemed to be held up with string in place of a belt, and what George could see of his face was a cheeky grin. A curl of black hair hung over the shadowed eyes, as if trying to escape from the cap.

'Sorry, guv,' the boy said, before continuing quickly down the street. George watched him for only a moment, then returned his attention to working out which way he needed to go.

In the end he asked for directions. The newspaper seller outside the station was happy to help, until he realised that George was not about to buy a paper as well. Then his attitude cooled, and George quickly bade him goodbye.

He now had no trouble finding Lorimore's house. It was set back from the road behind huge iron gates, which stood open as if expecting him. There was a man standing just inside the gates, and he certainly was not expecting George. But once George had explained his business, and shown the man his letter from Lorimore, he was allowed to pass.

A gravel driveway wound its way from the gates up through extensive grounds. As he made his way along it George began to wonder if he had not come to some public park instead of a private house. But then the drive looped again, and before him was an enormous four-storey house built of imposing red brick and pale stone.

The man who opened the door to George had been shoehorned into his dark suit. His neck bulged out over the stiff collar of his white shirt, though his face was in shadow and George could see almost nothing of his features. 'Yes?' His voice was a low rasp of disapproval.

'George Archer,' George said, trying to sound confident and unperturbed. 'Mr Lorimore asked me to call.'

The man stared back at him for several moments as if he had not spoken. Then he stepped back inside and gestured for George to enter the wide hallway.

'You'd better wait here, sir.' The last word sounded like an afterthought. 'I'll see if Mr Lorimore is expecting you.'

The butler's footsteps echoed off into the house and George waited close inside the door. The hall was wider than the biggest room in George's house, and had more furniture crammed into it than George possessed in total. But he was too used to the impressive space and furnishings of the British Museum to feel intimidated. Instead he spent the time he was alone looking with interest at the display cases that lined one whole side of the hall.

The first few were disconcerting. They were glass-fronted, mounted on the wall. Glassy eyes stared out. They seemed to follow George as he walked slowly along. From inside each and every case, a stuffed animal watched him. One was a fox, its teeth glinting sharply in the dark maw of its mouth. Then a family of mice, nestling in a home of straw. Cats, dogs, birds ... All manner of creatures were frozen within the glass cages. Each and every one stared at George in an uncomfortably accusing manner.

The last animal was another bird, which strutted somewhat precariously inside its relatively large environment. It looked ungainly yet somehow assured. It had a bulbous body and head, with a feathery tuft for a tail. Its beak was hooked and on another bird might have looked savage and threatening. But here it merely added to the whole faintly ridiculous shape. George examined the creature through the glass, wondering where it might have come from. There was no label or clue on the case.

Soon, George was standing before the last display case. From here on down the rest of the hallway, the wall was lined with low, narrow tables, each holding a display. At first he had thought that these too were bizarre examples of taxidermy. On the first table stood a figure about a foot tall which stared out at the world as if daring anyone to approach. It was a monkey, standing on its hind legs and dressed in an army uniform, complete with cap. In its tiny paw, the monkey was holding a cigarette.

But it was not a stuffed animal. George could see

now that it was made of wood and metal. A superb sculpture that caricatured the form of the real animal and emphasised the more human aspects. The figure stood on a small plinth, and in the plinth George could see a keyhole. An automaton he realised – once wound up the monkey would perform some trick or go through a series of predefined clockwork actions. He forgot his unease at the stuffed animals, and began to look forward to meeting Augustus Lorimore.

'It was constructed by a Frenchman called Thierry.' The voice was taut and nasal and quiet. It startled George.

He turned quickly to find a man standing beside him. The man was almost as tall as the butler, but incredibly thin. His suit fitted his skeletal form immaculately. His neck was sinewed, and the skin of his face was stretched like parchment over the bones so that the shape of his skull was distinctly visible. He was, George supposed, in his fifties. His hair was the colour of newly wrought iron. His eyes were almost the same colour, and seemed to burn with intelligence and passion.

'Mr Lorimore?' George guessed.

'Mr Archer,' Lorimore replied. 'They executed him, you know.'

'I'm sorry – who?'

'Thierry.' Lorimore was holding a key. The tiny piece of metal was almost lost in the man's long bony fingers as he slotted it into the plinth and turned it carefully. 'He was a murderer, of course,' Lorimore added as he wound the mechanism. 'But you would think that the ability to produce something as beautiful as this, as elegant and engineered . . .' He clicked his tongue, feeling round the base of the automaton for a switch or lever. 'Well,' he continued as he stepped back, 'you would think it should count for something, wouldn't you?'

'Er, yes,' George agreed, although he was not at all sure that he did. His attention focused on the monkey as its head turned and it looked around. Perhaps it was checking to see if anyone was watching, because then it raised its paw furtively to its mouth as if dragging on the cigarette. The mechanism was smooth and quiet, George noted.

'There is a facility,' Lorimore said, his voice quiet so as not to disturb the monkey, 'to light the cigarette, and also a wick inside the body. Then it blows smoke out of its mouth, to complete the illusion. It was a gift from Lord Chesterton, delivered only this morning. I am, I confess, still intrigued by its workings.'

As he spoke, the monkey looked round again. As if startled, its eyes widened with a click, and the paw holding the cigarette disappeared behind its back. A moment later, the other arm shot up and the monkey snapped a smart salute. George laughed out loud at the absurdity and cleverness of it.

'You too are impressed, Mr Archer,' Lorimore

observed. 'That is good. Very good. Now,' he held his arm out to allow George to precede him along the hall, 'let us discuss business.'

'I'm not sure it's really business,' George said as they walked slowly to the end of the hall. He was walking slowly so he could look at the other tables they passed. Each one had on it an automaton. Some were crude and simple – a musical box with a large key, for instance. Others were every bit as intricate and sophisticated as the monkey – a tiny carriage; skaters on a frozen lake of glass; a lady in a crimson, velvet dress – George could not guess what the mechanism did, but she looked perfectly sculpted and beautifully lifelike.

'Everything comes down to business,' Lorimore told George as they entered a large drawing room.

But George hardly heard him. It was as if the displays in the hall were merely the overture to a grand opera that opened out in the drawing room. The walls were all but covered with more display cases – animals, birds, unfathomable shapes floating in tanks of viscous liquid. Two sofas were arranged facing each other in the middle of the room, almost lost amongst the clutter. Beyond them, a large carved tiger was bearing down on the figure of a man who was trying to push it away. Every level surface seemed to have on it a metal or wooden model or apparatus.

'I apologise for the distractions,' Lorimore said,

smiling at George's evident fascination. 'A hobby of mine, I confess. I am a collector as well as an enthusiast. Flora and fauna, automata, historical books and papers . . . They all interest me.'

'I understand the fascination with automata,' George said. He bent down to examine a device that fed ball bearings down a chute after which they were channelled into different runs marked off with numerals. 'From what I understand, your factories produce industrial versions of machines almost as impressive and clever as these?'

'Almost?'

Perhaps there was a hint of annoyance in Lorimore's tone, but if there was, George did not hear it. He was tracing the possible paths of the tiny metal balls. 'Is this a clock?' he asked, realising how the mechanism must work.

'Indeed it is. You can tell that from looking at it?' There was no anger now, but surprise and perhaps a little respect.

George shrugged. 'That's the business I'm in.'

Lorimore nodded. 'And talking of business . . .' He motioned for George to sit on one of the large sofas that was almost lost in the huge room. He himself sat opposite, his hands resting on his bony knees, so that he looked like a spider hunched up ready to spring. 'What is it exactly that I can do for you?'

'It's very good of you to see me, and so promptly,'

George said, uncertainly. He was not really sure what Lorimore could do. 'Did you know Percy Smythe?' he asked.

Lorimore shook his head. 'No.'

'He suggested you might be able to help.'

Lorimore raised an eyebrow. 'Oh? He was the man who died last night, is that right?'

'He was murdered.'

'Indeed.' Lorimore was regarding George carefully. 'I have to confess I am now even more at a loss as to exactly what you expect from me. You offer to let me have a scrap of Glick's diary. The final scrap, or so you claim. Yet I have no idea what you are asking for in return.'

George was as confused as Lorimore now. 'I have a piece of the last page of the diary, yes,' he admitted. 'But I mentioned that only in passing. I thought you knew Smythe somehow. He told me you could help.'

'Help?'

'Help me find the people who killed him, the person responsible,' George said. He could feel his eyes pricking as the image of Percy's dying moments welled up in his memory. 'That's what I assume he meant.'

Lorimore's mouth moved as if he was literally chewing over what George had told him. 'Well,' he decided, 'perhaps if you allow me to see this page fragment, I might have a better idea of how your friend thought I could help.' He stood up and held out his hand. 'May I?'

'Of course.' George too stood up, reaching into his inside pocket. 'I have it here. In my –' He broke off, patting at his jacket in a sudden panic, reaching into each of the pockets in turn. 'My wallet.' He could feel the colour draining from his face and his stomach seemed to drop away as if he was falling from a great height.

Lorimore's long fingers snapped impatiently, like gunshots. 'Well?'

'My wallet,' George repeated. 'My wallet's gone.' He was checking his trouser pockets now, although he never kept his wallet anywhere but in his jacket. 'I can't find it.' He looked at Lorimore for help, aware that his mouth was open and his face pale.

Lorimore sighed, his whole frame moving with the sound. 'How much?' he asked.

George blinked. 'I'm sorry?'

'How much do you want?' Lorimore had no trouble finding his own wallet and opened it for George to see. He riffled through the folded bank notes inside.

'It's all right,' George said, thinking he must be offering to pay for his cab or train home. 'I'll manage.'

The large man's eyes narrowed. 'For the page,' he hissed angrily. 'How much do you want for the page from Glick's diary?'

George shook his head in confusion. 'I don't want

anything. I just want my wallet back.' He could not have left it at home – he had needed it to pay for the underground. 'Don't you understand?' George said, close to panic, 'I don't have the page.'

Lorimore all but ripped notes from his own wallet. 'Fifty,' he snapped.

'I beg your pardon?'

'All right – a hundred.' His eyes were wide with anger and passion. 'Name your price.'

George just stared. Part of his brain was struggling with the fact that the man was willing to pay a fortune for a scrap of burned paper. Another part was trying desperately to work out where his wallet had gone. His mind was retracing his journeys that day at high speed – to the Museum, out again to the underground, arriving at Gloucester Road station unsure of which way to turn . . .

'That boy,' he realised. 'He must have taken it. When he bumped into me.'

'Boy?' Lorimore demanded angrily. 'What boy?'

'There was a boy.' George tried to replay the events in his mind's eye. 'I thought it was an accident, but he must have meant to walk into me. Then in the tangle, as I stumbled, he took my wallet. My money.'

'Confound your money,' Lorimore's face was close to George's and the transformation was terrifying. His lips had curled away from his teeth and his eyes were red with anger. 'Describe the boy,' he snarled, grabbing George suddenly by the lapels of his jacket. 'If there was one.'

'Of course there was.' Lorimore let go of George and turned away. He was breathing less heavily now, more in control. George was relieved that the man seemed to have recovered his composure. He did his best to describe the boy, in faltering nervous tones. He recalled the grubby clothes, the cheeky expression, the comma of dark hair emerging from under the cap . . .

Lorimore nodded as if George's description was quite in order, and encouraged by this George asked cautiously: 'So, can you help me, sir?'

Lorimore frowned. 'What?' he seemed puzzled by the question.

'Can you help me find out who was responsible for my friend's death?'

A nerve ticked under Lorimore's left eye as he regarded George across the room. Then he walked quickly over to the fireplace and touched a button – a bell. 'I am afraid not,' he admitted as he turned back towards George. 'I really have no idea how – or why – your poor friend believed I could help you. I am sorry if I appear brusque, but you will understand that the possibility of seeing a page of Glick's diary was . . .' The nerve ticked again as he sought for the right word. 'Intriguing,' he decided. 'Please do not let my disappointment unsettle you.' He forced a thin smile.

The manservant was already standing in the doorway. Clearly, George was being invited to leave.

'Not at all. Thank you for your time,' he muttered, feeling his own disappointment keenly.

Lorimore waved a hand dismissively, not even bothering to look at George. He paced up and down, his head lowered, deep in thought.

The butler led George back past the automata and the display cases to the front door. He said not a word as he opened the door and let George step out into the cold of the day. All the while he kept his face turned away, his features obscured, as if trying to avoid letting George see his face.

George was annoyed – angry at his wasted journey and Lorimore's dismissal of him. Angry at himself for losing his wallet and not even noticing. Before he knew it, George had walked the length of the drive. He passed the man at the iron gates and turned out on to the main road, only distantly aware of the carved lizards on the gate posts watching him through sightless stone eyes.

Chapter 4

Gloucester Road was busy and noisy. Horse-drawn carriages clattered across the junction with Cromwell Road. Pedestrians struggled through the crowds. Shopkeepers watched from under their awnings and called out to any passer-by who looked like a potential customer.

The secret was to keep moving. Eddie knew the area better than the cabbies – all the side streets, all the possible escapes. He walked slowly, pausing only briefly before running across the road. A cart driver shouted at him to mind out of the way. Eddie didn't care about that, but he did mind that the man he had been following heard the warning, and stepped briskly aside. It meant that Eddie missed him, missed the opportunity to brush past and slip his hand into the man's jacket.

The man had seen him now. Just a glance, no notion that Eddie had been about to relieve him of his money or watch. But there was a chance he might remember if he saw Eddie again – might remember and realise the boy was following him. Time to move on.

Looking round as he kept walking, Eddie's practised eye lighted upon someone else who might be worthy of his attentions. The man had probably been tall and imposing, but was now bent with age and obviously frail. He wore a heavy coat, fastened tightly round his neck. But as he moved there was heaviness in the material at his chest that might signify money, or perhaps a silver cigarette case he could pawn . . .

Eddie matched his pace to that of the elderly gentleman, but kept several steps behind and to the side of him. Only now did he see that the man was not alone. There was a young woman with him. She was wearing a plain, pale green dress, and carrying a small bag. Eddie wondered if the bag might be a better target, but dismissed the idea almost at once. No, the man would have the money, and the woman would notice immediately if he took her bag. She might not be able to run as fast as Eddie, but he preferred that no one noticed him at work.

The pavement ahead was more crowded as several people came out of a shop. A carriage with an advertisement for Champion's Vinegar swept past. The sound of its wheels masked the sound of Eddie's running feet. As he approached the gentleman, Eddie could see his clerical collar inside the coat. He almost shied away then. Not that he had any qualms about robbing a clergyman, but the shape in his coat was probably a prayer book. Eddie had no use for prayers unless you could sell them.

But at that moment the man turned to say something to the young woman, and as he did so his coat fell slightly open. It was an opportunity too good to pass up. Eddie's hand dipped inside the coat as he bumped against the man, muttered an apology, lifted out the contents of the man's pocket, kept walking briskly. It was a wallet, Eddie could tell – the leather was warm and comforting in his hand, the shape bulged nicely as he stuffed it into his own trouser pocket. Perfect.

Except that the man had noticed. Perhaps he had checked his pocket, perhaps he had felt the light touch of Eddie's fingers. Perhaps he just knew from the way Eddie had collided with him. Whatever the case, he was shouting, pointing after Eddie. A glance back was sufficient to reassure Eddie that the man could never catch him. Soon he would be lost in the crowd, and no one would know who the clergyman was pointing at or shouting after. Eddie knew better than to run, and let everyone know for certain. Better to walk briskly, not look back, pretend it was nothing to do with him.

But there was another voice now – shrill, angry, determined. In spite of himself, Eddie did look back – to see the young woman racing down Gloucester Road after him. In that split-second he saw her knocking past several people, her dress gathered up so she could run more quickly, her eyes locked on Eddie in grim determination as she charged after him in a most alarming and unladylike manner.

She was quick. He could hear the slap of her shoes on the pavement behind him as he ran. He pushed aside anyone in his way, and pulled people into her path as he raced down the street. But whenever he stole a quick glance over his shoulder, she was still there. And every time she was slightly closer. It would not be long before she caught up with him, assuming no one grabbed hold of him first.

Eddie turned and raced across the street. A horse reared up in surprise. A cab lurched sideways. Shouts, gasps, the rattle of wheels close to him. His own blood thumping in his ears. But still the constant rhythmic sound of the woman's running feet close behind Eddie's own.

Eddie kept running, though he was slowing now. He turned into Stanhope Gardens, then immediately again into the street that led back up towards Cromwell Road where he hoped to lose her again in the crowds. He risked one more look back.

There was no one there. The street was empty, and Eddie drew a great gasping breath of relief as he slowed to a brisk walk. Almost immediately, he realised his mistake.

The woman was not behind him, because she had

caught up with him and was running alongside. He caught a glimpse of green out of the corner of his eye. But before he could react, he was pushed suddenly up against the wall close to the side entrance to a mews. Close, but not close enough to wriggle free and duck inside. She had him.

'What do you want?' Eddie demanded. 'I ain't done nothing.'

The woman was more composed than Eddie had expected, and she was not going to be fooled. 'I want my father's wallet back,' she said. 'And then I think we'll find a policeman.'

'Not the peelers,' Eddie protested. 'They'll send me away, they will. Off to the workhouse or worse.'

'They'll tell your parents,' she said levelly. There was no trace of pity in her face, and she was holding him to the wall with one hand while the other was held out for the wallet.

'I ain't got no parents,' Eddie said. He watched for any flicker of a reaction to this. She blinked, but nothing more. 'No home,' he added. 'Nothing. I live on the streets and wherever I can find shelter.'

The woman smiled thinly. 'Then perhaps the work-house would be preferable. At least you would have a roof over your head.'

Eddie said nothing. Instead he produced a leather wallet from his trouser pocket and slapped it into the woman's outstretched hand. She glanced at it, then put it inside her bag, which Eddie noticed was looped over her wrist. To do this, she had to let go of Eddie, and he almost ran off.

He stayed where he was partly because he was still out of breath, and partly because he was intrigued by the woman. Now he looked at her, she was not that much older than him really. Eighteen at the most, and possibly younger. Her face was red from running, but it was, Eddie thought, a pretty face beneath her anger. Her eyes were as startlingly green as her dress.

The wallet safe in her bag, she looked up at Eddie and to his surprise she smiled. 'Thank you,' she said. She stood looking at him for several moments, and Eddie guessed that she was deciding if she should try to march him off to find a policeman. He doubted she could hold him for long, but he was unwilling to find out.

'My father, Horace Oldfield,' she said at last, 'helps at a hostel in Camberwell. People go there when they have nowhere else to sleep. I can give you the address, you'd be welcome there.'

Eddie shook his head.

She sighed. 'You can get help, you know. So why do you do it?'

'Because I have to,' he blurted. He had not meant to say anything to her, but now it was easier to keep talking than it was to stop. And there was a policeman walking past the end of the street – he was sure that the woman had noticed.

'My mum died,' Eddie said, the words coming out in a rush. 'When I was twelve. She fell down the stairs. My father found her when he got in from the pub. Then there was just Laura and me and him. She's my sister. He didn't care much about me, but he loved Laura. She couldn't leave or he'd have come after her. But I did.'

'You ran away?'

He nodded, biting his lip at the memory.

'You can always go back. Remember the prodigal son. Even after all this time I'm sure your father would welcome you home.'

'I haven't got a home,' Eddie told her, wondering whose son she was talking about. He pulled away from the wall and stuffed his hands into his pockets, head down. 'Anyway,' he admitted, 'I did go back. A month after, I went back home.'

'What happened?' she asked gently.

He shrugged. 'Nothing. The house was empty. They'd gone. Moved away. Dunno where.' She wasn't going to call the peelers now, he could tell. 'So I've got no home, like I said. And I don't care.' He turned and walked away down Woodstock Street, leaving the woman standing alone.

Her father was waiting where Elizabeth Oldfield had left him, outside Grosvenor's Mourning Warehouse.

The shop specialised in clothing for the bereaved, and it seemed appropriate that an aged clergyman should be spending his time looking in at the window.

'There are so many of these shops nowadays,' he said distractedly as Elizabeth joined him. 'Death, it seems, is always with us.'

'So are the pickpockets,' she told him. 'At least I got your wallet back for you.'

'Thank you, my dear.' He smiled and shook his head as they continued their interrupted journey along the Gloucester Road. 'Although there's very little of value in it, it was given to me by your dear mother. I should be sorry to lose it.'

'There's the principle too,' Elizabeth said. She opened her bag and retrieved the wallet. She handed it to her father, who inspected it with interest.

'What is this?'

'It's your wallet,' she said gently. He was getting so very vague these days. 'Remember? The one mother gave you.'

'No, no, no.' He was shaking his head and offering it back to her. The dull brown of the leather was scuffed and well worn. He nodded back at Grosvenor's where he had waited. 'My wallet, the wallet she gave me, is as black as their mourning suits.'

Elizabeth just stared. 'You're sure?'

'Well, I ought to know my own wallet. Here, you have it.'

She took it, feeling the colour rush to her face as she realised what had happened. 'That urchin,' she hissed. 'He gave me the wrong wallet. He's kept yours. He didn't have time to take the money out, so he kept it. This is some other poor soul's.'

'Hmm, that's possible,' her father agreed. 'Relieved of its contents earlier, no doubt.'

'No doubt. All that talk about his mother dying, and running away from home . . .' She was breathing heavily, getting angrier by the moment at how he had tricked her – how he had played on her emotions. As she fumed she opened the wallet, knowing it would be empty.

Or almost empty. Certainly there were no notes or coins inside. But there was a handwritten card with a name and address, presumably the owner. Tucked behind the card, carefully folded in half as if to protect and preserve it was a small slip of paper. It looked as though it had been taken from a notebook. One edge of it was torn, leaving a tiny hole where the string of the binding had been threaded through. There was writing on the paper, faded black ink that started in mid-sentence, and was lost at the other side of the paper. The other edge was not torn, but ragged and charred, where it had been burned away.

Chapter 5

Elizabeth had not had cause to go to the police before, and she doubted she would hurry back. She had not expected them to be able to produce her father's wallet miraculously out of the ether. But neither had she expected the off-hand lack of interest with which she was greeted. Her father, perhaps anticipating how the visit would turn out, sat himself down on a chair near the entrance to the police station and waited for Liz.

Rather grudgingly, the policeman at the desk wrote down her name and address. At Elizabeth's insistence, he also scratched out a description of the boy who had taken the wallet, though he evidently thought this was a waste of time.

'Thank you for your help,' Liz said sarcastically. It was obvious there was no point in staying, so she turned to go. 'Oh,' she remembered, 'do you want this?' She reached into her bag and took out the wallet the boy had given her.

The policeman just stared at her.

'Well, what do you suggest I do with it?' she demanded.

'I suppose we *could* return it to its owner,' the policeman grudgingly admitted. 'You say there's a name and address inside?' He reached out tentatively for the wallet, as if it might be hot.

Liz sighed and pushed it back into her bag. 'Don't worry, I'll send it back to him. I expect your policemen are all too busy chasing pickpockets to worry about returning people's possessions.'

She felt she had at least made a point. But as she rejoined her father, Liz had no doubt the policeman would have forgotten all about her in a few minutes.

After his meeting with Augustus Lorimore, George walked the long way home. The loss of his wallet had unsettled him, but he was more upset by the way he had been more or less turfed out of Lorimore's house.

He kept thinking of Lorimore's strange behaviour – his changes of mood and the insistence that George and he were entering into some business deal. But then he was a collector – George could attest to that – and he had been led to believe George was bringing him something for his collection. Though how a tiny scrap of paper could be of any real value, George had no idea. Perhaps he should ask Sir William Protheroe his opinion.

George did not receive many letters, and very few if any ever arrived by the second afternoon post. So he was intrigued to find a plain white envelope on his mat. It had been posted, he noted, in central London just a few hours ago. The address was written with neatness and precision. The handwritten letter inside was every bit as elegant.

Dear Mr Archer

I have through somewhat circuitous means come into possession of a wallet, which I believe you lost recently. I am afraid that any money that was in it has been removed, but, my father having suffered a similar loss, I thought you might appreciate its return.

I am happy to deliver it to you in person, being loathe to entrust your wallet to the postal service. Please let me know, at the above address, if this is acceptable and convenient. I deem it a favour if we could meet, albeit briefly, as I feel you may be able to help me in my quest to recover my father's wallet which was given to him by my late mother as a gift and thus has a sentimental value. I am generally free during the day.

Yours faithfully

E. Oldfield (Miss)

George read the letter through carefully, wondering briefly what sort of woman would use words like 'circuitous' or 'albeit'. Probably some middle-aged spinster, he decided. Still living with her ancient father and desperate for an excuse to talk to anyone outside their immediate circle of acquaintances. He was tempted to write back and ask that she simply post him his wallet despite her qualms.

But reading the letter again, he decided that he might as well meet the woman. Also, it was possible that the fragment of Glick's diary was still inside the wallet – the card with his own name and address evidently was. As he sat down to write a brief reply, it occurred to George that following his recent encounter with Augustus Lorimore, it was obvious that the man was extremely keen to get hold of the contents of George's wallet.

Was he being over-cautious, he wondered? Or would it be better not to invite the woman to his house or the Museum. He would rather that Lorimore did not discover he had his wallet back – with or without the diary fragment. It was unlikely he was being watched, but it was safer, he decided, to be cautious without need. He dipped his pen in the ink and started to write a reply to E. Oldfield (Miss).

Returning to the British Museum the next morning, George made a point of informing Mr Mansfield that he would work through lunch but take an hour mid-afternoon, if that was all right. As before, Mansfield seemed more than happy to oblige him, and George wondered when the man intended to break the news of George's offer of a new job, if ever.

George's work that morning was further interrupted by a visit from Sir William Protheroe, wondering whether Mr Mansfield had indeed yet broached the subject of his offer of employment. He did not seem surprised to hear that Mansfield had not.

'I imagine he will put it off for as long as he can,' Sir William said. He seemed loathe to be more specific about the work until Mansfield had officially spoken to George.

When Sir William mentioned that he was in the process of examining Glick's diaries and researching the man's life and career, George was minded to describe his trip to see Lorimore. But he had not mentioned the surviving scrap of paper before, and he felt embarrassed at having to admit to its theft. Besides, he thought, the trip to meet Lorimore had been unrewarding at just about every level. So he said nothing.

Presently, Sir William bid George farewell and assured him he would once again press Mansfield to discuss George's career with him. George worked solidly through the rest of the day, wondering again what working for Sir William would be like and what it would entail. The combination of work and thought meant that the day passed quickly.

There was a tea room on the Charing Cross Road that George knew. He sometimes went there for a break from work. He had suggested to Miss Oldfield that they meet at three, since the tea rooms were invariably over-subscribed for lunch.

In his letter to Miss Oldfield, George had described where he would be sitting and how he would be dressed. He managed to get the table he wanted, and kept his eye on the door as he sipped at a cup of Earl Grey. There was no shortage of ladies of a certain age in the tea room, but none of them, mercifully, seemed especially interested in George.

Imagining that punctuality might be a particular trait of the lady whose handwriting was so perfectly formed and whose vocabulary was so correct, George kept careful watch as the clock on the wall reached three. He allowed himself a small smile as the door opened to let in the sound of a distant church clock chiming the hour, and a woman with steel grey hair scraped back from her face. She looked round the tea rooms with small dark eyes. Her nose was a hooked beak jutting out from a severe expression. George was tempted to duck under the table, and hope she decided he had not come and move on.

But incredibly, when she looked at him across the room, her eyes showed no recognition or interest, and she passed quickly on to an empty table nearby.

Relieved, George reached to pour himself more tea.

'Excuse me, but may I?'

There was someone standing on the other side of the table. A young woman was gesturing to the chair opposite. The light of the window was behind her, so George had to squint to try to make out her features.

'I'm sorry,' he said as her face dipped into view. 'I'm waiting for someone.' She had startlingly green eyes, he could now see. The ends of them curled slightly upwards, like a cat's.

'Yes,' she said. 'I know.' She pulled out the chair and sat down.

Taken by surprise, George started to rise politely. He was not sure quite what to say, and anyway she was already telling the uniformed waitress she would have a pot of tea.

'Well, it seems very nice here,' the young woman commented. 'Oh, and before I forget,' she went on, apparently oblivious to George's discomfort and reaching into a small handbag, 'here you are.'

George's mouth dropped open and the world round him seemed to take a tea break of its own. The young woman opposite was holding out a wallet – his wallet.

'You are George Archer, aren't you?' she said when he made no move to take it. She started to put the wallet away again. 'Oh dear, I must have made the most embarrassing mistake, please forgive me.'

'No, no,' George protested, finding his voice at last. 'I am indeed George Archer and that is my wallet, and I'm extremely grateful for its return.' He took the wallet and opened it, keen to check that the diary fragment was still inside. 'Thank you, Miss Oldfield.'

'You are welcome, Mr Archer.' She watched as he pulled out the slip of paper, looked at it, and visibly relieved carefully returned it to his wallet before placing that inside his jacket pocket. 'I am sorry that the contents are, I suspect, somewhat depleted. I did inspect the wallet to determine your name and address, of course. And I confess I found that piece of paper. From your evident delight at finding it, I assume it is important to you.'

She made it sound as if she was not interested. But George could tell from the way her eyes watched him over the lip of her teacup that Miss Oldfield was keen to know the truth. Her assessment of George's behaviour betrayed a keen intelligence as well as her obvious beauty. In fact, there was also something about her manner which made him instantly trustful of her, and he considered telling her everything. But anxious not to appear too eager, in case she misinterpreted his motives, he asked instead: 'You said in your letter that your father had lost his wallet?'

She set down her tea cup carefully on its saucer.

'That is so. A young boy, little more than an urchin, made it look as if he had accidentally collided with father in the street yesterday. He realised that his wallet was missing, and I chased after the boy and caught him.'

'Did you really?' George was unable to hide his surprise at this, and hoped she might interpret it as congratulation. 'Well done,' he added quickly.

'I demanded he return father's wallet. Stupidly, I thought he had. But in fact, he gave me yours in its place.'

George nodded thoughtfully. 'And did the police not find your father's wallet on his person?' She looked away, glancing round the tea rooms as if someone at another table might be better placed to answer the question. George gave a short laugh. 'Surely you marched the young scoundrel off to the police?'

She returned her attention to her tea. 'No, actually.' She took a sip, set down the cup, straightened it on its saucer. 'I let him go.'

Before George could reply, she was leaning across the table, her hands pushed out in front of her so that they almost sent her teapot flying. Her words came out in a rush. 'Oh I was stupid to do it, I know. But I suppose I felt sorry for him. I mean it can't be much of a life can it, for a lad like that. Having to steal to get the money for food, living out on the streets because his mother has passed away and he can't find his father and sister. Living hand to mouth.'

George sat back and folded his arms. He could not help but smile. 'So you had quite a conversation with the young criminal then, before you set him free.' He held up his hands to stop any protest. 'You asked me about that slip of paper . . .' He was leaning forward now, matching her pose. George wondered whether he should say nothing about the fragment of paper. But then again, just by having seen it Miss Oldfield might perhaps be in danger. Surely it was only right and proper at least to warn her of that possibility? 'People have died, quite possibly because of that tiny scrap of paper,' George said quietly. 'I myself may be in danger.'

They sat in silence for a moment after this. 'My goodness, Mr Archer,' she said at last, 'you make it sound as if we are caught up in the events of a penny dreadful. I think perhaps you had better tell me your story.'

She listened attentively as George spoke. It was, he found, a relief to tell someone finally about it. He started with the death of his poor friend Albert, who had died in his sleep – was it only last week? By the time he got to describe the break-in at the Museum and how the scarred man had lunged at him across Percy's desk, Miss Oldfield was sitting with her eyes wide and her tea quite forgotten.

He described how he had written to Augustus Lorimore, and told her of the strange reply he had received.

'So you determined to go and see the man?' she asked him.

George nodded. He was feeling rather parched and asked her if she wanted more tea.

But in reply, her hand flew to her mouth. 'Oh my goodness, look at the time,' she cried nodding at the clock on the far wall. 'I am supposed to be taking my father to visit his former parishioners this afternoon. He will be so cross if I am late.' She took a final, swift sip of cold tea, grimaced, gathered her bag, and stood up. 'He can't manage on his own. He needs me to help him with almost everything these days, I'm afraid.'

'That must be a burden,' George said, standing up.

She frowned. 'I suppose so,' she said quietly, as if the thought had never occurred to her. 'But I must know how your story ends.'

'If it has ended,' George replied. 'We could meet here again. Tomorrow perhaps?'

'I can't possibly wait that long to hear the rest of your adventures. Why not come to our house?' she said. 'Father won't mind. In fact if you come after eight o'clock this evening he won't even know – he needs his sleep. Oh, but it will all be quite proper, I assure you, Mr Archer,' she quickly added. 'I mean . . .'

'I know what you mean,' he said. 'And I should be delighted to call on you and finish my story, so far as it goes. I have your address from your letter. But I must not keep you, Miss Oldfield, though I do have one small request.'

She glanced at the clock again and frowned. 'Yes?'

'My friends call me George.'

She regarded him sternly for a moment. Then she smiled. 'Very well, George it is. My name is Elizabeth.'

'May I call you Elizabeth?'

'No,' she said in a matter of fact voice as she walked past him and headed for the door. She paused and turned. 'But you may call me Liz. I shall see you this evening, George.'

Only after he had sat down, his head swimming with visions of Elizabeth Oldfield's smile and the anticipation of seeing her again did it occur to George that his recently returned wallet was empty. He had no money at all.

Feeling foolish and anxious, he finally summoned the courage to gesture to the waitress who had served them as she walked past. 'Excuse me, but about the bill . . .'

'That's all right, sir.' She barely paused on her way to another customer. 'The young lady paid on her way out.'

They grabbed him as he was working the side streets near Kensington Gardens. It was a good place to finish up the day, and as night fell Eddie often found useful pickings in the area as people hurried home. That was how the two men knew he would be there, of course. Someone who knew Eddie's routine, such as it was, had told them – Smudgy Steve or Mike the Mouth. Possibly little Annie from the baker's who sometimes gave him one of yesterday's rolls.

The first Eddie knew of anything amiss was when a pair of enormous arms wrapped themselves round him from behind and pulled him backwards. He kicked out at once, shouting and struggling. But one of the arms was positioned so that a huge, sweaty hand clamped over his mouth. Someone else was approaching him, and Eddie's eyes widened. He hoped they would realise he was in trouble – help him or raise the alarm.

The street was in shadow, the sun already below the level of the buildings. The lamps had been lit, and as he approached Eddie, his potential rescuer's face caught the light. The man was smiling horribly, and Eddie could clearly see the thin, raised scar that ran down the whole side of his face. Scarface – the man who had been shadowing the old man Eddie had tried to help.

'I thought it might be you, from the description we were given,' Scarface said, grabbing Eddie's thrashing legs and lifting him up. The two men carried Eddie off into a narrow alleyway. 'So nice to meet you again. Eddie, isn't it?' His voice was rough as gravel.

Scarface set Eddie's feet down on the ground again, and the man holding Eddie from behind relaxed his grip slightly. Not enough for Eddie to have any hope of pulling free, but he could stretch round and see that it was 'Sidekick' – the man who had been with Scarface.

'I'm sorry I got in your way,' Eddie gasped as soon as the hand was removed from his mouth. 'I can give you me day's takings. To make amends.'

'You hear that, Davey?' Scarface ground out. 'Very generous I'm sure.' His face thrust close to Eddie's, the scar gleaming. 'But we don't want money off you, oh no. You've got something far more valuable than money, haven't you, Eddie the Dipper.'

Eddie swallowed. 'Have I?'

'Oh yes,' Davey – the man holding him – said with a high-pitched chuckle. 'Much more valuable, that's right Mr Blade.'

Something caught the light as Scarface drew it out of his jacket. A knife. He angled it so that the reflected light shone in Eddie's eyes. 'Bet you're wondering why I'm called Blade,' he said. The knife moved slowly closer to Eddie's eyes. 'Maybe you think it's on account of the scar?' And closer. 'Or perhaps you think it's because I'm so good with the knife.' Closer still.

The knife stopped just shy of Eddie's left eye. It was so close he could see the tiny flat dot of its point.

'But you'd be wrong,' Blade said. 'It just happens to

be my name.' The knife drew back, accompanied by Blade and Davey's laughter. 'Like Draper or Smith, it seems I'm named after my trade.'

'What do you want?' Eddie asked. His voice was husky and his mouth dry.

'Trade is a good word. 'Cos that's what we want. In return for your life, or at least your good looks such as they are, you give us something. How's that?'

'Anything.' He tried to pull away but the arms still held him tight. 'Whatever you want.'

'See?' Blade snapped at Davey. 'I told you he was a smart boy.' He reached out suddenly for Eddie, and Eddie squeezed his eyes shut, expecting to feel the prick of the knife on his face at any moment. But instead, Blade put his hand on Eddie's cap and rubbed it round his head, ruffling his hair. Then he slapped Eddie on the cheek. 'Good boy.'

'What do you want?'

'You lifted a wallet from a Mr Archer yesterday.'

'Maybe,' Eddie conceded. 'I lift lots of wallets.'

'Well this one, we want. Or rather, something that's in it.'

'What?' Eddie asked. He could read well enough to know which wallet had been Archer's. But why did they want the man's wallet – there hadn't even been much money in it. Just some loose change, a business card and a burnt scrap of paper. Hardly worth the effort, in fact.

'Well, that's for us to know and for you to mind your own business about.'

Eddie nodded slowly. 'Yeah,' he said. 'I got his wallet – Mr Archer – I lifted it yesterday. Still got it in fact. Nice leather one. Got nothing but a few coins and a pocket watch today, so I kept his wallet till I find something better.'

Davey let him struggle free enough to pull the wallet from his trouser pocket. He held it out to Blade, who snatched it at once.

With Davey leaning over Eddie's shoulder to watch, Blade opened the wallet and checked inside. 'It's empty,' he snarled, throwing it to the ground in anger and reaching for Eddie's throat with both hands.

'No,' Eddie insisted. 'No, it ain't. There's a scrap of burned paper inside, I saw it. Tucked away in the lining.'

Blade halted. 'Where?'

'I'll show you. Here let me show you.' So it was the burned paper they wanted, was it? But why? Eddie made to pick up the wallet, and Davey let go of him, watching closely. Eddie held up the wallet – the wallet he had taken from the old clergymen on the Gloucester Road and swapped for Archer's. He felt inside. 'Here it is, you see?' He pulled out his hand, then gave a gasp of annoyance. 'Oops,' he said loudly, 'dropped it. There – quick, before it blows away.'

Both men looked. They were not fooled for long, but it was long enough for Eddie. He was already running, the wallet jammed back into his pocket and his lungs bursting with the effort as he ran for his life. He could hear the sound of the men behind him – feet on cobbles, shouts of anger, threats . . .

As he ran, Eddie's mind too was racing. What could he do? Where could he go? They were desperate to find the scrap of paper, that was clear. So desperate that they would be after him again, they wouldn't easily give up. But what sort of scrap of paper was that important to anyone? Next time he might not escape so easily. Next time, Blade might bring the knife that bit closer to his face. Next time . . .

Half an hour later, Mr Blade's employer listened to his report without comment.

'But we'll find him, sir,' Blade concluded. 'He can't stay hidden for long, not with all the contacts and sources we have. We'll find him.'

His employer nodded. 'See that you do. With this and the mess at the British Museum I am not in the mood for any more mistakes.' He was angry and disappointed, but it would do no good to get upset with Blade. The man had at least established who the boy was and that he knew about the fragment of Glick's diary. If he did not still have it he would know where it was. In any case, Blade knew better than anyone the fate that awaited those who failed his master – and that was the best incentive that there could be.

The full moon shone in through the glass roof of the laboratory, augmenting the artificial light that illuminated the huge wooden work bench and the gears and cogs and components that were set out meticulously across it. The bare, pale flesh of a detached human arm seemed almost luminescent in the moonlight. The bottles of blood and jars of tissue reflected the glow.

The man rolled up the sleeve of his shirt and reached his bony hand deep into a tank of viscous liquid, feeling round inside. 'Mrs Wilkes, I gather, is telling some rather improbable stories,' he said to Blade.

'Indeed sir, so I gather. They're saying in the local pub that her dead husband went home and demanded tea and fruitcake. A somewhat fanciful account.'

'But nonetheless disturbing.'

'Indeed, sir. There is an old white-haired gentleman that has apparently been asking questions.'

'Just so long as he gets no answers,' the man replied sharply. 'Ah!' His hand closed on the thing he was hunting for, felt it give under the slight pressure of his fingers. He reached in with his other arm and cradled the grey mass of tissue carefully as he lifted it clear of the tank. 'This man might believe the stories, however improbable. He might think to investigate further if only to disprove them.'

'What do you suggest, sir?'

'I think it might be best, Mr Blade, if the dead were to stay dead. Don't you? And demonstrably so.'

Blade swallowed, and his master was amused to see that his manservant was trying not to look at what he now held in his hands. 'What about the body, sir?' Blade asked. 'It's hardly in a condition –'

'Yes, and I fear I have already used some of the components. When our friend failed to get us the diaries and instead went home to terrify his wife, I decided there was little reason to keep him . . . intact. But don't worry.'

'No, sir,' Blade said deferentially.

The man completed his examination of the slippery, grey brain and set it down next to the arm. 'I'm sure we can sort something out. I don't expect anyone will inspect it too closely, if at all.' He reached for an assembly of tiny gears and levers. 'Just put it back, best you can, Blade. Before this white-haired old man, or anyone else, goes looking for it.'

'Sir.' Blade hesitated only a moment, then he turned and quickly left the room.

They spoke quietly, although Liz knew that her father was sound asleep and would not easily be wakened.

There were two small armchairs in the front room, facing each other and angled towards the fire. Liz sat in one, George in the other. As he recounted his visit to Augustus Lorimore's house, the fire crackled and burned lower. George's fascination with the automata was obvious, and Liz found herself caught up in his enthusiasm as he described them. With him she felt a measure of distaste at the stuffed animals.

As George came to the end of his tale, Liz felt it was rather like listening to a ghost story, or being caught up in the excitement of a melodrama.

'And then I got your letter,' he finished.

'Yes,' she said. 'The question, I suppose, is what do we do now with this fragment of paper?'

'I suppose we must return it to Sir William to examine along with the rest of the surviving diaries. Unless you have another suggestion?'

Before Liz could answer, there was a knock at the front door. They both froze, looking at each other wide-eyed and fearful.

'They've found us,' George hissed. 'Those villains. They've come looking for the burned scrap of paper and I've led them to you.'

'How? They can't have, surely.' Liz got up, trembling at the thought that the man with the scar that George had described so vividly might be standing on her doorstep. She went to the window and gently pulled the curtain back just far enough to peep out into the murky street outside.

'Who is it?' George whispered.

'Well, it isn't your scar-faced man,' she told him. 'A

reformed criminal perhaps, though.' She went out into the hall, aware that George was following her.

As soon as she opened the door, the figure standing outside pushed his way into the hall and slammed it shut behind him. It was the boy she had chased down the Gloucester Road, and he was holding her father's wallet. He slapped it into Liz's palm.

'Look,' the boy said, 'you've got to help me.'

'Us, help you?' George said from behind Liz, the disbelief evident in his voice.

'You two know each other?' the boy asked, surprised at seeing George. He pulled his cap off and stuffed it into his pocket. 'You've got to help me because it's all your fault that's why.' He pointed at George as he said this, his eyes glinting with fear and accusation.

'What's his fault?' Liz asked.

'They're after me, that's what. Going to kill me too, if I don't give them what they want.'

'And what's that?' George demanded.

'The burned scrap of paper out of your wallet, that's what. I don't know why they want it, but they want it bad. And old scarface Mr Blade says he'll kill anyone that gets in his way.'

Chapter 6

Mist hung low over the gravestones like a shroud, almost glowing in the pale diffuse moonlight. The tips of the tombstones erupted from the soft blanket like broken teeth – angled, chipped, discoloured. Then clouds reached across the moon, and the scene faded to darkness and silhouette.

Two figures, made insubstantial by the mist that swirled round them, picked their way between the graves. Silent and pale as ghosts, they were caught for the briefest moment in a shaft of moonlight that escaped from behind the clouds. Between them they carried a large wooden box. They were a mismatched pair – one thin and wiry, the other taller and massively broad.

The struggling moonlight picked out a thin scar that ran down the length of the larger man's face as he turned to hiss instructions to his fellow. 'Just along here. Careful now, don't drop it.'

The smaller man did not answer, but he tightened

his grip on the wooden casket. The ground was uneven, broken up by the gravestones and by raised areas of thick, unkempt grass and by the ragged edges of fallen gravestones. The mist swirled round their feet as a breeze swept through the desolation, making the ground churn and undulate – as if it were about to give up its dead.

But neither of the men noticed. They were both used to being close to death.

'Here we are,' Blade said at last.

They set down the casket close to the mound of a new grave. Earth had been heaped over the grave, and the first spikes of grass were poking through the dark soil. There was no stone yet, just a simple small wooden cross to mark the place.

A wreath of flowers lay near the head of the grave. The smaller man picked it up and tossed it away. Leaves spilled from the wreath, leaving a trail across the grave. As the wreath fell against a nearby headstone, a shower of dry petals spilled like confetti across the ground.

Blade produced a knife from inside his jacket and used it to prise open the casket, wrenching the lid off the large oblong box. He blinked and coughed and cursed at the smell, and stuffed the knife back inside his jacket pocket. With a handkerchief clasped over his nose and mouth, he bent to reach into the box and pulled out a shovel. Blade dropped it to the ground, then reached back into the casket for another.

The smaller man helped him lift the wooden lid and they jammed it back over the box, covering its other contents.

'Let's make this quick,' Blade said. He was gasping from holding his breath as he pushed one of the shovels at the small man. He picked up the other one himself.

Together they began to dig into the loose topsoil, piling it in a mound beside the grave. The sound of shovels biting into the cold earth echoed off the impassive gravestones like some massive beast eating into flesh and bone.

The boy was frightened, that was plain. Liz had left him with George in the living room while she went upstairs to check her father had not been disturbed.

Now George and the boy were sitting opposite each other, neither of them willing to be the first to speak. George knew it wasn't just because they were wary of waking Liz's father, but he still could not think of anything useful to say to the boy who had so casually and expertly stolen his money.

As if guessing what George was thinking, the boy shuffled uncomfortably in the large armchair. 'I ain't got it no more,' he said quietly. 'I spent it. On food. Honest.'

'I'm not sure "honest" is the word I would have chosen,' George told him sharply.

The boy shrugged. 'You live here, do you?' he demanded. 'Or just visiting.'

'Just visiting,' George replied. 'Not that it's any of your business,' he added.

They sat in sullen silence for another minute, then George heard Liz's quiet tread on the stairs.

She stood in the doorway and looked at them both. 'George, this is Eddie,' she said, checking with the boy: 'That's right, isn't it?'

'Eddie Hopkins,' he confirmed. 'Didn't reckon you'd be seeing me again so soon, did you?'

'Indeed not. And I am a little puzzled as to how you found me.'

'You said your father did work at a hostel in Camberwell.' Eddie grinned. 'Wasn't hard to find out enough about him to get me here.' His grin faded and he looked nervous again. 'I tell you, they're out to kill me, or worse. I needed to find someone I could trust.'

'Trust?' George blurted in surprise.

'At least let's hear his story,' Liz said.

'Very well. I suppose, if what the boy says is true, it may also concern us.'

'I'll say,' Eddie agreed. 'There are people who want that bit of paper in your wallet enough to kill me. Reckon they'd kill you for it and all.'

George could feel the colour draining from his face. 'I think you'd better tell us your story, Eddie,' he said. 'From the beginning.'

The first glimmers of dawn were streaking the grey sky and struggling through the clouds. Police Constable Mark Skipper pulled his cloak tighter about his neck and stamped his feet to keep warm. It might be nearly morning, but the chill breeze was kicking up now, and wisps of damp fog still lingered in the air. Before long, the fog would be replaced by the smoke and smog of daytime London. In many ways, despite the cold, this was the best part of the day.

It was certainly a time that Skipper welcomed. Another hour and he would be off duty. Home to a large, hot breakfast and the chance to put his feet up. A cup of Rosie and then some shut-eye. Just time for one more walk round his patch, he decided.

The streets of London were never truly deserted, even at the dead of night. But here, away from the markets and the main shops, the early hours were as quiet as it got. Somewhere in the distance he could hear the sound of a carriage clattering through the cobbled streets. A dog barked, setting off another. He paused and leaned on the cast iron fence that surrounded the graveyard, staring out across the irregular arrangement of headstones, waiting for the first hint of the sun to edge over the horizon.

Now the light was streaming across the misty cemetery and the tombstones were black against the brightening sky. At first glance they seemed regular and similar. But Skipper knew that if you looked more closely you could see that every stone was different – the shapes and sizes, the way they had each angled and weathered gave every stone an individuality. Just as the people buried beneath had once been individuals. Now they were all equals – dust to dust.

He sighed and straightened up, ready to move on. But something caught his eye as he turned – a movement where he did not expect it. Between the stones, in the distance. Figures.

The black shapes of two men stood out against the tip of the rising sun. Two men making a slow and deliberate journey away from Skipper towards the far gate out of the graveyard and into Galsworthy Avenue. The policeman raised his hand to shield his eyes from the increasing glare of the sun. The men were almost out of sight now, over the slight rise and disappearing from view. But not before he saw that they were carrying something between them. A rectangular shape. Like a box.

Or a coffin.

'Oi! You there!' There was a gate further along the street, and Skipper ran for it as he shouted. Through the gate, cold air rasping in his lungs, the sun in his eyes making them water.

By the time PC Skipper reached the spot where he had seen the figures, there was no sign of them. Had he imagined it, he wondered? A trick of the morning light?

And as he turned, he saw the remains of a broken wreath lying haphazardly against a mossy gravestone. The grave itself was old and neglected. But next to it was a new grave. Skipper remembered it being dug, perhaps a week or so ago. He had walked through the graveyard and exchanged a few words with the men taking it in turns to dig. The next day he had seen that the grave was filled and covered, a wreath laid carefully at its head.

The wreath was now dead and had been moved aside. But the ground was still black and the soil loose. As if the grave had been dug and filled not a week or more ago, but in the last few hours. Skipper crouched down beside the newly turned soil. He scooped up a handful and let it trickle out between his fingers.

It was only when Liz drew back the curtains to allow the first light of the morning into the room that George realised how long they had been talking.

Eddie had told them how he had seen the man with the scar – Blade – a few days earlier. He recounted how he had seen Blade and his accomplice Davey grab the old man and drag him into the grounds of a house. George was impressed that the boy had tried to help the old man. Under the dishonest, insolent exterior it seemed there might be a heart and a conscience after all.

Then Eddie became quiet. He admitted he had not

been able to find Blade and the old man, that he had given up and left. George sensed there was more to it than this, and so it seemed did Liz. 'Why not go to that house for help?'

Eddie glared at him, his eyes wide with annoyance, and with something else. He held George's stare for a moment. Then he looked away again. When he spoke, his voice was so quiet that George could only just make out his words: 'Because of the monster.'

'Monster?' he echoed. 'What do you mean?'

'There's a monster,' Eddie said, more assured now, as if challenging George to disagree. 'In the grounds of that big house. I saw it, it chased me.' He held George's gaze for a moment, then looked at Liz. Then he looked away. 'You don't believe me,' he said. 'I don't care. I know what I seen.'

'Well,' George said after a moment's pause, 'I don't know about that. But I can understand you not wanting to tangle with the unpleasant Mr Blade. I've met him myself, I think. In fact, he killed a friend of mine.'

'Strewth,' Eddie said, at once involved and interested again.

So now it was George's turn to tell his story about the raid on the British Museum, and poor Percy's death. 'That's how I came to have that scrap of paper you think Blade is after,' he finished. George drew the scrap of charred paper out of his wallet and at once both Liz and Eddie crowded round to inspect it.

'. . . now know which came first, and I can prove it.
The answer lies in the Crystal . . .'

'So what's it mean?' Eddie asked.

'I don't know,' George confessed. 'But surely it must mean something, for Blade to be so keen to get hold of it.'

'And Lorimore too,' Liz added.

'Who?' Eddie asked. 'You mean the factory bloke?'

'Yes,' George said. 'But I'm pretty sure he is just a collector of curios and was interested because he thought I had something to sell.'

'You think he wants a complete diary?' Liz asked.

'Well if he does it won't be this one. The volume this paper came from is burned to ash,' George added. 'This is all there is now. Sir William Protheroe, at the British Museum, is examining the others.'

'They must want them bad to go stealing and murdering,' Eddie announced.

'Yes, and before that I think they tried to buy them,' George said. 'From poor Albert Wilkes before he died. He worked with my friend Percy,' he started to explain.

But Liz was looking at him in astonishment. 'You did not tell me your friend's name before,' she said. 'How curious. I wonder . . .'

'Wonder? Wonder what?'

'Yeah,' Eddie added, 'what is it?'

Liz frowned. 'Well, I can't think it is relevant,' she said. 'Though it was rather unsettling at the time. Father and I visited the man's widow just a few days ago. She lives on Clearview Street.' Liz was looking off into the distance as she remembered. 'The poor woman was in such a state. She must have been dreaming or something.'

'So what did she say?' Eddie demanded.

Liz was looking out of the window. When she turned, George could not make out her expression as the light was behind her now. 'She said that her husband, her dead husband, had come home and taken the dog for a walk.'

There was a moment's silence, broken by Liz's nervous laugh. 'Father did what he could to comfort the poor woman. But she was distraught.'

'As you say,' George agreed, 'a dream. A waking nightmare. She missed him so much she thought he had come back.'

Eddie was thoughtful. He stood up and walked round the room. 'What about the dog?' he asked at last.

'The dog?' George almost laughed out loud. 'Who cares about the dog?'

Eddie was looking at him excitedly. Then he turned to Liz. 'Was the dog there?'

'No,' she admitted. 'No, I didn't see a dog, I must confess.'

Eddie was almost breathless with excitement now.

'So maybe this Wilkes really had taken it for a walk.' He paused before going on: 'You see, that old man Blade was after had a dog,' he said. 'And that was on Clearview Street.'

George frowned. There was a coincidence here, but was it any more than that? He was trying to see the significance, if any, when he realised that Liz was no longer paying attention. She was looking out of the window again.

'There's a policeman coming to the door,' she said.

They had talked of going to the police, of course. But after her experiences with the relatively mundane matter of a missing wallet, Liz was adamant that without some solid evidence they would get no help.

'I was hoping to find the Reverend Oldfield,' the policeman said when Liz opened the door. 'I know it's early,' he admitted.

'Indeed,' Liz told him. 'He is still asleep. I am myself an early-riser,' she added by way of explaining how she came to be awake and up and dressed at the crack of dawn. 'Can I help? I am his daughter.'

'It isn't a pleasant incident, miss.'

'An incident? What can you mean?'

'Well, I'm not sure yet, miss. Probably nothing. I think I disturbed the men. I wasn't really sure what to do about it as it seems there's no real harm or damage done.'

'Some sort of damage?' Liz wondered. 'Where?'

'Well, not really *damage* miss. I saw two characters making off through the graveyard. Maybe they were just taking a shortcut. Only, well, one of the graves looks like it's been disturbed. I gather that Reverend Henderson is away, so I was advised to inform your father. I'm just going off duty myself,' he went on. 'But if the Reverend wants to take a look for himself, there'll be someone there until eight o'clock. We'd appreciate his professional opinion.'

'Thank you,' Liz said. The constable touched his helmet, and turned to go. Liz stepped back to close the door. 'Oh, constable,' she said quickly as a thought occurred to her. 'Which grave is it that has been disturbed?'

'It's a recent one, miss. Over towards the Galsworthy Avenue side. No headstone yet, of course. But I gather it's the grave of a gentleman called Albert Wilkes.'

Chapter 7

Eddie and George made their way to the graveyard while Liz went to wake her father. It seemed best to examine Albert Wilkes's grave as soon as possible, and George was conscious that despite his lack of sleep he was due at work at the Museum in a few hours. With luck he would be able to find a quiet store room and catch forty winks.

They walked briskly, Eddie leading as he said he knew the way. 'Do you live round here?' George asked him.

The boy glanced at George, a lick of dark hair poking out from under his cap. 'I don't live nowhere,' he said.

'Everyone lives somewhere.'

The boy grunted. 'Fat lot you know. You've got a house or something, I suppose.'

'Well, yes.' There was something in the boy's manner that made George almost ashamed to answer. 'It was my father's house,' he said.

'You got a father too. That's nice.'

'I did have,' George replied quietly. 'Not any more.'

Eddie looked at him – not a sideways glance of contempt, but with an intensity that made George feel even more uneasy. 'That's sad,' Eddie said. Then he looked away.

'I just meant you seem to know your way around here,' George said. It sounded more apologetic than he had intended.

'I know lots of London.'

'I suppose so.'

'What's that mean?'

Eddie had stopped, and George had to stop as well to answer. 'It doesn't *mean* anything.'

'I don't expect you to like me,' the boy snapped. 'I don't expect you to worry about what I do or where I sleep or where my next meal's coming from. You got a house and home, so that's all right.'

George stared at him. He had no idea how to respond to this sudden outburst. He could just agree with the boy and walk away – a lot of what he had said was certainly true, and George felt no pricks from his conscience about how he lived. But somehow, despite everything – even losing his wallet – he felt caught up in the boy's life. They were linked now, both entangled in a mystery that if the lad was right threatened their lives.

'I do like you, Eddie,' he said quietly, without even realising he was going to say it. It sounded trite and awkward, but he realised that it was true. There was something about Eddie Hopkins. If nothing else, the boy was a survivor, and while George didn't agree with the boy's morals, at least the lad had some.

Eddie stared at George for a long moment. His mouth moved as if he was about to speak. Then he glanced down at his feet before suddenly slapping George heartily on the shoulder and grinning at him. 'Let's go and see the grave robbing, then,' he said.

It was raining when Liz eventually got her father to the graveyard. A fine drizzle that was almost a mist, and which seeped into Liz's clothes. Her father seemed not to notice as he prodded at the turned earth with the end of his stick and muttered quietly to himself about what the world was coming to.

'You say that the constable was going to meet us here?' he said at last, his forehead wrinkling like a tortoise's.

'He was going off duty. But he said there would be someone.'

'Probably idling about somewhere,' her father decided. 'You stay here, I'll go and find the fellow.'

Liz watched him set off towards the nearest path, leaning heavily on his stick. She was tempted to follow, but she waited until her father's shape was blurred by the rain. Then she walked slowly over to where George and Eddie were sitting on the wall of the graveyard.

Being cold and damp was nothing new to Eddie. He could feel the rough brickwork of the wall through his trousers and shuffled slightly to get more comfortable. He watched the old man walking unsteadily into the mist, and then Liz came over. They had been forced together by circumstance, and he had stolen from both George and Liz. He quite liked them – well, the woman anyway. The man was quiet and dull and difficult to understand. But Liz was open and honest and she hadn't turned him over to the police when she could have done.

What worried Eddie was that neither of his new associates seemed willing to accept Mrs Wilkes's story. For Eddie it was simple – if the woman said her husband had come home, then she must have some reason for saying it. Even if she thought he was dead. And he was sure that he had seen the old man himself – dead and walking.

'We should dig this Wilkes bloke up,' he pronounced as Liz reached them.

'Why?' George wanted to know.

'To make sure he's still there,' Eddie said.

'And if the grave is empty?' Liz asked.

'Either he isn't dead at all, or . . .' Eddie shrugged.

'He is dead,' George said.

'People get buried alive,' Eddie protested.

'Not these days,' Liz said sharply. She bit at her bottom lip. 'At least, I don't think so.' The notion obviously worried her.

'Then we go to a medium and hold a séance,' Eddie decided. 'If he's really walking, we should find out what he wants. And to do that we have to talk to him.'

'A séance.' Liz's disapproval was obvious. 'You know that's all just nonsense, Eddie.'

'Just because your dad's a priest or whatever doesn't mean you know everything about death,' Eddie shot back. 'How do you know it doesn't work? God talks to us, doesn't he? He does miracles and stuff. And why do we say prayers if we can't talk to him up in Heaven, then, eh?'

Liz sighed as if he was six years old. 'That's completely different,' she said gently.

'Is it?'

'Look,' George interrupted, 'the whole thing's just ludicrous. Albert Wilkes is dead. His body isn't walking about, and he certainly didn't go home and take his dog for a walk.'

'How can you be so sure?' Eddie wanted to know. 'I saw an old man with a dog. I tried to help him, like I told you. It was on Clearview Street like you said and on the right night – I bet that was Wilkes, dead or not.'

'And you saw a monster,' Liz reminded him quietly.

'Yes, I did!' He was furious now. 'It tried to attack me. Spat at me too when it tried to bite.'

'Spat at you?' George made it sound like a music hall act. 'It must have been rain, or water dripping off a branch blown in your face by the wind or something.'

'It spat at me,' Eddie insisted. 'It stained my jacket – look.' He pointed to where the monster's saliva had dripped down him. He had to hunt round for the right stains – a spattering of dark, greasy patches in amongst the other marks on his threadbare jacket.

George leaned forward to examine the patches. He snorted in amusement. 'That isn't monster spit,' he said. 'It's machine oil. I've got enough of it on my own clothes before now to know that for a fact.'

'I don't expect you to believe me,' Eddie mumbled. 'But I still think we should go to a fortune-teller or a medium or someone. That paper out of the diary – it mentioned a crystal, didn't it.'

'What of it?' Liz asked.

'Could be a crystal ball, that's why. Could be it's telling us to look into a crystal ball.'

'It could be all sorts of things,' George said.

'Wouldn't do any harm to try it and find out though.'

'If there is an answer to be found,' Liz said, 'then I expect it is in the other volumes of the diary. Not in some old woman's tea leaves or crystal ball.'

'Or the entrails of a goat, come to that,' George added.

Eddie had no idea what goats had to do with it. But before he could ask, George jumped down from the wall. He stumbled as he landed, and took an involuntary step forwards – bumping into Liz. Eddie was amused to see their mutual embarrassment, quickly followed by nervous smiles and apologies.

George still sounded embarrassed as he said: 'I should go. I need to get to work. But I shall try to find an opportunity to ask Sir William if I can look at the surviving volumes of Glick's diary. He has them at the moment. Maybe he has found something.'

'An excellent idea,' Liz agreed.

'I'll meet you this evening and let you know what I discover, if anything. Shall I . . .' He hesitated. 'Shall I come round to your house again?'

'No. I have some business I need to attend to this evening. I shall come and find you when I am done, if that is convenient. I have your address from your card.'

George smiled. 'Of course.'

'I got business to do today and all,' Eddie said, partly to remind them he was there. 'I'll tell you all about it this evening.' They might have dismissed his idea of a séance, but Eddie wasn't to be put off that easily.

Liz was on her own again at the side of the grave when her father returned a short while later with a police sergeant. The two men had been talking, and once Oldfield had convinced him there would be no objection from the Church, the sergeant had agreed that he would arrange for the grave to be opened up.

'Just to check the coffin is intact,' he warned. 'Just so the poor soul is properly covered and can rest in peace.'

It was over an hour before two police constables started work with shovels. Liz was soaked through by then, and feeling cold and bedraggled. She must look a sight, she thought as she watched the men dig.

They scraped the wet earth from the wooden lid of the coffin.

'Well, it's still here at any rate,' the sergeant announced. 'All right, you can fill it in again.'

The constables both sighed audibly, and climbed out of the grave. One of them caught his boot on the coffin lid as he hauled himself out of the pit. The heavy wooden lid moved. Not much, but enough for the sergeant as well as Liz to notice.

'Hang on a minute,' he proclaimed. 'That should be screwed down, shouldn't it?'

'Indeed it should,' Oldfield agreed. 'I fear it may have been tampered with after all.'

The sergeant took a deep breath of misty air. 'You reckon we should open it up, sir? Just to check?'

'I think it would be advisable.'

Liz turned away as one of the policemen jumped back down into the grave. She could hear the scrape of the wood as the coffin lid was lifted clear. She did not want to look, but she strained to hear the reaction from the men watching.

'Well, he's in there all right,' the sergeant said.

'Bit odd though,' one of the constables said. 'I thought Albert Wilkes died in his sleep.'

'Indeed he did,' Oldfield's cracked voice replied.

'Looks like his legs are broken, or something,' the other constable said. Liz almost turned to see for herself.

But the sergeant said: 'All right, put the lid back on.'

'You're going to leave it at that?' Liz asked. Now she did turn round. From the expressions on the faces of the men, the body must have been a singular sight. Perhaps there was more wrong than broken bones.

'I really do think some further investigation . . .' Oldfield began.

The sergeant nodded, holding up a hand to stem the protest. 'I quite agree, sir. The way the man was lying, the way the legs were bent and all. That didn't look like any body I've seen, and I can tell you I've seen a few.'

'What do you propose?' Liz asked.

'Either this body has been tampered with, or this man did not die peacefully in his sleep.' The sergeant turned to Oldfield. 'I propose, with your agreement sir,' he said, 'to suggest to my superiors that we seek permission from the deceased's next of kin for an urgent post-mortem.'

Chapter 8

Her father was tired after his early morning exertions, and so Liz sat with him in the living room until it was time for her to get lunch ready. Once in the kitchen, she quickly laid out a plate of cold meat and some salad. She checked the clock, and seeing she still had twenty minutes before she needed to serve up the food, she opened a drawer in the kitchen table and took out a book.

It was not a novel, but a playscript. She sat down and checked that she could not be seen from the door. She did not expect her father to come looking for her, but if he did she would have time to push the book under the cushion of the chair. Not that there was anything untoward in the text. But she knew how much her father disapproved of the theatre. They had argued so often that Liz had given up trying to persuade him that plays were not the word of Satan and music halls the Devil's own choice of entertainment.

It was an argument her father would never let her

win, so instead she avoided it. And read her plays in the kitchen, or after he had gone to bed. With half an ear listening for the hall clock to strike one, Liz lost herself in Arthur Wing Pinero's world of *The Magistrate*.

The crust was hard and dry, but when Eddie broke it open, the inside of the roll was still moist and fresh. He gnawed at it, making it last, letting the hard flakes of crust soften in his mouth as Annie watched with obvious amusement.

'I don't reckon you've eaten anything for a week,' she told him.

'Maybe I haven't,' he admitted, sending crumbs flying. 'I don't know.'

She laughed at that. 'You want another one?' she wondered as she watched the roll disappear.

'You got one?'

'Can get one. But it'll cost you.' Her pale eyes glinted with mischief, and Eddie could guess what was coming.

'Got no money,' he admitted.

'A kiss then.'

He pulled a face and made a retching sound. Little Annie laughed again. But Eddie could tell that she was making light of her disappointment. She always did. One day perhaps he would give her a kiss, and see if she laughed then. Faint from the shock, more like.

Everyone called her little Annie, though she was as old as Eddie and slightly taller. But her dad, the baker, would tousle her hair with his floury hands and call her his little girl. Eddie liked Annie. He liked the way the flour flecked her dark hair, the way she half-smiled when she tried not to laugh. The way her eyes widened when she saw Eddie, and most of all the way she kept yesterday's rolls for him.

'Annie?'

She could sense he was going to ask her something serious, and frowned. 'Yes?'

'You know anything about talking to the dead?'

The frown froze on her face, lining her forehead and wrinkling the skin by her nose. 'You're weird, you are, Eddie Hopkins,' she said. 'Who do you know who's dead?'

Eddie grinned at her. 'Lots of people,' he said. He laughed out loud to see her flinch at that. But inside, he wasn't laughing.

A policeman called mid afternoon. He assured Liz and her father that a post mortem on Albert Wilkes was to be carried out that evening, and that the poor man's widow had been informed and the relevant permissions obtained. He made it sound very formal, and despite the way in which events had come about, Liz supposed it was.

That evening, after reading evensong from his battered Book of Common Prayer, Liz's father announced that he would retire early. Relieved, Liz helped him up the stairs. She did not want to be late meeting George Archer, and she had another appointment she intended to keep before that.

She sat on the top stair until the sound of her father's gentle snores was rhythmic and settled. Then Liz spent another fifteen minutes washing up the crockery and cutlery from supper and tidying the living room. She crept up the steps again, listening carefully to check her father was still settled and deeply asleep.

In the drawer of the kitchen table where Liz kept her playscript there was a sheet of cartridge paper. On it she had written a short message. The ink was faded from age and the paper was curling at the edges, but she saw no reason to write it out again. It was a short note to her father and he had never read it. Liz hoped he never would. She placed the sheet of paper prominently on the table in the living room where he would be sure to see it if he woke and came downstairs. It was not much of a letter, and while it did not tell the whole truth it was not actually a lie:

Dear Father

Since you were sleeping so soundly, I have taken the opportunity to go for a short walk. I feel the fresh air will do me good after such a long day.

Please do not worry, as I shall be back soon. I will look in on you on my return.

Your loving daughter
Elizabeth

The Chistleton Theatre was not an imposing building. Standing slightly back from the road, it was easy to miss unless you knew it was there. The frontage was narrow and bland, nothing like the decorated facades of the larger London theatres. It rarely boasted much of an audience, but the people who did come were keen and loyal.

Liz Oldfield barely glanced at the front of the building. It was dark and quiet – there was no performance this evening. A new play was in preparation, and Liz could just hear the sounds of the rehearsal. A deep voice was proclaiming loudly about the merits of afternoon tea, pausing at the end of each line of the script. She recognised it at once as the theatre's leading man – Nigel Braithwaite. He was loud and brash and not talented enough to have made it in the larger theatres. But he was also intelligent and modest enough to recognise the fact. Despite his bluff manner, he was willing to listen to the producer's advice and on the night he would be word perfect if not a hundred per cent convincing.

Braithwaite's volume increased when Liz opened the door, and continued to grow as she made her way through the narrow backstage corridor towards the auditorium. She stood in the flies, just off stage, hoping not to be noticed as she watched Marcus Jessop attempt to tone down his star's performance. Mary Manners was standing quietly beside Braithwaite on the stage, patient as ever.

'And Mary,' Jessop finished, 'that was fine thank you.'

The woman smiled thinly. She was playing the leading lady, which meant that both the main characters were rather older than the author had intended. But they complemented each other well, Liz thought. If she felt a moment's stab of regret that she had herself turned down Jessop's offer of a leading role – again – then she did not admit it, even to herself. One day, she had promised, one day she would take up that offer. One day she would have the time to commit herself to the theatre. But she scarcely dared think when that might be, or of the events that would have to take place to give her that freedom.

Until then, she would swell the crowd scenes, help with the props, perhaps even serve as prompter. Jessop had promised her a walk-on part, and she hoped and prayed she would not have to let him down. He seemed to have faith in her and she had earned a round of applause for her brief appearance in the last play – to

Mary Manners's distinct annoyance and Nigel Braithwaite's generous congratulation.

'You've got something I have to admit that I haven't,' Braithwaite had said quietly to Liz in the wings after the last night's performance. 'Talent. Skill. The audience responds to you.'

Jessop's voice jolted Liz back to the present: 'Is that Miss Oldfield I see lurking in the wings there?'

'Yes,' she admitted, stepping forward. 'I ordered the dresses and the hats. They should be delivered later in the week.'

'That's terrific, thanks ever so much,' Jessop told her. He ran down the centre aisle of the theatre from where he had been sitting half way back, and leaped on to the stage as if he was in his early twenties rather than his forties. 'Sorry you're reduced to helping with Wardrobe this time.'

Liz shook her head. 'That's all right. I'll do anything I can.'

Jessop nodded sympathetically. He had thinning dark hair and thin-framed glasses that caught the lights as his head moved. 'I know,' he said quietly. He had a bushy moustache that bristled and twitched when he spoke, and Liz always found herself watching that instead of meeting his eyes. 'Maybe next time, eh?'

'Maybe,' Liz said. It was what she always said, and at some point he would stop asking. 'I've got to go,' she told him. 'I have to leave in a few minutes, but I wanted to let you know that it is all in hand. And if there's anything else I can do to help . . . ?'

Jessop blew out a long sigh. 'Not unless you have any idea how we can make that ashtray . . .' He paused to indicate a silver-plated ashtray on a low wooden table on the stage beside them. 'Make that ashtray fly across the room and land in Mr Braithwaite's lap.'

Liz looked at the ashtray. Then she looked across the stage to where Braithwaite was sitting.

'No,' she said. 'Like the policeman in the play, I haven't a clue.'

'Pity,' Jessop said. He turned and made his way less enthusiastically back to the auditorium. 'Still, I expect we'll think of something.' He did not sound convinced.

The mortuary was little more than a hut with a wooden table standing unevenly in the middle of the damp floor. Doctor Jones washed his hands in a cracked tin basin in the corner of the room and then turned his attention to the final job of the day.

The body was already on the table. Jones was annoyed that the clothes had been removed. Someone had washed the corpse, which made Jones doubly-angry. How many times had he told them that the deceased was not to be touched save by himself. To have the clothes removed was to take away possibly vital evidence. To clean the body was to wash away more evidence. Even though this one had been in the ground for a week, he would still have liked to have met the man in his original condition. Preferably still in the coffin.

This was not morbid fascination on the part of Jones. Rather, it was typical of the methodical and meticulous way he approached his work. He did not pretend to enjoy his work for the police, and would have been happy to go home after finishing his general practice. But he suffered from a sense of duty, and he was very aware that if he did not help out when necessary then in all probability no one would.

The least he could expect, then, was that the body he was due to examine should not be tampered with. That this one had been was obvious from the moment he started his examination. He double-checked the notes he had been given, but there was no mention of a previous autopsy. Perhaps the notes were wrong – certainly surgery had been performed after death.

But, Jones thought, it would take a physician more dedicated and conscientious than himself to open up a cadaver and then sew it back together so carefully. And the places where incisions had been made – there was no sense to it at all. Jones stepped back from the table and surveyed the body of Albert Wilkes. The scars were obvious to anyone with any training. They seemed to run the length of the limbs. There was evidence of incisions in the chest and even under the receding hair-line. When he rolled the body on to its side he could see at once that the pattern of scars was repeated on the back of the corpse. But why? For what purpose?

Frowning and no longer tired or aware of the lateness of the hour, Jones set to work. Within minutes he was more puzzled than ever. After an hour he again stepped back from the table. He wiped his brow with his forearm. On the table beside the body was a long bone he had removed from the left leg. The flesh and skin that had surrounded it hung in loose flaps on the table. Jones just stared at it.

It did not take long for him to come to his decision. He opened the door of the small mortuary and called for the police constable who was posted to keep him company and lock up when he left.

'You all done, sir?' the constable asked hopefully. His hope visibly faded as he caught sight of Jones's expression. 'What is it, Doctor Jones?'

Jones turned and strode over to the small desk in the corner of the room. He took a pen, dipped it in ink, and scribbled furiously on a sheet of paper. When he was done, he folded it and wrote a name on it. He handed the stained paper to the police constable.

'I want you to take that to the station and have Sergeant Fisk or whoever is the most senior man on duty send it on to Sir William Protheroe at the British Museum.'

'Sir William Protheroe?'

Jones dried his hands on a discoloured towel and nodded at the body on the table. The constable made a point of not looking at it. 'I quote: "In the event of extraordinary results or findings that cannot be explained in the normal way of medical and anatomical understanding we are to inform Sir William Protheroe who will advise."' He tossed the towel into the corner of the room. 'So cut along, constable, and have him informed. And you'd best tell your sergeant that this matter is not to be pursued, unless Sir William specifically asks.'

'Right you are, sir.' The constable turned to go. 'Just out of interest, sir. Hope you don't think I'm prying. But, what is the problem with the dead gentleman?'

Jones smiled thinly at the man's deference. 'Apart from the fact that he is dead, which can't be a very satisfactory situation for him? Apart from that, the problem, as I have explained briefly to Protheroe in my note there, is that the bones in at least some of the dead gentleman's limbs are not his own. Not even human, come to that.' He sighed and looked back at the pale cadaver on the table. 'And if that doesn't run counter to our normal anatomical understanding of things, I don't know what does.'

Chapter 9

The body was laid out on a workbench in the room that Sir William Protheroe used as a laboratory. It was a large room at the back of the British Museum. To all intents and purposes this room together with Protheroe's rather smaller office, several large store rooms, and the persons of Protheroe himself and his assistant Garfield Berry constituted the entirety of The Department of Unclassified Artefacts.

Sir William had many skills, but he was not a professional pathologist. So rather than examine the body he turned his attention first to the notes provided by Doctor Jones. Each and every point the police pathologist made, Sir William himself checked with Berry's help on the corpse lying before them. Anything that Protheroe and Berry did not understand or could not verify, Berry noted down on a sheet of paper.

Finally, Protheroe came to the bones. From his knowledge of palaeontology and archaeology he had some understanding of how bone behaved after death.

He also had enough anatomical expertise to see at once that Jones had been right. The bone removed from Albert Wilkes's left leg was not a human bone at all.

Under Protheroe's direction, Berry weighed the bone, measured it, drew a scale diagram. 'What do you think is up with this chap?' Berry asked as he labelled his diagram.

Protheroe made a non-committal sound. He was examining the corpse's right arm, feeling along the scar that ran down it. 'Pass me that scalpel, will you?'

Berry put down his drawing and passed the surgical knife. He winced as he watched Protheroe open up the arm along the scar. Turned away as the elderly man folded back the dead greying skin and pushed his fingers inside. 'How very curious,' he murmured.

'What, sir?'

'I thought I was right with that bone from the leg. Now I'm sure.' He held the slippery bone for Berry to take. It was surprisingly heavy.

There was something else odd about it too, Berry realised as he rinsed it in the laboratory sink. It had run the entire length of the arm, yet it was a single bone. He turned to Protheroe, and saw that the man was watching him, nodding with encouragement, drawing out the obvious question.

'This can't be right,' Berry said. 'There's no joint. It's all one piece. Where's the elbow?'

'A very good question,' Protheroe conceded. 'Another good question is how this bone could ever have connected to the wrist. Or the shoulder, come to that.' He paused to consult a page of handwritten notes. 'This Doctor Jones is both very thorough and very astute,' he said quietly.

'I don't understand.' Berry laid the bone down next to the one taken from the dead man's leg. 'Are you suggesting this man had no elbow? That his joints were not connected?'

'I am not suggesting anything,' Sir William Protheroe said. He poked at the bone from the arm. 'But as Jones surmised this is most certainly not a human bone. In fact, unlike Jones, I recognise it quite distinctly.'

Berry just stared at the bones. 'Then what . . . ?' He wasn't even sure what question he should be asking.

'This man,' Protheroe said quietly, 'has the bones of a dinosaur.'

'You did what?' It was difficult to tell if George Archer was more annoyed or surprised.

Eddie had thought they would be pleased. He had waited until Liz arrived at George's house before stepping out from the shadow of an oak tree on the other side of the street. The door had opened immediately to his knocking, and at first both George and Liz had seemed pleased to see him.

Then he told them what he had done that after-noon. It provoked anger and disbelief from George. Liz went pale and quiet. There was silence for several moments, then both the adults seemed to slump into their chairs.

Eddie perched on the edge of George's threadbare sofa and waited for further reaction. When there was none, he decided that they must be waiting for him to tell them more. 'I didn't use your real names, of course,' he said, in case that was what worried them.

'Oh good,' George said weakly.

'No, they're expecting Mr and Mrs Smith.' Eddie grinned at his improvisation.

'Smith?' Liz said. Her voice sounded strained. 'I don't suppose they will believe that for a minute.'

'Couldn't you have chosen something less obvi-ously false?' George wanted to know.

Eddie sighed. 'It's all arranged,' he told them. 'There's some other people there too, but this Madame Sophia said she can squeeze you in.' Now came the bit they really wouldn't like, and Eddie cleared his throat and lowered his voice to add: 'for only three shillings.'

It looked for a second as if George was about to explode. 'Three shillings?!' He blinked and mouthed words that failed to appear, then shook his head. 'Three *shillings*?' he said again. 'For something I don't even want to go to – for a séance?'

'It's normally six,' Eddie said. 'I haggled them down to a shilling each.'

'Well, that's a mercy,' George said with more than a hint of sarcasm.

'If you don't go, you won't have to pay,' Eddie pointed out. 'But I think you should. If this Wilkes bloke is dead and you want to ask him what's going on and that, it's your only way.'

'It's Percy I'd really like to talk to,' George said quietly.

'Percy?'

'Percy Smythe,' Liz explained. 'George's other friend at the Museum. The man who was cataloguing the diaries. He's dead too,' she added.

Eddie laughed. 'There you are then. Two for the price of one. Bargain. What you complaining about?'

'I suppose it would do no harm,' Liz murmured. It seemed to Eddie that despite her earlier protests she was looking forward to the experience.

'You're serious?' George asked in surprise. 'You think we should go?'

Liz considered a moment, then nodded. 'What have we got to lose?'

'Three shillings.' George stood up thrust his hands into his trouser pockets as he thought about it. Slowly he turned towards Eddie. 'You said you got them down to a shilling each.'

'Wasn't easy.'

George held up his hand and counted on his fingers. 'Mr Smith, that's me. Mrs Smith, that's Liz.' He waggled the fingers. 'That's only two shillings.'

'You're forgetting young Master Smith,' Eddie said. 'That's me.'

Liz was on her feet now. 'Oh no,' she said. 'Oh no, no, no.'

Eddie leaped up too. 'What do you mean, "no no no"? Whose idea was this?' Eddie demanded. 'Who arranged everything? I'm coming.' Eddie folded his arms and sat down.

'No,' George said. 'No, you're not. This is your chance to get a good night's sleep. You can have the spare room. It used to be my father's.'

'I'm coming,' Eddie repeated, not looking at either of them.

'Either George and I go – alone,' Liz said sternly, 'or none of us is going.'

There was no changing her mind. George seemed to find the whole thing amusing, which just made Eddie all the more annoyed.

'I'll show you the room,' George said.

They all trouped up the narrow staircase and George led Eddie to a small room that contained a narrow bed and little else. The window gave a view of a tree, its branches dark and skeletal against the grey of the night sky. There was a key in the door and Eddie eyed it suspiciously.

'You're not locking me in.'

'I would hope we don't have to,' Liz said. 'Do we?'

Eddie looked at her.

'Do we?' she repeated.

'All right, I'll give you my word of honour,' Eddie told her solemnly. 'I'm not coming out of that door till you get back. Not unless I 'ave to. Happy?'

'What do you mean by "unless I 'ave to"?' Liz mimicked Eddie's accent, and he smiled despite himself.

'Well, if there's a fire, or someone comes to the door, or I need to go for a –'

'All right, that's fine,' Liz agreed quickly. She took a step towards Eddie, and for a moment he was afraid she was going to give him a hug. But she settled for: 'Goodbye. We'll look in on you when we get back and if you're awake tell you what happened.'

'I won't be asleep,' Eddie told her indignantly. 'And if I am, you can wake me up.'

Eddie waited until he heard the front door close behind them. Then he went to the window and looked out. The room was at the front of the house, so he could see the dark figures of George and Liz walking down the street outside. He glanced back at the door and sucked in his cheeks as he thought. He had given them his word he wouldn't go out the door, and Eddie was not one to go back on his promise. His word was his bond, and he sensed that they both knew that.

He waited another minute to be sure that Liz and George had reached the end of the street. Then he undid the catch and opened the window.

Chapter 10

The Atlantian Club was only ten minutes' brisk walk from the British Museum. Sir William Protheroe sat alone in the oak-panelled dining room, thinking carefully through the events and discoveries of the evening. No one joined him for dinner – the people who knew him well enough could also see that he was deep in contemplation. They knew better than to disturb him.

By the time he had finished dinner, Protheroe had already forgotten what he had eaten. He thanked Vespers the chief steward of the club, nodded in greeting to Sir Henry Walthamstow and a few other acquaintances, and made his way back through the chill of the night to the Museum.

He had several ideas about the body, and was ready to start putting them to the test. Protheroe had sent Berry home before he himself headed off to the club for dinner, so the few rooms that constituted the Department of Unclassified Artefacts were dark and empty. He lit the lamps in the main specimen room.

Their flames flickered in the glass doors of cabinets and cases, dancing across artefacts that should not, according to science, exist.

But the workbench was bare. The body of Albert Wilkes, and the bones that Protheroe had removed for examination, were gone.

'Is there anybody there?' The room was almost totally dark and Madame Sophia's voice was a ghostly wail that echoed in the gloom.

George had decided that the séance was a waste of time as soon as Madame Sophia greeted 'Mr and Mrs Smith' at the door and bustled them into her parlour. She gave almost every impression of being a scatty, eccentric lady of a certain age. But her sharp eyes gave her away. George could almost feel himself being sized up by the woman. If she had licked her lips in anticipation, it would not have surprised him.

Liz on the other hand seemed to be completely taken in. She sat carefully and attentively at the large round table in the middle of the cluttered parlour and seemed to hang on Madame Sophia's every word.

There were six of them in all. Madame Sophia's husband was a small man with a sharp nose on which was perched a pair of wire-rimmed spectacles. He was forever rubbing his hands together and had a permanent stoop that George thought made him look like a fictional money-lender. Madame Sophia introduced him as 'my husband Gerald'.

Mr and Mrs Paterson made up the six. Mrs Paterson was a small, timid, white-haired woman, while Mr Paterson was a huge, broad-shouldered man who was so fat he had to sit well back from the table. His hair was as black as his wife's was white, and slicked across the top of his head with oil.

'I do hope the spirits will be kind to us tonight,' Mrs Paterson said as husband Gerald turned down the lights. Her voice was shrill, like a bird pecking for a worm. Gerald was preoccupied with something on the dresser at the back of the room.

'Oh so do I,' Liz said, sounding eager and excited. 'It's all so enthralling.'

George said nothing. In the near-darkness, he was aware of Mrs Paterson's fingers coldly meeting his own as they spread their hands across the table. If they hadn't been twitching, he might have imagined he was touching a corpse. On his other side, Liz's fingers were warm and comforting.

'Is there anybody there?' Madame Sophia repeated.

George looked round, trying to see if everyone else was attentive. Something moved at the corner of his vision, a slight ripple of light in the emptiness. For a moment his heart flickered – a spirit? He stared, trying to make it out.

A bell rang. The sudden jangling made Mrs Paterson's hand leap away from George's in surprise. 'They are here!' she hissed. 'The bell!'

'What bell?' George asked, despite himself. He could see now that the dim light from one of the gas lamps had caught on a thread as it moved. A pale, thin thread that stretched across the back of the room.

'On the dresser,' Madame Sophia explained. 'The spirits have taken to ringing the bell when they are preparing to make themselves known to us.'

George grinned in the dark. 'How very convenient for us,' he said. The thread he had glimpsed stretched to the dresser, and he would be willing to bet it was attached to the bell. But before he could decide whether or how to tell Liz, he felt her hand shift too.

'Look!' she gasped. Liz had raised her arm, dark silhouette pointing across the room towards the door. 'A spirit,' she breathed. 'At the door.'

George shifted slightly to see the door. And sure enough, a pale, ghostly face was staring back at him.

'Don't look,' Husband Gerald whispered loudly. 'They don't like you to stare.'

'And please don't break the circle,' Madame Sophia said. 'That could be very dangerous indeed.'

'Of course,' Liz said, returning her hand to its position next to George's. He thought he could detect a hint of amusement in her tone, and as if to tell him he was right, her fingers tapped the back of his hand.

'Yes,' Madame Sophia was saying. 'Yes, I can hear

you . . . You wish to speak to someone here?' Her voice had taken on an ethereal, sing-song quality. The bell rang again. 'You do!' Sophia exclaimed in delight. 'And your name is . . . Edward.'

'Edward?' Liz's voice was shaking with emotion. 'Not Edward?'

'You know an Edward? Someone who has passed over?' Husband Gerald asked. There was a glimmer of satisfaction in his voice.

'Why, no,' Liz said. 'It just sounds such a nice name. For someone who is dead.'

George stifled a laugh. 'I don't know any Edward either,' he said helpfully.

'It's a small world,' Liz told him in apparent seriousness.

'No wait,' Sophia interrupted quickly. 'Edward is his spirit name. Here on Earth he would have been known as . . .' She hesitated, for all the world as if listening to a voice that George and the others could not hear. 'As . . .' she added impatiently after a few moments.

'It isn't,' Mrs Paterson said in a squeak. 'I mean, it couldn't be – could it?' She gave a table-jolting sigh. 'Not little Andrew?'

'Why yes.' Sophia seemed surprised. 'That is what he says his name was. Andrew. There is another name . . .' She made no effort to give it.

'Griffiths,' Liz said with conviction.

'Andrew Griffiths,' Sophia agreed. Then she realised

that it was Liz who had spoken. 'Er, is not the name,' she finished.

'Andrew Jones?' George suggested.

'Do we all have to guess?' Mr Paterson asked. He sounded bored.

'My brother,' Mrs Paterson explained with an oblivious sob. 'He . . . passed over when we were children.'

'It *is* a child,' Madame Sophia confirmed, as if this was something that she had simply forgotten to mention in all the excitement.

'We were hoping for an Albert,' Liz said sternly.

George sensed she had had enough of this. 'Or a Percy,' he added, trying to sound equally stern.

'The spirits are not at our beck and call,' Husband Gerald reprimanded them.

'Oh, aren't they?' Liz murmured, just loud enough for George to hear. Then a moment later: 'Look!' she gasped.

Their eyes had grown accustomed to the darkness now, and everyone looked where Liz pointed. They all saw a white shape, formless and ethereal, hanging in the air above the table. It shimmered and twisted as if trying to become real, dancing across the room towards the dresser. It disappeared into the darkness and the bell gave a startled jangle.

Mrs Paterson clapped her hands together in delight. 'A ghost. Oh, do say I have seen one of the spirits.'

But Madame Sophia did not answer. She was staring

open-mouthed across at the dresser. 'I don't . . .' she muttered. 'I never . . .' She turned white-faced towards Husband Gerald. But he too seemed pale and shocked.

'Is that the end?' Mr Paterson demanded. 'Show over, is it? Can we go home now?'

George was about to say that he thought they probably could. But then, the table levitated. He was not actually aware of it happening until Liz gave a startled gasp. 'The table,' she cried out. 'It's moving. Can't you feel it?'

Her eyes were wide and pale in the gloom as she looked round at them. 'There it goes again. Oh, my goodness – it's rising up. You must be able to feel it.'

George could indeed. And by the ashen expressions on the dimly lit faces of everyone else so could they.

'You can tell it's moving, can't you, Mr Smith, dear,' Liz said to George. He nodded dumbly, really nervous for the first time since they had sat down. But despite her apparent anxiety, she winked at George. 'Oh my goodness,' she said as she did so. 'Here it goes again.'

The new delivery boy was charming, if rather scruffy, Mrs White decided. She was surprised he had been sent out so late, but the lad insisted that this was his last delivery of the day and he would be off home soon. But could he beg a quick cup of tea before he went – just to keep out the cold of the night?

Mrs White was the cook, not a maid, so she wasn't

in the habit of making tea for delivery boys. But he seemed so cold and exhausted that she made an exception. And after all, he had come out late in the night to her kitchen. He was a chatty boy. Well, he didn't talk an awful lot, but he was interested.

He told Mrs White that he had heard that the house was used for séances and the like. 'Are you a believer in the afterlife and all that?' he asked her.

So she told him. Yes, she thought there was probably something in it. So many people thought so, after all. Not that you would want to come here to find proof, she told him.

'Oh?' He seemed surprised.

Mrs White shook her head. 'Madame Sophia, she calls herself. Sophie Southgate's her real name, but she never uses that. No, nothing's real here.'

'What do you mean?'

But Mrs White refused to be drawn. 'It's not my place to say, young man. More than my job's worth.'

'That's all right,' the boy assured her. He finished his drink. 'Thanks for the tea.'

The boy handed her his cup, and Mrs White took it over to the sink. When she turned back, the boy was gone. Funny, she thought – she had not heard the outside door. He was a strange one, working all hours, demanding tea, then just slipping away like that. Still, it was kind of him to bring the . . .

Mrs White frowned. What was it the boy had

delivered? For the life of her she could not remember. She blew out a long breath. It had been a tiring day. She locked the outside door before making her way up to the servants quarters, and bed.

Liz was having fun. She had realised almost at once, just as she assumed George had, that it was all a fake. At first she had considered going along with it, appearing to be impressed, then making as early an escape as possible. But soon she decided that if she was wasting her time she might as well enjoy herself while she did it.

Husband Gerald was sitting next to her, and Liz could see his leg jerk every time the bell rang. It did not require much imagination to work out that there was – literally – a connection. The face painted on the door had provoked a quick frisson. But again, she knew all about luminous paint from the theatre.

Confusing and misleading Madame Sophia was almost too easy, so Liz tried to think what else she could do to liven up the proceedings. It was a challenge, to see if she could beat Madame Sophia and Husband Gerald at their own game – could convince them that they were experiencing genuine spiritual moments through the simplest of tricks. Throwing her handkerchief across the room with the same movement as pointing had worked well. The lacy material seemed almost to hang in the air before landing on the dresser and – with a stroke of good fortune – knocking the bell. But Husband Gerald had glared at her, evidently not convinced.

So she turned her attention to the table. It was not really levitating. She nudged and jiggled the heavy wooden table with her knees, just enough for the séance participants all to feel some slight movement. In the darkened room, their minds attuned to the possibility of mysterious happenings, Liz's insistence that the table was levitating might be enough for their imaginations to do the rest.

It worked better than she had hoped. Even Husband Gerald gasped in surprise, and seemed to be trying to push the table back down – into the floor. George too seemed taken in, bless him. His eyes were wide with amazement. Mrs Paterson was shrieking with a mixture of delight and fear. Mr Paterson was grumbling as if bored with the whole thing, but Madame Sophia herself was rocking backwards and forwards and keening like a child at Christmas.

After a while they seemed to decide that the table had stopped moving and some semblance of order was restored. Husband Gerald suggested in a strained voice that perhaps they might try something else. He excused himself from the table for a moment, and turned up the lights. Liz guessed this was as much for his own peace of mind as anything.

Madame Sophia was also in something of a state,

but in her case it was closer to euphoria. The notion that the spirits actually *had* visited her séance seemed almost too much for her, turning her into a bundle of nervous excitement and bubbling enthusiasm.

'The glass, Gerald dear, the glass. And the cards. I shall do the cards.'

Gerald soon gave up trying to persuade her that perhaps they had entertained enough spirits for one night, and fetched a glass tumbler. This was placed upside-down in the middle of the table. Then Gerald, with help from everyone else, arranged a set of cards – a letter printed on each – in alphabetical order clockwise round the table.

'Now,' Madame Sophia said in a stage whisper, 'who shall we contact?'

Liz glanced at George. This was obviously a complete waste of time, but George was watching with interest and enthusiasm. There was no way to tell him that she, Liz, had orchestrated much of what had happened while the rest was simple stage trickery.

'Albert Wilkes,' George said. 'We want to make contact with a gentleman who recently departed this life named Albert Wilkes.'

Madame Sophia smiled confidently. 'And so we shall,' she said. 'Do you have any small thing, some personal possession or other that I may use to focus my communications.'

Liz sighed. Probably she wanted it to glean any

clues about the dead person. Perhaps, since George had nothing that had belonged to Wilkes, this would soon be over.

But to Liz's surprise and horror, George had taken out his wallet. He passed the scrap of paper from Glick's diary carefully across the table to Madame Sophia. She inspected it somewhat dismissively.

'It's worth a try,' George mouthed to Liz. She sighed.

'I suppose this will have to do,' she decided, and set it down on the table in front of her, next to the letter 'A'. 'Fingers on the glass,' she instructed. She kept one of her hands pressed down on the fragment of paper. Her eyelids fluttered.

'Don't be disappointed if we fail to make contact,' Gerald warned.

'We won't,' Liz assured him.

But her words were drowned out by Madame Sophia's sudden shriek. 'He is here,' she exclaimed in surprise and delight. 'Albert Wilkes. His spirit is still in the land of the living. He is with us now!'

In the laboratory at the back of a large house, Albert Wilkes sat up. His movement was stiff, his eyes were unseeing pearl-like marbles.

'The vocal cords have atrophied,' the man standing beside the workbench said. 'But he should still be able to write.'

'We got no sense out of him last time, sir,' Blade observed. 'That was why we sent him off to the Museum for the diaries. Except he ignored us and went home instead.'

The other man was nodding. 'I am aware of the problems. But despite Sir William's meddling, I am optimistic. Now that we have a little more time, the bones have been properly replaced, and while they are not actually his own they will more than suffice. The brain has been subjected to an improved form of electrical stimulation which I hope will this time have shocked it into some semblance at least of sense as well as life. I need sentience as well as instinct.'

'Speak to us,' Madame Sophia intoned. 'You are troubled, I can sense that. Do you have a message for anyone here? For Mr Smith perhaps? Anything?'

Beneath her fingers, Liz felt the glass tumbler tremble. She looked round at the others seated at the table. They all seemed equally surprised. Then the glass began to move.

'A pen, sir?' Blade offered. He was unable to take his eyes off the dead man.

'If you please. Of course,' his master went on as Blade took a pen from the desk and dipped it in an inkwell, 'despite my best efforts, the brain may be damaged beyond the point of repair.'

'He has been dead rather a long time, sir.'

The lifeless fingers closed coldly on the pen, and Blade

suppressed a shudder. He placed a sheet of paper on the
workbench under the poised, dead hand.

Liz was as sure as she could be that it was not movement caused deliberately by anyone there. The glass
quivered and shook like a struck tuning fork. It circled
slowly, as if trying to make up its mind which letter it
wanted.

'Yes?' Madame Sophia hissed excitedly. 'Yes? Tell us,
please. What is your message, you poor tortured soul?'

'Now, Mr Wilkes,' the man said gently, 'you are quite aware
of what I want to know. Be so good as to write it down
would you?'

Nothing. No flicker of understanding or tremor of move-
ment from the corpse.

'Write it down!' the man shouted with a ferocity that
made the windows rattle. 'Or would you rather Blade
returned you to the ground?'

Slowly, deliberately, the pen stroked at the paper.

The glass paused, then trembled again. It moved directly
across the table towards George, stopping by the card
imprinted with the letter 'O'. It hesitated only a
moment, then it moved again. Not far, just a few letters clockwise round the table: 'R'.

Wilkes's fragile hand continued to move slowly over the

paper. His dead eyes did not look down. Another letter was slowly inked on the page.

Next was 'I'. Liz could almost feel the tension in the room. Everyone seemed to be holding their breath.

'O R I,' Gerald said quietly. 'What can it mean . . . Origin?'

'Hush,' Madame Sophia said, surprisingly gently. The glass trembled again.

'Thank you.' The man's breath misted the cold night air. It didn't do to mix warmth with death.

Blade waited for Wilkes to finish. Then he took the sheet of paper. He swallowed dryly when he saw what was on it. He handed it to his employer without comment.

Next was 'M'. Liz's throat was dry. It was just a trick, she kept telling herself. But both Gerald and Madame Sophia seemed as caught up in it as anyone. Just a trick – surely it was just a trick.

The glass moved again, heading for another letter.

The man stared at the paper for several moments, breathing deeply as he struggled to keep control. Five uneven characters were scratched into the paper. Ragged and useless:

O R I M O

'Another O,' George said out loud.

The glass stopped. It wasn't trembling any more. The strange life it had taken on seemed to have deserted it again.

As if to confirm this, Madame Sophia let out a long, deep sigh. 'He has gone,' she announced. 'He has left us. The link is broken.' She lifted her hand from the table and carefully passed the scrap of paper back to George. But despite the disappointment of contact being lost, she was smiling.

He crushed the paper into a ball and hurled it across the laboratory. The man was trembling with anger, but when he spoke his voice was cold and controlled.

'Dead too long, it seems. There is something lingering, but not enough. I think, Mr Blade, we shall have to try a different approach.' He snapped his fingers impatiently. 'Paper and pen. Quickly, man.'

Blade hurried to oblige. He took the pen from Wilkes, dipped it in the ink again, and returned it to the dead man's grasp.

'Not for him, you dolt! Give it to me.'

'I'm sorry, sir. I thought—'

'You are not paid to think,' Augustus Lorimore said, snatching the sheet of paper that Blade offered him. 'Now leave me in peace for ten minutes. Then I will have a letter for you to deliver.'

Chapter 11

Madame Sophia seemed still in a daze. Mrs Paterson was pale and shocked, her husband blinked when the lights were relit, as if he had just woken up. Without ceremony, Husband Gerald ushered the Patersons to the door and out into the hall. Liz could hear him talking to them in a low voice – accepting their money or making an appointment for a further consultation no doubt.

'The table,' George said in disbelief. 'That was incredible.'

'Thank you,' Liz said with a smile.

But before she could explain, Husband Gerald was back. He stood in the doorway, staring at Liz and George. He did not look happy, and he had undergone a transformation. No longer was he the dithering, ineffectual little man dancing to his wife's instructions. To George, the man seemed bigger than before. His eyes were cold and hard.

'How much of that was real?' he asked.

George frowned. 'What do you mean?'

'You know very well what I mean,' he snapped back. 'But I wasn't asking you. Sophia?'

'Oh the spirits came,' Madame Sophia told him. She still seemed to be in a state of near rapture. 'No doubt about it. They touched my mind – just like in the old days. Just like they used to.'

'Are you telling me you really used to be able to communicate with the spirit world?' Liz asked.

'But of course. Though you must be very powerful, my dear.' She got up from the table and walked slowly towards Liz and George. There was something menacing about her movement. 'Very powerful indeed to levitate the table like that. I know it wasn't me.'

'It wasn't me either,' Liz said quietly. 'The table didn't levitate.'

Husband Gerald was nodding as if he had guessed as much. But it was news to George.

'People will believe what they want to,' Liz admitted. 'I told you the table was levitating and that was what you, and that poor gullible Mrs Paterson wanted to hear. It didn't lift at all really.'

'Oh,' Madame Sophia said quietly. 'So it was a trick. That really is most unfair.'

Liz gave a short humourless laugh. 'It's all right for you to trick Mrs Paterson, though isn't it? How much did you want from her? How much does it cost to believe you're communing with the spirits of lost loved ones?'

'That's no concern of yours,' Gerald told her sharply. He was standing in the doorway and he did not look like he was going to move for them.

'I think it's time we were leaving,' George said. He wasn't quite sure what to make of the evening, but he was sure he wanted to get out of this house as soon as he possibly could.

'Oh I think you should stay a while yet,' Gerald said. His voice was low and threatening. 'My wife has some questions she would like to put to you. If you really do have the ability . . .'

'We don't,' Liz said. 'Look, I'm not sure what happened there with the glass and the letters, but it was nothing to do with us.'

'His spirit felt so strong,' Sophia said. 'I could feel it here, almost in the room with us. You have to tell me how you made such close contact.'

George was beginning to think he would have to physically move Gerald out of the doorway. He hoped the man wouldn't call for help from some burly servant or claim he had been assaulted. 'Let us pass, please,' George said in what he hoped was a menacing voice.

'No,' Gerald insisted. 'You came here under false pretences, and obviously under false names. You are not leaving until we have a satisfactory explanation of your conduct this evening.'

George looked at Liz, and he could see in her face that she was ready for whatever unpleasantness might follow.

But before either of them could do anything, there came an urgent shout:

'Fire!'

George flinched. For a moment he thought Gerald was ordering them to be shot. But the shout had come from outside the room – loud and urgent.

'There's a fire. Everyone out, quick. Get the brigade! Hurry!'

Distracted, both Sophia and Gerald turned towards the sound. Coiled up and ready to move, George did not waste the moment. He shoved Gerald aside, out of the doorway. Liz was with him immediately, and together they ran down the hall to the front door. A maid was already there, pulling the bolt across and unlocking the door.

'Where's the fire?' she asked, her eyes wide with anxiety. She looked deathly pale. 'Where's Mrs White?'

George did not pause to answer. He heaved open the door and dragged Liz through. They did not stop running until they reached the end of the street.

~

'Theatre?' The surprise was evident in George's tone.

'What's wrong with that?' Liz demanded, at once on the defensive.

'Nothing. I was surprised, that's all. Though . . .' He shrugged and walked on.

'Though what?' she asked suspiciously.

'Though, I suppose I shouldn't be. Not after tonight's performance.' He paused under a lamp-post, grinning in the diffuse light. 'I was quite taken in by that table routine, you know.'

Liz glanced back as they walked on. Just for a second she had thought there was someone behind them. Someone following. But she could see no one, and hear nothing save the distant chimes of a clock and the clatter of a carriage in a nearby street.

'I've never really been interested in the theatre,' George was saying. 'Well, not really. Not the plays anyway. I'm interested in the mechanisms.'

'Mechanisms?'

'The way the curtains are operated. The manner in which scenery is changed, backcloths dropped in. Trap doors. That sort of thing. I am an engineer, after all.'

'You might be able to help with a theatrical mechanism of ours, actually,' Liz realised. 'Mr Jessop, our producer, is having some trouble with an ashtray.'

'An ashtray?'

'A silver ashtray. It has to fly across the stage from a table and land in a person's lap several yards away. It is presenting something of a problem.'

George thought about this for several moments. 'I would need to know the size and weight of the ashtray,' he decided. 'And the distance it must travel. But I imagine a simple spring and a hair trigger release would do the trick.'

At some point during their conversation, Liz had taken George's arm. She was not sure exactly when this had been. She squeezed it to be sure that he had noticed.

George stiffened. 'What was that?' He pulled his arm gently free from hers and held up his hand to silence her. 'I heard something. Behind us.'

'I did think we were being followed earlier,' Liz admitted.

'Yes. There's someone there, in the shadows, look.' He raised his voice, calling: 'Come on out, whoever you are.'

'We know you're there,' Liz added, trying to keep the nerves out of her voice.

A small dark figure detached itself from a different shadow to the one Liz had been shouting at. 'Cor blimey!' it exclaimed. 'It's taken you long enough, ain't it?'

'I thought you promised not to leave the room,' George spluttered.

'I promised not to go out the door,' Eddie corrected him. 'And I didn't. I climbed out the window,' he explained, as if this was completely reasonable. 'How was the séance then? Did you talk to the spirit of Mr Wilkes?'

'I'm not really sure,' George admitted. 'It was most peculiar.'

'The business with the glass did seem genuine

somehow,' Liz agreed, 'though the rest of the show was trickery and illusion.'

Eddie nodded. 'Lot of it about. So what's this glass business, then?'

'It spelled out letters,' George explained. 'Though they don't make much sense.'

'O R I M O,' Liz told him.

'Well, that's something, innit?'

'Hardly,' George said, 'we were lucky to escape an unfortunate situation.'

'Luck was it? Eddie asked. He seemed to be trying not to laugh.

'Yes,' Liz told him. 'A rather unpleasant gentleman was keen to know how to contact the spirit world. Luckily there was a fire somewhere in the house, and he was distracted.'

'There weren't no fire,' Eddie said.

'How do you know?' George asked. 'You weren't there.'

Eddie coughed. 'There weren't no fire,' he repeated. 'Someone shouted fire as a distraction.'

Liz frowned. 'But who would . . .' She stopped as she realised what Eddie was telling them.

'You *were* there?' George had realised too. 'After all we said, after what we agreed? How can we ever trust you again after this?'

'There's gratitude,' Eddie complained.

Eddie had a point, Liz thought. She was angry with

him too, but it was lucky that he had been there with his wits about him. She sighed, trying to explain. 'Look, we're grateful for the help, really we are.'

'Don't sound it. You never do. If Blade finds you he's going to want his bit of paper. If he finds me, he'll likely cut my throat. Now it seems like we got a clue from this séance and I get not a word of thanks for the idea nor for saving you at the end of it. You don't believe I can do anything to help, though I'm in just as deep as you are. Don't even believe I saw a monster either, do you?'

'You were scared,' Liz said gently. 'It could have been a tree or anything.'

'I know what I saw,' Eddie said. 'You weren't there. But I was. You just don't trust me.'

'Leave him be,' George told Liz. 'If he's got it into his head there's a monster, we won't talk him out of it.' They continued down the street in uneasy silence.

The moon was a pale sliver of light that danced in and out of the scudding clouds. Crouched in amongst the trees, Eddie began to wonder if this was a good idea after all.

He had been angry with George and Liz when they laughed at his story about the monster. George had told him it was all his imagination. Although Liz had been sympathetic, she had agreed with George. But Eddie knew what he had seen.

Yet Liz and George weren't interested. George had offered to walk Liz home and they had agreed to meet again tomorrow when George had a day off from the Museum. There was a mystery here that he could solve, Eddie was certain, but they just weren't seeing it. There was a monster, and it lived near where Albert Wilkes had disappeared – in the grounds of the house where those men had taken him. That wasn't just by chance, there had to be some connection. Well, he'd show them. He would go back, he had decided, and get proof. He didn't know what sort of proof, but he'd find it.

That had been the plan. Now he was not so sure. He had to climb over the wall because there was a man on guard at the gate. Now he found there were more men patrolling the grounds. Eddie was shivering in the cold, hiding behind a tree and hoping the moon stayed hidden until the second man, the one guarding the house, had gone.

Eddie had seen him walking first one way then the other. The man paused to stamp his feet in the cold or to light a cigarette. In the brief flashes of thin moonlight, Eddie could see him clearly on the gravel pathway. He was stocky, his bulk emphasised by his heavy coat. A cap was pulled down low over his eyes, and over his shoulder was slung what Eddie had at first thought was a fishing rod.

But as he crept closer, he saw that it was a shotgun. Eddie quickly slunk back into the trees and wondered if he had been foolish to come here. Perhaps he should have waited until morning and tried to convince George and Liz to come with him.

'They didn't believe me before, they wouldn't believe me then,' he murmured to himself. No, it was up to Eddie to investigate on his own. He held his breath as the guard walked close in front of him and didn't exhale again until the guard was long gone. He watched the guard disappear into the mist, waited until he could no longer hear the crunch of the man's feet on the gravel. Then Eddie ran quickly and quietly in the opposite direction. Towards the place where he had seen the monster.

The more he thought about it, the more he thought that maybe George was right, about the monster at least. What had he really seen? A tree blowing in the breeze, its branches clutching like claws? Dark clouds hurrying across the sky?

He was running on the grass so as to make no noise. The house was a dark shape across the gravel drive that ran around it. As he came round the side of the house, Eddie could see a large room jutting out of the back as if recently added. Light was seeping round the edges of huge blacked-out windows. A thumping sound made him stop abruptly. The sound stopped too, and he realised it was his feet. He was no longer on grass.

Eddie stopped and looked down. He was on a narrow gravel path which seemed to run from the house towards the trees. Or rather, as the moon dipped out from behind the clouds, he could see it led to a small hut positioned just at the edge of the wooded area.

As he drew closer, he could see that the hut was much bigger than he thought. The whole of the front was a large wooden door with a heavy iron bar resting across brackets to keep it shut. It was too heavy for Eddie to lift.

What was behind the doors? A coal bunker perhaps? Storage for garden tools? Eddie pressed his ear to the rough wood. There was something inside. He could hear it. He strained to work out what it was. A puffing, rasping, regular rush of sound. It lasted several seconds then stopped. After a pause it came again.

The clouds parted to reveal the moon, and in the increased light Eddie glanced back – to see the guard with the gun coming round the path from the front of the house. Quickly and quietly, he slipped round the side of the hut. It was built of brick, he realised – solid and substantial. He waited a moment, then made a dash for the trees.

The man continued his patrol, oblivious to Eddie's presence. But Eddie was not watching him. He was staring back at the dark smudge that was the hut. What had he heard? Was it the sound of a train on the underground perhaps? Maybe there was a tunnel close to the coal chute or whatever was behind the doors. Or maybe it was water rushing through a sewer.

But no matter what Eddie thought it might be, nothing could displace his first impression. The thought that it sounded like something breathing.

Chapter 12

Eddie was exhausted when he finally climbed into bed. He fell asleep almost at once, dreaming of fog and monsters and men with guns.

He was wakened by the light streaming in through the open window and the sounds of London. Carriages clattered past in the street outside; paper boys shouted headlines; someone cursed loudly. And an enticing smell of bacon wafted up the stairs. It was the smell that revived Eddie and which reminded him where he was. He hadn't bothered even to take his jacket off, so he went straight downstairs.

There was a small kitchen at the back of the house. 'Something smells nice,' Eddie announced as he went in.

George was standing by a little stove. He flinched visibly at Eddie's voice and almost dropped the frying pan he was holding through a wrapped tea towel.

'Dear Lord, you gave me the fright of my life,' George said when he had recovered a little. The bacon hissed and sizzled in the pan.

Eddie was laughing. 'I could see that.'

'How did you get in here?'

Eddie frowned. 'You gave me use of the room. Said I could sleep in there.'

'Yes, but you weren't there last night when I got back from escorting Miss Oldfield home. I thought you'd be waiting outside.'

'Can't help that.' Eddie leaned over the stove to inspect the bacon. 'There's not much in there. You not having breakfast, then?'

George moved him aside. 'I didn't know you were here.'

'Must have got back after you then,' Eddie said. 'You can get in through windows as well as out of them.' He pronounced it 'win-ders'.

George was about to respond to this when he was pre-empted by a loud knocking from the front door.

'Might be the postman,' Eddie decided. 'I'll go and see.'

'You will not,' George told him firmly. 'You will stay and finish cooking my breakfast.'

'What about *my* breakfast, then?' But George had already gone. So Eddie picked up a dirty fork from the wooden table in the middle of the small kitchen and helped himself to a rasher of bacon out of the pan.

Augustus Lorimore paced up and down in front of a display case of stuffed birds. His face was pale and drawn with anger. 'This Protheroe,' he snapped, 'is making enquiries about Glick. And he has seen the body. He is a nuisance.'

Blade kept his expression neutral. 'Yes, sir.'

'Him and his friends.'

'We don't know that they are friends, sir. It could be a coincidence. Archer works in a different Department at the Museum.'

Lorimore paused, turned towards Blade, gave a snort of derision and then continued his pacing. 'Of course they are in league. You saw Archer and Protheroe together at the Museum the night you failed to retrieve the final volume of Glick's diary, did you not? And Archer has been here – to this very house.'

Blade knew better than to argue. He had also caught the emphasis on 'failed' and he knew his life hung by a spider's thread at this moment.

'No,' Lorimore continued, 'they are in this together. And this street urchin who deceived you. And possibly others.'

'But what do they want, sir?' Blade hazarded.

'The same as I, of course. They want it for themselves, or to deny it to me. It doesn't matter which. I must have it.' His eyes burned as he fixed them on Blade. 'And they have this page from the diary. A clue, it must be, to where Glick hid it. I have spent years tracking it down, tracing it to Glick, realising the clue would be in his private diaries. I must know what he did with it, and for that I must have the diary page, Blade – you understand?'

There was an old man at the door. He was wearing a full-length dark coat, and silver hair poked out from under his hat. Sir William Protheroe peered at George through his small round spectacles.

'I'm glad to find you at home, Mr Archer,' he said. 'May I come in?' He did not wait for a reply, but pushed quickly past George and made his way into the living room. 'Is that breakfast I can smell? Capital. I feel as if I could eat a cavalry charge.'

Somewhat bemused, George closed the door and followed his uninvited guest. He found Sir William making himself at home in George's favourite arm-chair. His hat and coat lay discarded over the back of the small sofa.

'I'm sorry,' George said, 'is this about the job you mentioned? I'm afraid I've not had time to give it much thought.'

Sir William waved his hand dismissively. 'No hurry, dear chap. It is the weekend after all. And I don't suppose that dolt Mansfield has even mentioned it to you yet, has he?'

'Well, no, sir, actually he has not. Do you think

perhaps I should mention to him that I have spoken with you?' George wondered.

But Sir William Protheroe seemed preoccupied. He sniffed, his forehead crinkling as he frowned. 'Is that burning bacon I can smell?'

George left Eddie in the smoke-filled kitchen with instructions about clearing away and washing up. It had not actually been the bacon that Sir William had smelled burning, as that had all been eaten by Eddie. But he had simply replaced the empty pan on the stove, and the fat heated up until it burst into flames, which Eddie thought wonderfully exciting. George had remained calm enough – just – to throw a wet tea towel over the pan, and lift it off the heat.

'And you stay in there and clean up the mess,' he told the boy. 'I have things to discuss with Sir William Protheroe.'

If Eddie replied, his words were lost in the drifting smoke.

The armchair was empty when George returned to the living room and George saw that Sir William was standing by the bookcase in the corner of the room. He was examining the spines of the books there.

'You read a lot, Mr Archer?'

'Most of those were my father's,' George confessed. 'I do enjoy reading, but I fear that many of those volumes will remain unread for a while.'

'A pity. There are some interesting books here. And speaking of books . . .' He turned from his inspection of the bookcase and returned to the armchair, settling himself back into it. 'I wonder if you have given any more thought to the identity and motivation of those ruffians who were after Sir Henry Glick's diary.'

'Well, I have been rather busy,' George said. He sat down on the sofa, carefully avoiding Sir William's coat and hat. 'And I think some of what I have been up to does indeed relate.'

'So have I. Busy researching our friend the late Sir Henry Glick. But we shall come to that in a moment. First, perhaps you can tell me what you have been busy with, if you believe it is relevant.'

George paused, wondering what he should say. There was something about the man sitting opposite him that inspired confidence. 'I have been spending much of my time trying to discover who was so desperate to get hold of Glick's diary. And why they want it badly enough to resort to murder.'

Sir William replaced his glasses. 'Alas, poor Percy,' he murmured. 'And poor Albert too, come to that.'

'You knew Albert Wilkes?'

Sir William adjusted his head. 'Until last night I had never knowingly set eyes on the poor man.'

'Last night?'

'I didn't even realise who he was until the body disappeared, then I made some enquiries and found he had worked with Percy, who I did know slightly.' Sir William paused, staring off into the farthest corner of the room. 'I'm sorry,' he went on after a moment, 'I'm probably not making much sense to you, am I?'

George nodded. Vaguely he could hear a noise, and it took him a moment to realise that it was another knocking on the front door.

It was Liz. George led her into the living room and introduced her to Sir William, who shook her hand solemnly before turning to George and raising an eyebrow meaningfully.

'Miss Oldfield,' George explained, 'has been helping me investigate the strange case of Sir Henry Glick's diaries. She has been most helpful.'

'I fear that we have not discovered much,' Liz admitted. 'The desecrated grave of Mr Wilkes, a slip of charred paper, and a peculiar but largely fake séance. Little else.'

'That may be more than you think,' Sir William said slowly. 'Let me tell Miss Oldfield about who I am and what I do. Mr Archer already knows,' he told Liz. 'And he also knows that we may actually be investigating different aspects of the same mystery. Since he appears to trust you, and I value his judgement, there are things that you should know.'

George moved the coat and hat so that he and Liz could sit together on the sofa. Sir William Protheroe leaned forward in his armchair. His fingertips tapped rhythmically together, and he began to speak. He told Liz much of what he had told George that night after the break-in and Percy's death. He explained the Department of Unclassified Artefacts, and he told them both how he had read through the surviving volumes of Henry Glick's diary and also researched the man's career and life.

'And it seemed to me that a recent investigation of my own might be related in some way,' he went on. 'From what Mr Archer tells me of your own exploits it seems I was right. You see, last night, I performed a brief examination of a body that was brought to me. An elderly man called Albert Wilkes. Yes, you begin to see the connection. You know that Wilkes was initially responsible for cataloguing Glick's diary, and you know that he died – apparently of natural causes. Mr Archer tells me his grave was perhaps opened, and that I find especially intriguing. Because I found, before it mysteriously disappeared, that Wilkes's body had been tampered with.'

Sir William paused, took off his glasses and polished them on the corner of his jacket. 'There is a mystery here, Mr Archer and Miss Oldfield,' he told them. 'Something is happening that may challenge our understanding of the scientific world. And, with your help, I mean to discover what.'

There was silence for several moments after Sir William had finished. Sir William regarded his audience carefully, the light glinting on his spectacles as he replaced them and waited for their reaction.

Liz spoke first. 'It is very generous of you to take us into your confidence, Sir William.'

'And we do appreciate the need for complete secrecy,' George added, looking at Liz.

Sir William nodded seriously at this. But his manner changed in an instant as a voice called from the doorway:

'So who was this Glick bloke, anyway?' Eddie stepped into the room. 'I only ask 'cause it seems like his diary's the key to all this.'

Sir William stared at Eddie for several seconds.

'What?' Eddie demanded.

'Have you been out there for long?' Sir William asked, his voice quiet and strained.

'Oh yeah, I heard everything,' Eddie assured him. 'No need to go over it all again.'

'This is Eddie,' George said quickly.

'He's, er, he's been helping us,' Liz added.

'If you can call it that,' George muttered.

'Indeed?' Sir William pulled a large white handkerchief from his pocket and dabbed at his forehead. When he returned it to his pocket he seemed to have recovered. 'And you can vouch for Eddie?' he asked.

'Well,' George said, 'he's a pickpocket and a rogue, but I think he's trustworthy.'

'He seems to have his own moral code,' Liz said.

'Honour amongst thieves or something.'

'Like I said,' Eddie interrupted, 'who's this Glick?'

Sir William fixed Eddie with a steady gaze, as if summing him up. 'Sir Henry Glick was a palaeontologist and geologist.'

'What?'

'He was a scientist,' George told him.

'And a very eminent one,' Sir William agreed. 'He was destined for great things, or so it was thought.'

'So what happened?' Liz asked.

'According to my sources, he died young. Very tragic, before he could realise his potential. His diaries are useful as they catalogue his discoveries and theories and give us some insight as to the mental processes he went through on his journey of enlightenment.'

'So why does someone want the last volume?' George wondered. 'If his work is already known about.'

'I really cannot imagine. His early years were apparently his most productive, before he became ill. He continued to work, of course. In fact he was one of the twenty-one scientists invited to dinner at the Crystal Palace on New Year's Eve 1853. It was, by all accounts, quite an occasion though I was not myself invited.' He sniffed, as if irritated by this apparent oversight.

'What was the occasion?' Liz wondered. 'Just the New Year?'

'No, it was to celebrate the creation of the dinosaur

statues that are now in the Crystal Palace Park. In fact the dinner was held inside the Iguanodon statue before the top was lowered. There was a drawing of the event in the *Illustrated London News*, I remember. Sir Henry Glick was due to make a speech which was eagerly anticipated. But on the evening his illness took a turn for the worse. It was, I think, the beginning of the end for him. He made his apologies and left early. Perhaps,' Sir William said with a sad smile, 'he was sickened by the rather self-serving speech that I gather the eminent palaeontologist Richard Owen gave.'

'I've seen a monster that looked like a dinosaur,' Eddie offered.

Sir William was impressed. 'You have been to the Museum of Natural History?'

'Course not. I saw it in the grounds of a big house. Monstrous it was. Huge, with great teeth.'

'Not this again,' George sighed. 'I told you – it's all in the imagination. All you saw was the branch of a tree blowing in the wind or something.'

'George is right,' Liz said gently.

Eddie stared back at them defiantly. 'Maybe,' he said. 'But I went back there last night, and I heard it breathing. In a big shed at the edge of the lawn.'

'You did what?' Liz said, aghast.

'Where was this?' Sir William asked quietly.

'Just off Clearview Road. The place where they

nabbed your mate Albert Wilkes. Place with lizard things on the gate posts,' Eddie told him.

'Nabbed Albert Wilkes?' said Sir William in surprise.

'But that's Augustus Lorimore's estate,' George said. 'It has to be.'

'The industrialist?'

George nodded. 'Funny thing, you know. But that's who Percy told me to go to for help.'

'Not that he was much help, was he?' Liz said.

Sir William was frowning. 'How would Percy Smythe know Augustus Lorimore, I wonder. And what's this about Albert Wilkes being there? Tell me, what exactly did poor Percy say?'

George struggled to remember. 'He said Lorimore's name. And he said "help" I think. He was telling me Lorimore could help.'

Sir William's face was grave. 'But the man was dying,' he said quietly. 'He was asking *you* for help, for himself. Mentioning Lorimore's name under those circumstances . . . Well, isn't it just as likely that he was telling you who was to blame for his death?'

George felt suddenly cold. 'I suppose it's possible,' he admitted. It was not something that had occurred to him, but now it seemed to make sense. And it explained Lorimore's strange behaviour when they had met – how he had wanted the last surviving page of the diary. 'But, Augustus Lorimore? There was something else nagging at him too, something at the edge of his mind.

'Lorimore,' Liz said. She was staring at George. 'If you were spelling that out to someone, and they missed the first letter . . .'

'Orimore?' George said, bemused.

Liz went on. 'And if they were interrupted or the contact was broken.'

'What contact is this?' Sir William asked.

'I dunno,' Eddie told him. 'Think she's going barmy.'

But George understood now. 'If you just spelled out the middle part of his name,' he said. 'O R I M O.'

'What you said that glass spelled out at the séance,' Eddie said jumping about in excitement. 'Albert Wilkes told you, his spirit told you. Like I said it would.'

'Well, something did,' Liz said. 'Unless it's just a coincidence?'

'It sounds like a big coincidence,' Sir William said. George explained quickly what had happened at the séance, and the older man nodded. 'We live in strange times, Archer. Though of course it *could* be just coincidence.'

'Don't sound like coincidence to me,' Eddie said. 'Specially if this Lorimore lives in the lizard house where the monster is. The house where Wilkes was dragged off by Blade.'

'Monsters or not,' Sir William decided, 'it does seem at least a possibility that Lorimore is indeed behind these macabre events. But we should be wary of jumping to conclusions without sufficient evidence.'

'And I went to see him,' George groaned. 'I went and told him about the surviving fragment of the diary, and what I was doing. He knows everything.'

At that moment, in Sir William's office at the British Museum, Garfield Berry was hunting through the papers on the desk. He found the notes from the examination that Sir William had performed on the body of Albert Wilkes, and quickly and efficiently set about making a copy.

When he was finished, he replaced the papers exactly as they had been. He put his copy in an envelope together with a short covering letter that explained that he had received the request and hoped that this was what was wanted. He also included the address of another employee of the Museum – a man called George Archer. It had not been difficult to get into Mansfield's office and find the information he needed. Berry sealed the envelope and quickly wrote the name of the recipient on it: Augustus Lorimore.

Berry locked the office behind him with a duplicate key that Sir William knew nothing about. He did not expect Sir William back for a while yet, but he was still in a hurry. The man with the scar was waiting.

Chapter 13

Mr Blade waited patiently and silently while Augustus Lorimore read Berry's letter. Clutching the paper in spindly, spider's leg fingers, Lorimore read it through twice. His lips twitched as he reached the end for the second time. Then he bunched the letter into a tight ball and hurled it across the drawing room.

Blade did not react. But he noted where the letter had fallen so he could recover and burn it later.

'You wish me to deal with these people, now that we know where Archer lives, sir?'

'I don't care what happens to them, Blade.' Lorimore turned away, studying the sightless birds that stared back at him from behind the glass. 'Just so long as I get what I want, and they never interfere with my work again.'

'I shall be happy to arrange that, sir,' Blade assured him. He was smiling thinly, his mouth a knife-slash across his face. 'It will be dark early this evening. We can move then, without fear of being seen.'

Lorimore turned back from the display case. 'I can't wait until this evening, you dolt.' He nodded at the window on the other side of the room. A thin mist was already pressing up against it, filtering the pale winter sunlight. 'The smog is thickening already. I'm sure your thugs can run fast enough to escape any interference. And in half an hour you'll barely be able to see your hand in front of your face.'

There were springs and cogwheels and screws and oddly shaped bits of metal all over the table. Eddie watched with interest as George arranged the bits and pieces. He had a magnifying glass mounted on a metal bracket so he could see what he was working on. When Eddie tried to peer through, George pushed him out of the way with a grunt of annoyance.

'What you making, anyway?' Eddie demanded for the third time.

'It's only a prototype,' George mumbled.

'A type of what?'

George sighed and put down the tiny wheel he had been examining. He hunted for another with the tweezers, eventually selecting one that looked to Eddie to be identical to the first.

Liz had left them soon after Sir William Protheroe. That had been hours ago now. Eddie reckoned it must be getting on for lunchtime, but he was fascinated when George got out his collection of tools. They were so tiny – like proper carpenter's tools, only much smaller. There were screwdrivers, knives, tweezers, clamps, and even a miniature saw.

'You a jeweller?' Eddie asked.

'No,' George told him. 'I mend clocks and watches.'

Eddie had quite a collection of pocket watches stashed away. He considered offering them to George, but he might not approve. Anyway, most of them worked, if he bothered to wind them up.

'I still don't know what it is,' Eddie said, watching closely as George started to assemble various components he had built into a single compact unit.

'It's for Liz – Miss Oldfield. She wants me to work out a mechanism for sending a silver ashtray flying across the stage.'

'What stage?'

'At the theatre. She indulges in amateur dramatics.'

George sat back and inspected his work. The spring was fixed between two metal plates. One kept the whole contraption stable on the top of the table. The other was fixed to the top at an angle. A small key emerged from the side of the device, and George wound it carefully. As he did so, the spring contracted and the top plate, which was slightly indented, lowered and levelled.

'Pass me that ball bearing, will you?'

Eddie did so. 'It isn't an ashtray,' he pointed out.

'This is just to test if my design will work.' George

placed the ball bearing on the top plate. The small steel ball sat easily in the middle, where the plate had been hollowed slightly. 'If it does, I can build a larger version that will catapult the ashtray.'

George turned the device so it was pointing across the room towards the door and reached for a hinged sliver of metal that was protruding from the edge of the device. He hesitated just before his finger reached it. 'Come here, Eddie. You do it.'

'Do what?' Eddie joined George at the table, and George pointed.

'Press that trigger.'

'Trigger? You mean, this is like a gun?'

George sighed. 'Not really. Just push it. Gently, mind, so you don't jolt the thing.'

'Like this?'

Eddie gingerly pressed on the bit of metal. It was sharp and bit into the skin on the end of his finger, but it moved easily enough. There was a dull click as the spring suddenly expanded. It forced the top plate rapidly upwards, pivoting it around a metal rod so that the ball bearing was flung off.

The steel ball was hurled across the room like a bullet. It hit the door, embedding itself in the wooden panelling with a splintering crunch.

'Wow!' Eddie exclaimed with delight.

George was grinning too. 'Maybe a bit fierce,' he noted. 'We need to angle it so the ashtray is lobbed up in the air rather than shot out like that.'

'It worked though,' Eddie said. He was impressed. For the first time he realised that George Archer was maybe not just a boring grown-up who delighted in telling other people what to do.

While George set to work adjusting the spring slightly, Eddie started to tidy away the tools and spare components. George was winding up the device once more when there was a knock at the front door.

'That might be Liz,' George said eagerly. 'Have a look, will you?'

Eddie went to the window and peered out into the street. The fog was thick now, and all he could see was a grey blanket hanging across the world. There were several darker patches that could be people. He leaned forward until his forehead was against the cool glass and tried to make out who it was outside.

'I meant, answer the door,' George said irritably.

'Keep your hair on, I'm going.'

Eddie leaned back from the window. But he did not go to the door. For at that moment, a face loomed out of the mist. Someone was leaning towards the window, trying to look in. The face was contorted, grinning horribly as it saw Eddie on the other side of the glass. It was a face Eddie instantly recognised, even before he saw the pale scar running down one side of it.

'Cripes!' Eddie yelled. 'It's him – they found us.'

At the same moment, the knocking at the door

became a hammering. Then a splintering as the wood around the lock gave way.

'Come on,' Eddie shouted at George. 'Let's get out of here.'

'But this is my home,' George protested.

Eddie did not wait to argue. He pushed George across the room towards the door.

'Wait.' George struggled free of Eddie's grasp and ran back to the table. He scooped up his device and several ball bearings. Then he was running back across the room and together they tumbled out into the hall-way.

The front door was shaking and shuddering as the men outside put their shoulders to it. A strip of wood flew off and spun down the hall, just missing Eddie. The lock had almost broken away. Another few seconds . . .

'Let's get out of here,' Eddie said. 'Come on, through the kitchen.' There was a kitchen door leading to the yard and the alley at the back of the house. Eddie had opened it earlier to let the smoke out.

'We need to slow them down,' George shouted back at him as the door finally crashed open and a swirl of fog and dark shapes fell into the hall.

Eddie saw that George had the clockwork device in his hands and was winding it up furiously. He set it down on the hall floor, dropped a handful of ball bearings on to the plate on the top, and then adjusted the angle – aiming it along the length of the hallway.

Three men were advancing slowly, the fog drifting behind them so they were silhouetted against the cloudy grey. One of them was Blade, and he was holding a long knife. The other two men hefted wooden cudgels.

'Hurry up,' Eddie urged, bouncing from one foot to the other as he prepared to run for it.

George did not reply. He waited, timing the moment, then gently pressed down on the trigger. As soon as he had done so, as soon as the top plate of the device had whipped upwards, George stuffed the contraption back into his jacket pocket and ran after Eddie.

Eddie was also running. But he had waited just long enough to see the ball bearings smash like shotgun pellets into the approaching men. Blade had been caught on the arm, dropping his knife with a cry of pain. One of the other men seemed to have escaped, perhaps shielded by his fellows. But the third had taken several ball bearings in the face. He collapsed backwards with a shriek of pain. He clutched and clawed at his face, the cudgel he had been carrying clattering to the floor.

'Gotcha!' Eddie cried. Then he was gone.

The last thing he heard as he fled was Blade's laughter.

'I don't know what he finds so funny,' Eddie told George as they slammed the door behind them.

George had taken the key from the inside of the door, and he locked it behind them. 'Won't hold them for long, but it all helps.'

Eddie wasn't listening. 'Unless there's someone waiting for us out here.' He stared at George through the thickening air. 'That's it – they're chasing us out of the house for someone else to catch.'

'They'll never find us in this pea-souper,' George said. He grabbed Eddie's hand and pulled him across the small yard to the gate. 'Keep hold of me, or we'll both get lost. No one in their right mind will be out in this.'

The alley was thick with smog. Grey-green and acrid, it caught at the back of Eddie's throat as he gasped for air. They looked both ways along the alley before George set off to the left, still pulling Eddie after him.

The fog deadened the sound of their feet slapping against the damp cobbles. It muffled the sounds of splintering wood as the back door gave way. It deadened the cries of the men who gave chase.

But it did nothing to mitigate the sudden roar of sound from ahead of them. Eddie skidded to a halt. It was a sound he knew.

'Come on!' George urged. 'It's just a tram or a train or something.'

Eddie shook his head, almost speechless with fear. 'That's what anyone else will think. But it's not . . .' As if to confirm his nightmare realisation, a shape solidified out of the fog above them.

Hot steam-like breath blew the fog from around them, whipping it into a vortex. Half-glimpsed jaws snapped inches from George's face as Eddie pulled him backwards. With a snarl of rage, something lunged towards them again. Enormous feet slammed down on the ground; claws scraped and clinked on the cobblestones. From behind them came the shouts of Blade and his fellows.

'We're trapped,' George gasped. 'God help us, we can't go back.'

'Then we'll have to go sideways.'

'There's a wall.'

'No,' Eddie said. 'There's a gate.'

The gate was locked. Together they battered at it, without success. The reptilian head had lost them in the gloom. But an ear-shattering roar told them the creature was not far away. A massive claw slashed through the air, splitting the fog apart.

At the last moment, George pushed Eddie aside. The claw smashed into the gate, shattering it and sending planks and splinters and hinges flying into the small yard beyond. Immediately after them went George and Eddie. They fled down the narrow path that led along the side of the house.

Terrifying roars echoed round them as they raced down the passageway and out into the street. Eddie was almost crying with relief as they emerged.

'We were lucky to escape,' George gasped.

Eddie was about to answer when a dark figure stepped out of the fog. Strong arms wrapped round him and dragged him backwards.

'Not as lucky as you think,' Blade's voice rasped in Eddie's ear.

He didn't think, just acted. He kicked out backwards, struggling to break the man's grip. But Blade was holding on tight to his coat.

'Run!' Eddie shouted to George. 'I'm right behind you.'

Blade grunted and gripped Eddie all the more tightly.

Eddie fought and kicked, and with a sudden, fluid movement, he ripped his arms out of the sleeves of his jacket, leaving Blade to fall backwards, holding only his coat.

Eddie caught up with George, and together they ran as fast as they could down the road. They did not stop running until they both collapsed, gasping for breath. The pale fog closed in around them like a shroud.

'What are you doing here?' Liz was surprised to see George and Eddie. She was helping Marcus Jessop work out the design for the backdrops when her two friends ran into the auditorium.

Excusing herself from Jessop, Liz climbed down from the stage as decorously as possible, and made her way up the aisle to where George and Eddie were looking around with interest.

She listened with mounting amazement and anxiety to their story. She glanced at the small contraption with its two metal plates and winding key which George proudly showed her. None of them noticed the sound of the back door of the theatre opening distantly and then banging shut again.

'So you thought I might be in danger?' she said when they had finished.

Eddie and George were sitting together in a row of seats, near the back of the theatre. Liz was in the row behind them, facing towards the stage as they talked.

'Well, of course,' George said. 'After they came for us, we worried they would also be looking for you.'

'We tried your home, but your father said you were out,' Eddie told her.

'So we guessed you'd be here,' George finished, proud of his deduction.

Liz nodded. 'Lorimore knew who you are because you went to see him. He knows you have, or had, the page of Glick's diary. But until now he didn't know who I am, or even that I exist.'

George sighed with relief. 'I suppose that's true.'

Then he realised what she had said. 'What do you mean, "until now"?'

Liz was looking past George and Eddie. 'The man with the scar is talking to Marcus on the stage,' she said.

They turned to look, just in time to see Marcus Jessop nod and point down into the auditorium, to where they were sitting. As the man with him turned, the stage lights caught and illuminated the pale scar running down his face.

'Run!' Eddie shrieked.

Blade was already leaping down from the stage and heading rapidly through the theatre.

George and Liz leaped to their feet and stumbled into the aisle. Eddie was over the seats and waiting at the back of the auditorium.

'But, how did he find you?' George asked as they ran through the foyer.

Liz opened the main doors, slamming them behind after they had all come through. 'He didn't,' she said angrily. 'He followed you.'

'Oh.' George was crestfallen. 'I thought we'd escaped.'

Liz led them across the road and they ducked behind the end of a wall almost opposite the theatre. After a few seconds, Blade emerged from the theatre. He looked up and down the street, peering into the fog. They heard him curse out loud, before hastening away.

'They let us run to see who we'd go to. Once we'd

escaped they thought it was easiest just to follow,' Eddie realised.

'So now they know where you live, and where I live as well as about the theatre,' Liz pointed out.

'We could go to Sir William, at the British Museum,' George suggested.

'That's where you work,' Eddie said. 'So they'll know to watch there too.'

'And they could very well be watching Sir William anyway,' Liz added.

'There must be somewhere we can go until they stop looking,' George said.

'If they ever do,' Eddie mumbled.

Liz did not reply. Somewhere in the distance, muffled by the fog, she heard the roar of a train. Except that somehow she knew it was not a train at all.

Chapter 14

Sir William had his hand on the door knob before he realised there was someone already in his office.

He hesitated, hand poised ready to turn the knob. It was Garfield Berry that he could hear – the distinctive nasal tones. He did not know why Berry should be in his office, but it was no matter. Except . . .

Except that Berry was talking to someone. And not even Berry was permitted in Sir William's office without his permission. And now he came to think about it, Sir William had left the office locked, the key was still in his pocket. Berry had no key, not that Sir William knew about anyway.

As he stood there, trying to make out the muffled voices from behind the door, several things occurred to Sir William. He remembered how he had thought his papers had been moved yesterday. How on several occasions he had wondered if things on his desk had been examined. How he had once found Berry in his office when he was sure he had left it locked. Berry

had insisted the door was open and he had been looking for Sir William.

His hand dropped as he made out some of Berry's
words:

'. . . back soon. He won't be expecting us . . .'

The other voice was low and gruff. It was harder to
make out, but Sir William caught odd snatches of
what it said:

'. . . can't go back to the theatre, or to Archer's
house . . .'

Sir William stiffened at this. He pressed his ear to
the door, struggling to hear more.

'What about the woman?' Berry was asking.

'We're watching her house too. That urchin doesn't
live anywhere so far as we can tell. But we have
another way of finding him, don't you worry.'

'So you think they might come here?' Berry said.

'It's where Archer works. And we are pretty sure
that Sir William High-And-Mighty Protheroe is also
involved with them.'

Sir William smiled at that. He certainly was
involved, and getting more involved by the moment.

'Mr Lorimore got my letter?' Berry asked. 'About
the body, with the copy of Sir William's notes? And
Archer's address?'

The smile faded from Protheroe's face. Lorimore –
so now he knew for sure. And he was right, someone
had been through his papers. He had suspected that

idiot Defoe, not the apparently loyal Berry. He stepped back from the door and considered his options. To confront Berry and the other man now would perhaps be to overplay his hand. As it was, they did not realise that he knew Berry was working against him.

No, he decided, better to leave them to their intrigue while he decided how to help Archer and his friends. But first he would have to find them – before Lorimore did. Sir William made his way back out of the British Museum and towards the Atlantian Club. The night was drawing in and he could do with a spot of dinner. He lived alone in a big, old house some miles away so the club was convenient and he had no one expecting him at home. Dinner, and a glass of wine to lubricate the brain while he considered where George Archer might be found. If necessary he could stay overnight.

He continued to pursue the problem as he sat alone in the club dining room and tucked into his steak and kidney pie. It was clear that Archer could not go home, nor could he go to Miss Oldfield's house. The theatre – wherever that was – was also off-limits. The boy Eddie was of no fixed abode, so that was no help. He might have all kinds of dens and haunts where he could take George Archer and Elizabeth Oldfield, though he doubted any of them would be very salubrious.

He tried a different approach – considering their characters. Archer was a proactive man. That was one of the things that had drawn Sir William to him – the fact he liked to be busy, to be doing something rather than sitting around looking important like so many of his colleagues. He was sure Miss Oldfield was the same. And the boy Eddie was nothing if not impulsive and energetic. They would be actively searching for clues and solutions to the puzzle – hoping to gain the upper hand rather than simply trying to avoid capture.

In fact, he realised as he drained the last of his wine, there was only one place they could end up. Sir William dabbed at his lips with his napkin. They might not have worked it out yet themselves, of course, but eventually they would have to go there. They really did not have any other choice.

'Thank you, Stephen.' Sir William smiled at the doorman on his way out. He paused on the foggy threshold to put on his hat.

'Getting thick again, sir,' Stephen commented.

'Indeed it is.' Sir William hefted his cane. 'I was going to walk, but perhaps you could find me a cab?'

'Of course, sir.'

'Oh, and Stephen?'

'Sir?' He raised a hand, almost lazily.

'If anyone comes looking for me . . .'

Somehow a cab had clattered up outside the club, though it seemed not to surprise Stephen. 'Yes, sir?' he prompted.

'I was never here.'

Stephen nodded in understanding. He stepped forward to open the door to the carriage. 'I will make sure that no one else has seen you either, sir.'

'I still think this is a daft idea,' George protested in a hoarse whisper.

'We all agreed,' Liz told him, also whispering. 'If you have a better suggestion, then please do tell us.'

'Just along here's a good spot to hide and watch,' Eddie said.

He led them through the foggy night into a small wooded area. George was glad to be off the driveway and out of sight. Even with the thick fog, he had been afraid that any moment Blade or one of his thugs would appear in front of them. It had seemed like a good idea to come to Lorimore's estate to hunt for clues when they were hiding behind the wall outside the Chistleton Theatre. But now they were actually here, George thought it was the most absurd notion.

'If Lorimore is behind this, then this is the last place they'll think of looking for us,' Liz reminded him as they followed Eddie into the trees. 'If he isn't then it should be safe. And as you have pointed out, we need more evidence – any evidence – if we are to go to the police.'

The branches were sweating where the fog condensed on their bark. The very air itself dripped with the damp, and it was bitingly cold. Eddie was huddled down on the ground pointing through a gap in the trees.

'You can see his house from here. Well, nearly. You could if it wasn't so foggy.'

George and Liz sat down beside Eddie. He could just make out a blurred shape that might be Lorimore's house. A faint light glowed at the back of it.

'So where's this monster live?' Liz asked. From her tone, George guessed that she was still dubious that such a creature even existed. But he wasn't, not any more.

'Over there.' Eddie pointed across behind the house. 'There's a big shed near the trees. I reckon that's where the monster lives.'

'In a garden shed?'

'They wouldn't want to attract attention,' George told her.

'Apart from sending it through the streets of London to attack you two, you mean?'

'It was foggy,' George protested. 'But even so, they must have brought it most of the way in a special carriage or something.'

'We might find out if we watch,' Eddie said impatiently.

'We're as safe here as anywhere, I suppose,' Liz admitted.

'That's true enough,' George agreed. 'Like you said, this is the last place anyone would expect to find us.'

He froze as behind them in the fog, someone cleared their throat.

'I must beg to differ,' a voice said.

George turned so fast he sent the fog swirling. Liz gave a gasp of astonishment, and Eddie scrambled for cover.

'I'm so sorry,' Sir William Protheroe said, 'did I startle you?'

'I'd be lying if I said you didn't,' George told him when he had recovered.

'What are you doing here, Sir William?' Liz spoke in a loud whisper.

'Well, believe it or believe it not, I was waiting for you.'

'How d'you know we'd be here, then?' Eddie demanded, reappearing from a clump of foliage.

'I overheard an unpleasant gentleman talking to my assistant Mr Berry. I gathered several things from their conversation. One of those was that the three of you were on the run, sought after by Lorimore's thugs.'

'Lorimore – so we're sure he is behind this?'

'Oh yes. Quite sure.'

'But how did you know we were *here*?' Liz asked.

Sir William smiled. 'It seemed the most likely place.'

'But why?'

'Because, Mr Archer, it is the best place to gather clues and evidence, and the last place that Lorimore would expect to find you. I think we all want answers to the various questions that Lorimore's behaviour and actions have posed. This seems the most likely place to discover those answers.'

Eddie only half listened while between them George and Liz explained to Sir William what had happened since that morning. He stared into the fog, trying to make out details of the house.

Last time he was here – was it only last night? – there had been a guard patrolling with a shotgun. But tonight there was no sign of him – perhaps he had been sent to look for Eddie and the others. That would be a hoot, what with them all right here where the guard should have been.

But Eddie kept a careful watch in case the man was simply taking a break or lingering round the other side of the house. His ears strained to catch the telltale sound of boots on gravel.

What he did hear was the sound of voices. They drifted faintly through the fog. Eddie strained to hear, leaning forward. They seemed to be coming from the house – voices, moving now across the lawn. He could make out the vaguest of shadows through the heavy air.

Behind him, the others were discussing what they should do next. Eddie waved at them to be quiet.

'What is it?' Sir William whispered, crawling forwards to join Eddie at the edge of the small wood.

'People. From the house. I think they're going to the shed.'

'I wonder what they're up to,' George said quietly.

'We won't find out just by hiding here,' Liz hissed. 'Why don't we go and see?'

'An excellent notion,' Sir William said quietly. 'I for one should like to know a lot more about this creature. It sounds fascinating, to say the least. But I would suggest that rather than all four of us trying to get close without being seen, we send one of our party to scout out and report back.'

'I'll go,' George said at once, to Eddie's relief.

But he could see that Sir William had his hand on George's arm. 'I'm sure you would do magnificently, but there may be someone here better suited to the job. Someone who knows exactly where this shed is located. Someone used to creeping about without being noticed and with a good turn of speed should they be spotted. Someone,' he added, turning to look at Eddie, 'small.'

Eddie stared back indignantly. 'Who you calling small?'

'He's right,' Liz said before Sir William could answer. 'Eddie's the best person for this.'

'For what?'

'Just creep over,' George said, 'and see what they're up to over there. Find out what they're talking about. Then you can come back.'

Eddie was furious. Why should he be the one to risk his life creeping up on Lorimore's killers and the monster? 'No way!' he protested.

He felt a gentle touch on his shoulder, and turned to find Liz looking down at him. Her eyes were wide and appealing.

'Please,' she said softly, 'we need your help, Eddie.'

Eddie crept towards Lorimore's men. The problem was, that if he was close enough to see them clearly, then they could see him. He edged as close as he dared – until their voices were audible through the fog. Then he dropped to the ground and crawled slowly forwards.

There were four men. He could already tell that one of them was Blade. He was talking to a tall, spindly figure who seemed to be directing them – Lorimore himself, Eddie guessed. The other two were further off, standing by the shed. The door, Eddie saw, was open. With the figures outside to show how big it really was, the building looked more like a coach house.

'It's gone down the tunnel,' one of them said. 'But it's on its way back now.'

'It comes when I call,' Lorimore said in his high-pitched whine. He sounded smug and self-important.

'Expecting to be fed, probably,' Blade replied. 'It'll be a bit agitated after all the excitement.' Something was draped over his arm, but Eddie could not make out what it was. 'You sure this will work, sir?' Blade asked.

'Your incompetence has left us few options, Mr Blade,' Lorimore replied caustically. 'But the olfactory systems remain preserved and should function, at least well enough for our purposes. The idiot's brain I put in it should manage that. You say yourself that you believe the boy was in the street outside, possibly even in the grounds when you retrieved Wilkes. Find the boy and we find his friends. Find his friends and we find what remains of Glick's last diary. Or at the very least someone who can apprise us of its contents.'

Blade nodded, but if he spoke the sound of his voice was drowned out by the roar from the open shed behind him. It was a sound that Eddie had heard several times before. The fog round the shed door swirled and thickened as smoke or perhaps steam billowed out. Slowly, terrifyingly, the grotesque shape of the creature's head appeared as if from the ground inside the shed. The monster was hauling itself out of a huge pit that was hidden inside the building.

Eddie could see now that two men were standing either side, holding heavy chains that reached up and round the creature's neck as it emerged into the open. Its head swung to and fro as if it was sniffing the air, as if it was searching for food.

'Gently now,' Lorimore said. His voice was soft as if he was talking to a child. 'There's nothing to worry about, my beauty. Mr Blade has a small task for you to perform.' He turned to the big man. 'Mr Blade?'

Blade handed him the thing that had been draped over his arm. As Lorimore took it and opened it, Eddie could see through the gusting smoke that it was a jacket. Lorimore held it out at arm's length.

After a moment, the monster's head dipped down. Steam erupted from its nostrils. It nudged the jacket with its nose, teeth glinting in the suffuse light.

'Fetch,' Blade said, and laughed. His men laughed too, until Lorimore turned on them.

'That's enough,' he said. 'It has the scent. Lead it to the gates and let it pick up the trail there.'

'What if it's seen?' Blade wondered.

'There won't be many people out in this. And those who are won't be certain. They will just see shapes and shadows, unless they get very close. And if they do . . .' Lorimore laughed now – a nasal whine of amusement.

But Eddie hardly heard. He was staring at the jacket, now lying discarded on the ground at Lorimore's feet as the smoke and steam swirled round it. The jacket that the monster had sniffed at to get the scent of its prey.

Eddie's jacket.

In front of him, the monster was lowering its head to sniff at it again. Eddie shuddered as he remembered the creature's own oily, acrid smell. He sniffed, expecting to catch a whiff of it again. But there was nothing. Just the bitter, smut-filled smell of the smog.

The creature slowly raised its head and swung round. Towards Eddie. Towards the scent it was picking up on the breeze. It looked like an enormous skeleton, papered over with thin metal plates. Metal and bone glinted through the mist that shrouded it.

With a colossal roar and the sudden snap of teeth, the creature lunged. One of the men was swept off his feet as the chain went tight. The other fell backwards, the chain wrenched from his grasp. Blade leapt back, pulling Lorimore with him.

But Lorimore seemed elated. 'It has the scent!' he shouted with delight. 'Already. Just think how much more efficient my next prototype will be.'

'Prototypes again,' Eddie mumbled, bracing himself ready to run.

'That vermin must have been here that night, in the grounds,' Lorimore was saying to Blade. 'Wait until I see Higgins again – he was supposed to be keeping guard. When I catch up with him . . .'

Eddie did not wait to hear what would happen to Higgins. He was already scrambling to his feet and running for all he was worth back towards the wood and his friends.

Behind him, claws slashed through the foggy air as the monster roared in triumph. The ground shook as it stamped its way towards Eddie.

Chapter 15

Eddie's only thought was to get away. His only hope was that the huge creature lumbering after him would be unable to follow into the trees. He looked back once – a quick glance over his shoulder. The thing must be twenty feet tall, but as it ran, its head was down almost level with Eddie's. Steam snorted out of its nostrils and mouth and even the fog shrank away from it.

He dived into the trees, stumbling, falling. Strong hands pulled him to his feet.

'This way,' George said. 'Quick!'

Liz and George ran with him into the deepest part of the wood. As he risked another look back, Eddie saw Sir William standing at the edge of the wood watching the foggy shape of the monster with interest. He turned slowly, and made his way unhurriedly towards them. Amazingly, the monster did not seem to be following, but had crunched off down the driveway.

'Hurry up,' Liz hissed. 'It'll be after us in a moment.'

'Oh I don't think there's any rush just now,' Sir William said. He was smiling thinly. 'What an extraordinary creature. I should like to take a closer look at it. Examine it properly.'

'You will if you hang about here,' Eddie told him. 'It's sniffing me out. They gave it my coat to smell.'

'And you have been here before,' Sir William said, nodding. 'It isn't you it's after Eddie. Or rather it is, but at the moment it is following the trail you left on your last visit.'

As if to confirm the point, a distant roar split through the foggy wood.

Sir William smiled, and patted Eddie on the shoulder. 'You know, it may not have fancied struggling through these trees, but actually I don't think its sense of smell is quite what it should be, my boy. Now why is that, eh? I should very much like to find out.'

'Let's hope it keeps going along the old scent for a while,' Liz said.

'Giving us time to get away,' George agreed.

'Good gracious me, no.' Sir William seemed astonished at the suggestion. 'Giving us time to take a look at this shed where it lives.'

'There's a tunnel,' Eddie said. 'I heard them mention it.'

'A tunnel.' Sir William clapped his hands together in delight. 'Then perhaps that is how they transport it from place to place without being seen. Right then, we'll give them another minute to get clear with their pet monster, then we'll take a look shall we?'

Sir William treated the short walk across the lawn like an afternoon stroll. He looked round with interest, peering into the fog, and all the while swinging his cane.

'Is it a dinosaur?' Liz asked him as they paused for Eddie to get his bearings.

'Possibly, possibly. But I think it's rather more unusual than that. Something more than *just* dinosaur, if you take my meaning.'

Eddie didn't, but he could now see the dark shape of the shed. Before he could point it out, another hideous roar wrenched through the night.

'That was closer,' George said in alarm.

'It's coming back this way,' Liz realised.

'You said it was heading out, following where I went the other night.'

'Yes,' Sir William admitted. 'And so it was. But I fear it may now have picked up your rather fresher trail coming in this evening.'

Eddie could feel the ground thumping under his feet. 'What do we do?'

'Run,' George suggested.

'Too late!' Liz shrieked. Over her shoulder, Eddie could see the fog swirling away from the monster as it charged towards them out of the night.

'This way!' Sir William was running – surprisingly

fast for such an old man, Eddie thought. But then he was, like the rest of them, running for his life.

'Not that way!' George cried after them. 'Head back to the trees.'

But Sir William either did not hear or ignored him. He was leading them across the lawn. Had he seen the open shed? Eddie raced to catch him up, hoping to reach him before he fell into the pit just inside the shed. Just as it seemed Sir William would fall into the dark opening, he skidded to a halt at its edge. He looked down into the blackness, nodding with satisfaction. There was no sign of Lorimore, and Eddie guessed he and Blade had either followed the creature or returned to the house.

'Yes this should do,' Sir William announced. He grabbed Eddie's hand. 'Come on.' He jumped, pulling Eddie with him.

Moments later, Liz and George fell after them. They all landed in a crumpled heap in the blackness.

'Good grief!' Liz exclaimed. 'It stinks!'

'I was right,' Sir William said. 'See, where it is even darker, there is a tunnel leading off. That and the smell would suggest that this pit connects in some way to the main sewers. Now, let's see what we can discover about this creature. What it eats, if it sleeps – everything.'

Eddie tried to make out the patch of blackness that Sir William had mentioned. But he could see nothing except the grey square above him that was the open shed outside the pit. The grey darkened as a shape closed over it. At first he thought someone was closing the shed door. But then the darkness was shattered by the roar of the creature. Its silhouetted head swung back and forth as it struggled to find them in the blackness, snuffling and snorting as it caught Eddie's scent.

'I don't think we should stay here,' George said. 'Or we may find out first hand what it eats.'

'But we can't see where we're going,' Liz pointed out.

Sir William was unperturbed. 'Hold hands,' he said. 'I'll lead the way. This is fascinating, absolutely fascinating.'

Eddie felt a hand close on his. He didn't know if it was George or Liz, but he allowed himself to be pulled towards the back of the pit. The darkness deepened, and he felt the damp brick-lined walls of the tunnel with his free hand as they picked their way through. The sound of the monster's snufflings slowly died away.

'Right hold on a moment, let's see where we are.' There was the scrape of a match on sandpaper, and a tiny flame flared into life further along the tunnel. 'That's good,' Sir William said.

The tunnel stretched away beyond the reach of the flickering light. 'What's good?' Eddie wondered. 'We're trapped down here now. And that monster will be after us soon.'

'Yes, I'm afraid he will. But there is a lot of methane in the air down here – hence the smell. I was just grateful it didn't ignite.'

Eddie could see now that it was Liz holding his hand. Her grip tightened as she thought about what Sir William had said. But before any of them could reply, the whole tunnel began to shake. Dust fell from the arched roof and the match went out.

'The creature,' George said quietly in the darkness. 'It's coming after us.'

'Then let's keep moving,' Sir William said. Another match flared into life and he led the way along the tunnel. 'We may have to postpone a detailed investigation for the moment.'

'Where're we going?' Eddie wondered.

'Wherever it leads. But ideally I should like to find a narrower side tunnel.' Sir William paused as another bellowing roar echoed round the tunnel. 'And soon.'

They went as fast as they dared, hoping they could stay ahead of the monster. The tunnel was narrow – maybe it wouldn't want to follow too far in case it got stuck. But each time Eddie thought they had gone far enough and it might have given up, another roar rang off the brickwork and brought dust down into their hair and mouths and eyes.

At one point they reached an intersection of tunnels. Their tunnel was joined by two more – a choice of directions. Sir William led them down one of the side tunnels, perhaps hoping that Eddie's scent would be lost in the smell of the sewers and the monster would instinctively go straight on.

'You think it can hear us?' George asked.

'Probably. But remembering how weak its smell was, let's hope all its other senses are equally dulled.'

'Some chance,' Eddie muttered.

'You know I really think we must be making good progress,' Sir William announced after several more minutes.

'You think we've come far enough to be safe?' Liz asked.

'Oh I shouldn't think so for a moment. No, no – I mean if Lorimore is desperate enough to risk sending this animal or whatever it is through London to find us, then he must consider us to be a real threat of some sort.'

'And that's a good thing?' George asked, his voice strained.

Another match flared, illuminating Sir William's craggy face and deepening the lines across his forehead. 'Oh I think so. What is he worried about, hmm? Something he is afraid we can do or discover or work out.'

'The only clue we have is the fragment of Glick's diary,' George told him. 'It's meaningless.' He had to shout to be heard above the almost continuous roar of the approaching creature. 'We have to get out of here.'

'No it isn't meaningless,' Sir William went on calmly. 'That's his mistake, do you see? If Lorimore had ignored us, we might well have come to that conclusion. But as it is, by his actions, he is telling us that the diary fragment is a vital clue. He is afraid that from that clue we can make some fundamental discovery. Presumably the same discovery as he himself is hoping to make. The difference is that he knows what he is looking for while we are working in the dark. In more ways than one,' he added as the match sputtered and went out. 'I do think someone should invent an everlasting match,' he grumbled, striking another. 'However, Lorimore is evidently afraid that we might deduce what he is after from that fragment.'

'Which means,' Liz said, glancing apprehensively back down the tunnel, 'that we can do just that.'

More dust and ancient mortar fell from the ceiling. The tunnel was shaking in time with the creature's thumping steps. Eddie could hear the rhythmic thud of its feet and the rasping of its breath. It had not taken the obvious route where the tunnels joined, and now it was almost upon them. 'If we live long enough,' he said nervously.

'Let's try through here, shall we?' Sir William said, and disappeared into the tunnel wall.

Eddie could see it now – the huge creature was bent almost double. It filled the tunnel as it charged towards them. The match-light faded as Sir William disappeared, and Eddie was left with the impression of huge teeth snapping at him in the darkness. He could smell the monster's oily breath as he scrabbled at the wall, desperately trying to find where the others had gone. Jaws clamped shut close to his face, as he finally found the opening and fell shrieking into it.

There was a narrow gap – a short passageway leading into another parallel tunnel. Eddie was barely through when another roar echoed after him, followed by a frantic scrabbling and scraping. He could imagine the monster slashing at the entrance of the passage with its knife-like claws – gouging out chunks of brick as it widened the passage so it could follow them.

'Let's hope it isn't clever enough to realise that these tunnels probably join up further on,' Sir William said.

'I think it's time we found a way out of here,' George said.

'Indeed it is. I'm down to my last couple of matches.'

'Perhaps there isn't a way out,' Liz said quietly.

'There must be an inspection hatch or something somewhere,' George told her. 'Probably up that way. The tunnel slopes slightly, and a hatch is likely to be at a higher point.'

'Good thinking,' Sir William said. 'Let's take a look shall we?' He led them up the tunnel in the direction George had indicated. To their relief, the sound of the monster's frantic scraping and scratching gradually faded into the distance.

'So let's recap on what we know,' Sir William suggested. They were walking slowly in darkness now, their feet splashing through the thin stream of foul-smelling water that was washing down the tunnel. 'Lorimore wants the final volume of Glick's diary. Presumably for some entry he believes is in it. An entry that means nothing in itself, but provides a clue to what Lorimore is really after. Some clue that no one else has yet managed to decipher.'

'He approached Albert Wilkes to get hold of it,' George said. 'Maybe he murdered Albert when he refused to help.'

'Or maybe he died of natural causes,' Sir William said.

'What about Wilkes's body?' Liz asked.

'Yes, a rum do,' Sir William told them. 'It sounds fantastic, but I believe that Lorimore somehow reanimated Wilkes in the hope he would retrieve the diary, or at least show them where it was kept. Instead of which poor old Wilkes surprised them by settling back into his usual routine. They thought he'd gone to his house to get the diary, and instead he went home for tea.'

'That's why Blade was trying to get him back,' Eddie realised.

'So they somehow switched him off, as it were, when that didn't work. And then they replaced the body, rather hastily, when there was a possibility it might be dug up again,' Liz said. 'When Mrs Wilkes told people her husband was walking.'

'A very hasty job indeed,' Sir William agreed. 'In fact they didn't have time to put him back together properly after whatever they had done to him. They were forced to use bones that came from elsewhere, for example. They hoped no one would notice. I shudder to think to what use Lorimore had put the poor man's own limbs.'

'And now we find he has this . . . creature at his beck and call,' George said.

'Yes,' Sir Wiliam agreed. 'I should like to learn more about that. How Lorimore has managed to reconstruct a dinosaur, if that is indeed what it is.'

'A question for another day, perhaps,' Liz suggested. 'I don't fancy trying to examine the brute down here.'

Eddie was running his hand along the crumbling bricks of the tunnel wall as they shambled along. As Sir William was speaking, Eddie's hand hit something – a rusted metal bar running down the tunnel wall. He suppressed a cry of surprise and pain.

There was another bar close after the first. The rust was brittle and sharp, flaking off under his palm. He was about to move on, when he realised what it must be.

'Hang on! It think there's a ladder here.'

'Good work, young man. I have just one match left for this contingency.'

A moment later it flared into life, and Eddie could

see that it was indeed a rusty iron ladder, set into the wall of the tunnel.

'It doesn't look too secure,' George said. He pulled at it experimentally and dust and lumps of old cement showered down from above.

'Beggars can't be choosers,' Sir William said.

'And it must go somewhere.'

'So long as it isn't locked or sealed off,' George pointed out.

'Well, let's find out shall we? Eddie.'

'I know, I know.' He took hold of the ladder and pulled himself up to the first rung, testing it carefully with his foot in case it was ready to give way. 'I'm the lightest so I get to see if it's safe.'

'Good lad.'

'The question, then,' George was saying as Eddie hauled himself up the ladder, 'is what was Glick writing about in that diary? What we have seems meaningless. *The answer lies in the Crystal . . .*'

'Maybe he went to a séance with those creepy people,' Liz said. 'Saw something in a crystal ball, like Eddie said.'

Eddie had reached the top of the ladder. It ended in a heavy metal grating, and through it he could see the foggy world outside. Poking his fingers up through the grille, he could feel the cold of the night air.

'Just that one page survived?' Sir William was asking.

'Lots of pages survived,' George replied. 'But most

of them were blank. There can only have been that one entry in that last volume.'

'You didn't tell me that,' Liz said sharply.

'It's hardly important.'

Eddie heaved at the grille. He could feel it move slightly. Rust and crumbling cement rained down on his head and he coughed and blinked before trying again.

'Hardly important?' Liz echoed. 'Did it not occur to you that if there was only one entry in that diary, then what Lorimore is after might well be at the end of the previous volume?'

With an almighty effort, Eddie managed to heave the metal grating up and out. He shoved it sideways until there was room to squeeze past and out into the deserted street above.

George's voice sounded small and quiet as it followed Eddie out of the sewer. 'I never thought of that.'

Chapter 16

It seemed to Eddie that if there was a job that needed doing and which was important or dangerous, then he was the one who got volunteered to do it. The British Museum was a large building, true. But he was sure he could get inside and be able to find his way to wherever Glick's surviving diaries were stored. He had offered to climb in through a window or sneak round the back or anything.

But no. George and Sir William and Liz had other ideas. Better ideas. It was all made to seem like a discussion with Eddie as an equal partner. Except he never got his way, while everyone else got theirs.

Which was why Eddie was outside the imposing main entrance to the British Museum, looking round for whoever Lorimore now had watching the place following Berry's treachery. They weren't hard to spot. Two of them – Eddie recognised the type. Large men with beer bellies who would knock you down and steal your wallet and your watch as soon as look at you. Not quick, but strong. If they got hold of him he would be in trouble.

Despite himself, Eddie found he was relishing the moment, enjoying himself. The two thugs were standing together on the corner of Museum Street, and since they were together they could not keep an eye on the back of the building. Perhaps there was someone else there. It didn't matter.

One of the men was smoking a clay pipe. He blew out a stream of smoke that was soon lost in the mist that lingered from the earlier fog. Away from the factories, the air was clearer. They would see Eddie easily. He would make sure of that.

Hands in his trouser pockets, Eddie set off past the main entrance. He paused under a street lamp, making sure his face was in full view for several seconds. Then, bracing himself to run at any second, he walked slowly past the two men.

The man with the pipe was knocking it out against the heel of his hand. He looked up as Eddie passed, watching the boy with a bored expression. The other man glanced across too, to see what his fellow was watching. Now Eddie was close enough to hear them. He held his breath, kept walking slowly past.

'Reckon it'll rain tomorrow,' the man with the pipe said.

'Never,' the other man countered. 'No sign of that.'

The men lapsed into silence again. Eddie sighed and

continued on his way. At this rate he reckoned he could probably walk into the Museum, retrieve the diaries, and walk out again without either one of them paying him any heed.

But that wasn't the plan. So he crossed the road and walked back along, whistling. When he reached the two men, he stopped in front of them. The whistling had disturbed their reverie and they both looked at him, bored. One of them glared at Eddie as if to say: 'Go on, get out of here.'

Eddie sighed, clearly they weren't going to realise who he was without help. He dropped his mouth open in an expression of horror and fear. 'Oh my good God,' he said loudly.

The men stared at him, mildly surprised at this outburst.

'Oh my cripes,' Eddie went on quickly. 'It's you, isn't it? You're the ones Lorimore's sent to find me, ain't you?!'

Realisation slowly dawned on the pipe-smoker, and his pipe fell from his fingers and shattered on the pavement.

'What?' said the other man, seeing his fellow's reaction.

But Eddie was already running – not so fast they had no hope of catching him, but fast enough to stay out of reach. He could hear their uneven gasps as they came after him.

And at the other end of the street, two shadows detached themselves from the gloom and made their way unseen towards the entrance to the British Museum.

They went straight to the written archives. George had no idea what had happened to the books that Percy had been working on after the break-in, the fire and his death. But Sir William seemed to know exactly where they would be, having, he explained, returned them there that morning.

The few volumes that had survived were stacked in a cupboard. George recognised the remains of the final volume with its blackened pages and one curled cover. The other cover was missing entirely. They gathered it up together with the half dozen volumes that had survived unscathed, and several more that had been damaged to a greater or lesser extent by the fire.

'I don't want to spend too long here,' Sir William said. 'The longer we are here, the more of a risk that that scoundrel Berry will clap eyes on us and go running to Lorimore himself.'

George found a Gladstone bag full of pages of a manuscript in the bottom of the cupboard. He took out the loose pages and stacked them on the shelf where the diaries had been. Then he put the diaries into the bag.

'We don't want to advertise the fact that we are removing them,' he said.

Sir William nodded. 'I suggest we take them all and examine them back at the club.'

They had left Liz at the Atlantian Club. While it only admitted gentlemen as members, and learned ones at that, Sir William was allowed to bring in Liz and the others as guests. The chief steward, Vespers, had shown no trace of surprise at their dishevelled appearance, though his nose wrinkled inadvertently as he got too close.

'May I suggest a private room for your meeting?' he had offered, and Sir William had been pleased to agree at once. 'I'll see if we have one with a washroom nearby,' Vespers had promised.

As soon as they approached the club, the door was opened from inside.

'The young lady is installed in your room, sir,' Vespers told Sir William. 'I have taken the liberty of having the chef send up a selection of cold platters. I gather from the young lady that she and the gentleman here have not yet dined.'

'We were rather busy,' George said as Vespers led the way through the foyer and to a small door.

'Back stairs,' he explained. 'I gather there is a need for discretion, even here.'

'I am afraid so, Vespers. Rather tiresome, but unavoidable I fear.'

The stairs were bare polished wood, and emerged from a narrow and inconspicuous door on the first floor of the club. Vespers led them down an oak-panelled corridor to a rather more imposing, heavy wooden door.

'The Plato Suite, sir.' He leaned forward, and added quietly: 'There is a washroom attached. I can organise a change of clothes if that is required.'

'Good notion, thank you.' Sir William beamed. 'Yes, very kind of you.'

'Not at all, Sir William. I'm not sure what we can do for the young lady, especially as it is getting rather late, but rest assured we shall make every effort to accommodate.'

'And discreetly, if you would, Vespers,' Sir William implored.

'Discreetly' was hardly a description of Eddie's arrival at the Atlantian Club.

He had led Lorimore's two thugs round most of Holborn and twice down the Charing Cross Road before he grew bored and decided that he had given George and Sir William more than enough time to retrieve the diaries from the Museum. He put on an extra burst of speed, rounded a corner, and ducked into a narrow alley.

Almost a minute later, the two men passed the end

of the alley. They were struggling to draw breath, close to exhaustion. Neither of them noticed the dark opening where Eddie was hiding in the shadows as they puffed past like steam trains.

'Where's he gone?' one of them gasped.

'Must be round the next corner. Come on, or we'll never catch him.'

Eddie gave them plenty of time to get clear before slipping out of hiding and setting off back down the street in the opposite direction. Sir William had given him the address of the Atlantian Club, and Eddie knew the road. But he was unprepared for either the imposing entrance or the tall uniformed doorman who stepped out as soon as Eddie approached.

'Can I help you?' the man asked. His tone implied that he doubted very much that he could.

'Yeah,' Eddie told him from several steps lower down, 'I'm meeting me mates here.'

'Mates?' The man's nose wrinkled.

'George and Liz,' Eddie said. The man seemed unmoved. 'And Sir William Something-or-other.'

This had an effect. The man came down the steps to meet him. 'You're with Sir William's party?' he asked quietly, looking round to make sure no one could hear them.

Eddie nodded, surprised at the change in the man's attitude.

The doorman sniffed, and made a face. 'Yes,' he said,

'Now you mention it, I can tell that you are. Will you come with me please, sir? Sir William is expecting you.'

Inside, Eddie was impressed by the foyer with its panelled walls and marble floor. The doorman led the way, and finally he was shown into a large room dominated by a huge oval table that was so highly polished that the ornate ceiling was reflected in its wooden surface.

'I gather this young gentleman is with you, Sir William,' the doorman said.

Sir William, George and Liz were seated together at the table. Half a dozen leather-bound books were piled up in front of them. Others were lying open. Sir William rose to greet Eddie.

'Indeed yes, Stephen. This is Eddie – a vital member of our team. Thank you so much for showing him up.'

The doorman smiled and left them to it. Sir William beckoned Eddie over to join them at the table. Eddie noticed that they had all changed their clothes, but he said nothing. They might offer him starched, uncomfortable clothing too. Or worse, a wash.

But the others were more keen to explain what they were doing than to worry about how Eddie looked or smelled.

'This is the penultimate volume of Sir Henry Glick's diary,' Sir William said, pointing to one of the books open on the table. 'The last entries must come soon before the contents of the destroyed final volume. Here,' he said pointing to a fragment of charred paper which Eddie recognised, 'is all that remains of that volume, apart from blank pages. And we can draw several conclusions concerning what Glick was writing about.'

Eddie read the fragment aloud – to prove he could read as much as anything.

> *'. . . now know which came first, and I can prove it.*
> *The answer lies in the Crystal . . .'*

'Now,' Sir William went on, 'if we look at the previous volume we find that the final entries concern preparations for a dinner on New Year's Eve 1853 in the Crystal Palace Park.'

'Which came first . . .' Eddie repeated, barely paying attention to the others. 'Sounds like a riddle.'

'It is a riddle,' George agreed. 'But the answer is not as straightforward as "Which came first, the chicken or the egg." We'd thought of that.'

'So what does it mean?'

'It's the word "Crystal" that we think is important,' Liz said.

Sir William was nodding enthusiastically. 'As Miss Oldfield pointed out, it is odd that Crystal should be capitalised. Unless it refers to a proper noun.'

'A what?'

Sir William waved aside Eddie's question and pushed the last surviving volume of the diary in front of him.

He jabbed his finger at a piece of card that was gummed on to one of the pages. There was a drawing on it – a large bird with huge leathery wings stretched out in flight. Its beak was more like a crocodile's mouth, filled with sharp teeth.

'A pterodactyl,' Sir William said. 'A flying dinosaur, from the time before history even began.'

There was writing on one of the outstretched wings which Sir William read aloud. 'Mr Waterhouse Hawkins,' he paused to explain: 'He was Director of the Fossil Department at the Crystal Palace.'

'Crystal,' Eddie realised. 'You think—'

But Sir William was reading again:

> *Mr Waterhouse Hawkins requests the honour of Sir Henry Glick at dinner in the belly of the Iguanodon at the Crystal Palace on Saturday evening December the 31st at five o'clock 1853 – an answer will oblige.*

George leaned forward and turned the page. 'And here,' he said to Eddie, 'Glick writes that he was asked to address the guests at that dinner, and he seems excited. He has something he says will "astonish and astound" them.'

Eddie nodded. He could see why they thought the scrap of writing from the final diary might relate to this same event. 'So what,' he asked, 'is an ig-wan-o-dan?'

'An iguanodon,' Sir William corrected him.

'It's a sort of dinosaur,' Liz said. 'A huge reptile, like a lizard only enormous, from prehistory.'

'And you eat dinner in them?'

Sir William laughed. 'Generally not. But following the Great Exhibition, several life-size models of recently discovered dinosaurs were cast and are still now situated in the Crystal Palace Park. That creature that pursued us earlier this evening was I believe derived in some way from a dinosaur.'

'Where do they live?' Eddie asked, amazed. He had never heard of such a thing, let alone seen one. Not until that week anyway.

'They died out many many years ago. Perhaps millions of years ago. We don't know much about them, even now eighty years after the discovery of the first dinosaur bones and skeletons. We don't even know how they reproduced.'

Eddie was struggling to make sense of all this. 'So this Glick bloke knew something about dinosaurs. And he was invited to dinner in one where he told everyone else what it was?'

'Not quite,' Sir William corrected him. 'You see, while Glick did indeed attend the dinner, it seems he was taken ill and left before he could make his speech. Though in fact his diary gives a slightly different interpretation.'

George was holding the diary and turned to the very last page.

'That scoundrel Richard Owen antagonised me so very much with his rather self-satisfied account of his achievements I felt physically ill. Not once did he spare a thought for Messrs Mantell or Buckland, or even Cuvier, much less give them any iota of praise or any hint of acknowledgement. It quite put me off my food. And by the time it was my turn to say a few words I had decided not to waste my breath on these selfish fools. I made my apologies and left, explaining with as much irony as I could muster, that I felt quite ill. To my subsequent dismay I left in such a hurry that I neglected to be sure I had with me the very item I had gone there to present. And when I checked the next morning, I found that in my haste, I had dropped it. Though of course it is not lost for I know precisely where it now is, and the irony makes me smile.

So, instead, I shall present my startling discovery within this diary. Or rather the next volume of this diary for as you see we have reached the final page. So the next volume will bear witness to the matters that Owen and his cronies forfeited that night.'

'So what was it?' Eddie asked, excited now despite not really following everything he'd been told.

'That is the question,' Sir William replied.

'And the answer,' Liz said, 'is in the Crystal.'

Eddie frowned. 'Does he mean the park? Or the Crystal Palace itself?'

'Just what we were wondering when you arrived,' George said.

'And I was about to say that I believe it is neither,' Sir William said. He stood up and walked slowly round the table as he spoke. He tapped his index finger against his chin, deep in thought. 'Now Sir Henry died soon after that. He had been ill for a while, so that is probably why no one seemed surprised he had to leave early. But we know from this extract that he took something with him to the dinner that evening. Something that would demonstrate in some way the astonishing and astounding information he had to impart. Something that will tell us what it is that Lorimore seeks so desperately to discover.'

'And he says that he lost it,' George said.

'Not exactly. Because he also says he knows exactly where it is.'

'But if it's important, why didn't he go and get it back then,' Eddie wanted to know.

'Or was he too ill for that?' Liz suggested.

Sir William shook his head. 'He did not retrieve it, because while he knew where it was, it wasn't possible to get it back. Think – where is he most likely to have accidentally left it?'

They all thought. And they all reached the answer at the same moment, their faces slowly clearing into realisation. It was Eddie who put it into words:

'It's still there,' Eddie said excitedly, 'whatever it is.

The answer lies in the Crystal Palace igu-whatsit-thing.'

Sir William nodded vehemently. 'Literally it does. After the meal, the statue was completed. The top was lowered into place, and sealed. The tent around the statue was dismantled and the iguanodon still stands guard in the Park. It still keeps Sir Henry Glick's secret safe inside. As he himself says: ironic.'

There was silence for several moments while they all thought about this.

'So what do we do?' Liz asked at last.

'Why I should think that was obvious. We must go at once to the Crystal Palace, and find out what is hidden inside the iguanodon.'

Once again, Stephen managed to get a cab within seconds, despite the fact it was now gone midnight. George, Liz and Eddie piled into the carriage. Sir William paused to give instructions to the driver before he squeezed in beside them.

The driver cracked his whip, and Stephen watched it depart into the lingering shreds of fog. Then he turned and walked back inside the warmth of the Atlantian Club.

Had he hesitated just a few moments, he might have seen two figures standing in the shadows on the opposite side of the street. One of them turned to the other.

'Mr Blade was right,' he said. 'Sir William's club – obvious place for them to come really.'

'Just luck, that's all,' the other replied.

'Doesn't matter. Let's find Mr Blade, fast as we can. He'll want to know where they're headed: the Crystal Palace.'

Chapter 17

Mist still hung heavily over the sloping ground of the park. It shimmered and shivered in the light breeze, like a moving blanket of smoke. The grass was wet with dew and the moon struggled to find its way through the thinning clouds. The Crystal Palace stood majestic in the moonlight. Its glass walls glinted and glistened, reflecting pale ghosts of the hazy parkland.

Sir William led them along one of the paths that swept down the hill and round the Crystal Palace towards the lake. Despite the fact that they were probably the only people in the entire park, they still spoke in hushed whispers.

'Do you know where we're going, sir?' George asked.

'It has been a while,' Sir William admitted, 'but yes, I think I can recall the way.'

'What are we looking for?' Eddie asked.

'An iguanodon,' Liz told him. 'A dinosaur.'

'What's it look like?'

'I expect you'll know it when you see it,' George replied.

'Big and lizard-like,' Liz said. 'Remember?'

Eddie did remember. 'And it's a statue, right? And somehow we have to get inside it?'

Sir William paused. 'Yes,' he said slowly. 'You know I hadn't really considered that. I wonder how we can get it open.'

'It depends how the thing is put together,' George said. 'We may need to come back with tools.'

'Or we could smash our way in,' Eddie suggested.

'With our fists?' Liz said. 'What's it made of, this statue?'

Sir William led them off the path now, over the wet grass and into a thicker patch of mist. 'Cast iron, brick, stone . . .' His voice faded with him into the night. Eddie and the others hastened after him.

'We won't need tools,' Eddie muttered to George. 'We'll need a gang of navvies.'

The ground rose, disappearing into the mist. They were skirting a small lake when Eddie heard the noises. The bank was steep and the grass was slippery, so they were all concentrating on keeping their balance.

'It's just along here somewhere, I feel sure,' Sir William called back to them.

But Eddie had stopped. 'What's that?'

They all stopped and listened. The sound was muffled by the heavy air, but in the silence they could all hear it – the distant sound of people talking, of undergrowth and branches being forced aside.

'They're looking for us,' Eddie knew instinctively.

'We can't be sure of that,' George replied quietly.

'Why else would they be here?' Eddie said. 'In the middle of the night?'

'It does seem likely that somehow we have been traced or followed,' Sir William admitted. They were all talking in hushed tones now.

'Then let's get moving,' Liz whispered.

They hurried on along the bank for several minutes, and it seemed – to Eddie's relief – that the voices and sounds receded into the night behind them. After a while, Sir William stopped, pointing up the steep slope. A large dark shape loomed up above them, barely more than a charcoal silhouette in the mist that rose from the lake beside them.

'Ah, here we are.' Sir William stepped aside, at the base of the rocky outcrop. Above him, through the mist, a shape was forming – gaining substance as Eddie got closer. A scaly, reptilian head thrust out of the gloom. A vicious spiked horn protruded from the creature's nose, and large glassy eyes regarded Eddie suspiciously.

'The monster!' Eddie gasped.

'What? Oh nonsense,' Sir William told him. 'It's just

the statue of an iguanodon. And not terribly accurate at that, from what we now know. The iguanodon was a dinosaur that lived on our Earth many years ago, Eddie. Despite what we have seen tonight, or think we have seen, the last dinosaurs became extinct long, long ago.' He paused to examine the monstrous head, towering above him, glistening with condensation.

Sir William walked slowly round the statue, tapping at its side, its belly, its back with his cane. 'Yes, here, I think,' he decided. He was kneeling at the back of the creature, almost hidden in the undergrowth that sprawled out on to the rock. 'Bring that stone, will you?' he said to George, gesturing to a large, heavy lump of rock lying at the base of the outcrop.

'We don't have long,' George said as he picked it up.

'They'll hear us trying to break in,' Liz pointed out.

Sir William suggested that George use the heavy chunk of rock to try to break through the underbelly of the statue. 'Here, you see?' he pointed out the spot to George. 'You can feel where the metal is worn slightly smooth, and there is a joint where the plates do not quite meet. The elements have begun to take their toll.'

'Let's get a move on then,' Eddie said. The cold was getting to him now. He had no jacket and the damp mist had eaten into his clothing so that he was shrouded in a chilly aura.

The first blow echoed metallically round the park, bouncing back from beyond the lake. The faint sounds of the distant search stopped at once. Then they started again, immediately louder and closer.

'Let's hope it takes them a while to get a bearing on us,' Sir William said as George laid into the underbelly of the beast with renewed urgency and vigour.

'The echo may help,' Liz said, between blows.

Eddie was stamping his feet to try to keep warm. 'We might have to leg it,' he said.

'It is possible we were followed from the club,' Sir William said. 'So if we do have to make a run for it, and we get separated, then I suggest we meet back at the British Museum. It should be empty by now. They will have let poor old Berry go home to his family once they discovered where we were.'

The next blow made a different sound – cracked and discordant.

'I felt it give,' George said excitedly. 'I think it's going.'

After several more blows, George set down the rock and worked at the ragged metal with his bare hands. It had torn along the joint and he managed to wrench a whole plate of metal free, revealing a dark opening in the underside of the statue. 'I can get my arm right inside,' he said. 'It *is* hollow.'

'Excellent, excellent.' Sir William clapped his hands together in delight. 'Can you feel anything?'

'No, nothing.'

'We shall have to get right inside to search,' Liz said.

'Or,' she added, turning pointedly towards Eddie, 'someone will.'

'No way,' Eddie said at once. 'Really no way. At all. Not ever.'

George had emerged from under the statue. He was listening carefully, head cocked to one side. 'They must have heard the noise. I think they're coming.'

'We can't just leave,' Liz said desperately. 'Not now.'

'How big is the hole?' Sir William demanded. 'Maybe I can –'

'You can't,' George told him.

Now they could hear running feet, trampling through branches and long grass. Shouts of anger and elation as the hunters found their trail.

'We've got about half a minute,' George hissed. 'At the most.'

Everyone was looking at Eddie. His arms were folded and his expression was set. He stared back at them. 'Half a minute,' he muttered. 'Oh give us a leg up, will you?'

'What am I looking for?' he asked as he scraped and scrambled through the jagged tear in the statue.

'I am afraid I really don't know,' Sir William whispered.

Eddie stifled a cry of pain as his knee caught on a curl of sharp metal. He slumped forward into the darkness, his every move echoing hollowly round the black interior of the creature. The belly of the beast.

Slowly and carefully he crawled forward. There were bracing struts – like roof girders – running round the inside of the statue. Heavy, sharp bolts held them in place. They were painful when you crawled over them, as Eddie quickly found.

'Anything?' Liz's voice hissed up through the hole.

'No,' he hissed back. He reckoned he had crawled round a good part of the interior by now and found nothing inside it at all that was not part of the structure.

Then a shout – not a voice Eddie recognised. 'They're here!'

'Oh corks!' he heard George exclaim.

Then Sir William's urgent: 'See you back at the Museum, Eddie. We'll try to lead them away. Good hunting.'

'Get Mr Blade,' the voice shouted again, so close that Eddie thought it might be inside the statue with him. Running feet, the clatter of pursuit. Eddie lay as still as he could, not daring to move, not daring even to breathe.

After what seemed for ever, he turned round carefully, staring into the close blackness in the hope of making out the hole where he had come in. But he could see nothing.

His hand touched something. Something hard and round and heavy. It rolled away from him, sounding like a large glass marble inside a tin can. The noise was louder than thunder in the confined space.

'What was that?' said a voice that sounded uncomfortably close. 'Where did that come from?'

Eddie's hand found the stone again – it was about the size of an orange, and he lifted it carefully, gently, silently. The only weapon he had. The moon must have broken through the clouds again, for now he could see the uneven hole in the floor about four feet in front of him.

And as he watched and held his breath and grasped the stone tightly, first a large hand, then a whole arm reached in through the hole. Searching, feeling its way towards Eddie as he sat and shivered in the darkness.

Chapter 18

They soon lost their pursuers in the dark, the voices and the sounds of Lorimore's men falling behind.

'Let's hope they don't much wonder what we were doing,' Sir William said quietly. 'We don't want them examining the statue too closely or they will uncover poor Eddie.'

'You think that's likely?' Liz asked, concerned.

'I doubt they're clever enough to realise the significance, my dear.'

They moved as quickly and quietly as they could through the misty night. Sir William led them towards the back gate of the park. With luck it would not be guarded. The path sloped upwards, past the lake, and before long, a dark shape loomed out of the mist ahead.

'Is that the gates?' Liz wondered.

'Looks more like another statue,' George said, the apprehension heavy in his voice.

As they edged cautiously closer, George could see

that it was a figure – a large man, stretching out as if it was waiting to enfold them all in an enormous bear hug. A sudden gust of wind scattered the mist, and the moon shone down for the briefest of moments before the clouds could regroup.

But in that moment they could see the massive ape of a man stood waiting for them at the top of the slope. His face was scarred and pockmarked, and several days' growth of dark stubble added to the ape-like image. His eyes were deep-set and black as tar. With an inhuman roar he leaped down the slope towards them.

George moved quicker than even he would have thought possible. The huge man had hurled himself at Sir William, but George got there first, intercepting the man. The two of them slammed together and rolled down the slope. George was tall not broad, but sinewy. He was no match for the enormous figure that rolled him aside and started back up the slope. George grabbed at his legs, dragging him down. But the man swatted him away like an annoying insect. George rolled with the blow, stumbled, and pulled himself painfully back to his feet.

Liz was staring, shouting anxiously to George to see if he was all right. Sir William looked on with a mixture of anxiety and interest at the bear of a man who was now lumbering towards him. As he came closer, Sir William stepped down to meet him, raising his cane. He whipped it down on the man's head, so hard that George heard the crack of the splintering wood.

The man seemed hardly to notice. He gave a grunt of annoyance, but did not even slow down. Three more steps and he would be on Sir William. His hands were outstretched ready to snap the old man in two like a dead branch.

Without even thinking about it, George launched himself again at the ape-like man who was now reaching for Sir William.

The force of the impact as George crashed into him sent the man stumbling sideways. George found himself slipping away down the bank, and collided with something heavy and jagged and painful. A lump of rock.

George was back on his feet now, hefting up the rock. He stumbled once more towards the attacker who was pulling himself slowly to his knees. But before George got there, Liz stepped smartly forwards and kicked the man hard under the chin. His head snapped back and he groaned in pain and anger. But his hand whipped up and grabbed Liz's foot – twisting and pulling so that she slipped to the ground with a cry.

The man was on his feet again now, his hands clasped together as if he held a sword. He was poised, ready to bring his double fist smashing down on Liz's head.

Sir William barged into the massive figure, shoulder down, in an effort to knock him off balance. But he might as well have run into a brick wall. He glanced off, stumbled, and fell to the ground.

He was too far away to reach Liz. But George brought his arms up above his head, and hurled the large, heavy lump of rock. It caught the assailant in the chest, the force of the impact forcing him to take several steps backwards. Liz scrambled rapidly out of reach, the rock thudding to the ground where she had been only seconds before.

'Sorry,' George gasped as he pulled himself up the slope. He stooped down beside Liz, not to check she was all right, but to lift the heavy lump of stone once again.

But the ape man was too quick. With a desperate effort, Sir William scrambled forwards, rolling into the man's legs. He grabbed and pulled, scrabbled and was somehow able to slow the man just enough for George to stagger back out of the way, the rock again clutched to his chest.

As the man started to run heavily and ponderously straight at George, Sir William grabbed his bent cane and threw it like a spear between the man's legs. Caught between one leg and the other, the cane shattered with a bullet-like crack.

But it had done its job. The man stumbled. Off balance, and heading down the steep hill, he had to run faster to prevent himself from falling. George's eyes widened as he saw the giant figure hurtling towards him.

Then a ball of crinoline and limbs rolled itself in front of the attacker – who stumbled, tripped, crashed forwards over the top of Liz and thumped massively into the ground, skidding muddily down the slope to come to a halt face-down at George's feet.

Without a word, without thinking, George smashed the rock down on the back of the man's head. But incredibly, he heard the man cry out. Slowly but inexorably he was stumbling back to his feet.

'Again!' Sir William cried.

George did not need telling twice, and smashed it down again on the man's head. And again.

Eventually, the figure was still. George let the rock fall to the ground, before collapsing exhausted to his knees beside it.

'I'm afraid the noise may have alerted this man's colleagues,' Sir William said breathlessly. 'If,' he added as he stooped beside George to examine the body, 'he really is a man.'

'What do you mean?' Liz was picking herself up and brushing unsuccessfully at the muddy stains down the front of her dress.

'Is he dead?' Eddie asked. He half hoped the man was, though he shuddered even to think of it.

'He should be,' Sir William said. 'Just one of those

blows should have shattered his skull.' At this point the huge man snored, loudly. Sir William was feeling round the top of the man's head. Apparently satisfied, he turned his attention to the rest of his body – prodding at the arms and legs and mumbling to himself. 'Yes, yes, yes,' he decided at last. 'Just as I thought.' He looked up at George and Liz as they stood watching. 'Just as I feared.'

'We should hurry,' George said, alerted by the sounds of cries and shouts from somewhere behind them.

'Yes.' Sir William got to his feet and retrieved the pieces of his broken cane. He looked at them sadly. 'I think the gates must be just up here. He was probably left to guard the exit.'

Sir William led them quickly along the path and they soon reached the back gate out of the park. It was locked, but Sir William produced a small metal tool from inside his jacket, and in moments the gate was open. It creaked ominously in the still of the night, and Liz froze, half expecting hordes of Lorimore's strongmen to descend on them out of the darkness. But all remained silent.

'You think we'll find a cab?' George asked.

'Later, perhaps. I'd like to take a short walk first.'

'A short walk?' Liz was appalled. 'Poor Eddie will be heading back to the Museum looking for us, possibly with all manner of blackguards on his tail, and you feel the need for a constitutional?'

Sir William smiled. 'All in a good cause, I promise. But if you want to go straight back to the Museum, please don't let me stop you.'

'Where are you thinking of going, sir?' George said before Liz could reply.

'It's only a short way to Lorimore's main foundry,' Sir William explained. 'I have a notion it might be worth a quick look, since we happen to be in the vicinity.' He looked from George to Liz. 'What we have seen tonight, the incredible strength of that man for instance – and I do mean incredible – has somewhat piqued my interest. The back of his head, for example, seemed to be made of metal. And where do you suppose Lorimore would have the facilities to make a metal headpiece, hmm?'

The probing hand felt round the hole, scrabbling at the rough metalwork inside. Eddie watched it, transfixed as if by a cobra. He held his stone poised, ready to slam it down on the hand should it come too close, or if the owner tried to pull himself through the hole in the underside of the statue.

Time seemed to have slowed down – it took an age for whoever was attached to the other end of the arm to decide that he was wasting his time and withdraw it. Eddie had to force himself not to sigh out loud with relief. He could hear two men outside talking, but their voices were muffled now and indistinct. Perhaps because they were facing away, perhaps because of the fog, perhaps because they were leaving.

Even when it was completely silent outside, Eddie remained frozen in position. He could feel the rough metal through the material of his trousers. When he did move his knees would be embossed with a relief map of the inside of the statue. Gently and silently he edged closer to the hole. He clutched the rounded stone as if it was a talisman, reassured by the way it fitted so well in his hand, ready to strike at anything that moved.

But the only movement was the slow drifting of the wisps of fog between the underside of the statue and the ground several feet below. Cautiously, Eddie lowered his head through the gap, looking all round to be sure there was no one in sight. The mist had rolled in again as the air near the water warmed with the approaching threat of dawn. He waited a full minute to be sure he was indeed alone. Then he allowed himself to fall forwards through the hole, his arms outstretched in front of him to take his weight.

The ground was slippery rock, and he was hampered by the stone he still held in one hand. He slipped and crashed to the hard ground, grunting in pain and annoyance as the air was knocked out of him. Eddie lay there, staring up at the underside of the dinosaur as he got his breath back. He was also thinking, trying to remember the way back to the park entrance. Could he retrace his steps? Would Blade have left anyone on guard at the entrance? Come to that, was it the only way out of the park? If there were others, maybe Eddie had a better chance of avoiding Lorimore's men and making his escape.

Eddie knew he had to get moving, but he did not want to. He wanted to stay here, in the shadow and safety of the dinosaur. The best way to break the spell, he knew, was not to think about it but just to do it.

So without really picking the moment, Eddie got to his feet and stumbled out from under the statue. He made his way cautiously back down the slope towards the lake, peering into the mist in an effort to make out his surroundings, listening carefully as he hurried back to the path. He could hear nothing, but did that mean that Blade and his men had given up? Or were they hiding, waiting for him?

This was the path back to the main gates now, he was sure. Eddie hastened his pace. Just another couple of minutes and he would be out of the park and safe. Getting back to Holborn might take him a while, but maybe he could get a ride with a milkman heading that way to start his rounds, or a postie . . .

The smoke from Lorimore's huge foundry thickened the fog for miles around. The noise of the machinery inside was almost deafening as they approached it. The enormous building straddled several streets – massive and grey and featureless, its chimneys rising out of sight above the building.

George and the others ducked into the shadows as a large man walked past, his massive, ape-like silhouette easily visible through the mist.

Sir William nodded grimly, before leading them to a side door. Like the park gate, he set about opening it with the metal tool from his pocket. In moments, they had slipped inside and closed the door behind them before the guard could return.

It was as if the fog had crept inside the great foundry, thickening and billowing. Smoke and steam mingled, clawing at the back of George's throat as he followed Sir William. He held tight to Liz's hand, so as not to lose her. Sir William was as faint as a figure behind a muslin curtain, all but swallowed up by the heavy air.

Struggling not to choke on the hot, acrid fumes, George followed. He could hear Liz clearing her throat beside him, but could barely see her through the yellowed mist. Then, in a moment, they were through and the air cleared enough to see the great factory floor stretching out in front of them.

'An updraft of some sort,' Sir William said. He almost had to shout above the rhythmic metallic thump of the machinery. It seemed to have increased as they emerged from the smog. 'Deliberate ventilation,

I imagine. It would be no good if the workers couldn't see what they were doing.'

'Even if they can't hear themselves think,' Liz remarked.

George was surveying the scene in front of him. 'What *are* they doing?' he wondered.

There were several dozen men working in the factory. So far none of them had noticed Sir William and his friends. But soon someone was sure to spot them, George realised. If there was anything to be learned here they needed to do it fast, and then get away. He pointed this out, and Liz nodded in agreement.

'We need to get up higher,' she said.

'Why?'

'So we can see what they're doing. Like seeing the stage from the gallery – you get a better view of the whole layout. It is easier to make out what is happening.'

'Splendid idea,' Sir William agreed. 'What do you have in mind?'

There was a metal gantry running round the wall, perhaps twenty feet above their heads. A ladder led up to it from several yards away. Liz led them over to it, and George went first, then Liz, with Sir William bringing up the rear.

The ventilation Sir William had described was drawing the smoke and fumes up from the clanking machinery on the ground and high into the structure of the building to be vented through open skylights in the lower part of the sloping roof. Soon George found himself climbing through a moist, warm mist. Looking down, the foundry floor was wreathed in thin clouds of smoke. The huge iron machines rose up above the swirling fog, reminding George of the gravestones in the cemetery.

They reached the gantry, and George led them along to where they could get a good view out over the entire enormous space below. Slightly further on, another ladder led up to another gantry high in the roof space. There were dozens of the steam-driven engines on the floor below, each working away. Smoke and steam rose through the metal grille of the gantry, swirling round them as they watched. Pistons slammed in and out, and chains clanked as they were drawn through the machines, emerging with glowing metal components hanging from them like washing from a line. The glow dulled as the chains moved along and the metal cooled.

The chains seemed to link groups of the machines together, daisy-chaining them so that components manufactured by the first engine were modified by the next, refined by another, finished by a fourth. Finally, the chains all met and together were hauled through a huge vat of oily water. The metal hissed and spat as it sank into the churning depths, to emerge blacked and smudged with oil on the other side.

Here men took the metal components – rods, wheels, bolts, casings – and assembled them. George peered through the drifting steam in an effort to see what they were constructing.

'It appears to be some sort of exoskeleton,' Sir William said, pointing to the nearest group of assembly workers.

'A what?' Liz asked.

'A frame, to hold something inside it together,' George explained. It was difficult to make out the exact shape, but Sir William was right. There were dozens of the completed frames standing in lines at the side of the work area. 'What can they be for?'

'I don't know,' Sir William confessed. 'But I have several very unpleasant suspicions.'

'Relating to that man's head?' Liz asked, remembering why they had come here.

'I thought we were never going to stop him,' George admitted. He was still shaken by the experience.

'I think we are very lucky that we did,' Sir William told them as he watched the activity below. 'He was no ordinary thug. His cranium, as I say, had been plated with metal. The end result was so thick I doubt it left much space for the brain. And his limbs were lengthened and heavy. From a very quick analysis, and of course I am no expert, I would say that the man's bones were larger and considerably more dense than human bones.'

'He wasn't human?' George asked, trying to understand what Sir William was telling them.

'I believe he was, once. But just as poor Albert Wilkes's bones had been replaced, albeit in a somewhat rudimentary manner, here the transition was rather more advanced. The process had been completed.'

'But what process?' George asked.

Sir William nodded at the men toiling below the gantry. 'A process to replace a man's brain with something less sophisticated, something with a much reduced reasoning capacity. The ability perhaps merely to understand and carry out simple instructions.'

'And the bones?' Liz asked.

'Intriguing, isn't it?' Sir William said. 'A man whose bones had been replaced, I believe, with the bones of a long-dead dinosaur. But,' he went on, 'there is no reason why they should not be replaced by metal too. Or even,' he added significantly, 'by an entire metal frame.'

'But why?' Liz demanded. 'What is he doing this for?'

'I can only speculate,' Sir William offered. 'But everything here would seem to support my theory. He is, as we can see, an industrialist. He runs factories like these where workers manufacture goods, or smelt metal. How much more efficient if he could staff those factories with labourers each of whom has the strength of ten men, and who doesn't have the mental capacity to complain about the working conditions, or demand more pay? Human machines.'

George was about to ask whether this was really possible when there was a shout from the floor below. One of the workmen was pointing up at the gantry – up at George and the others. More of the men turned to look. There was a stiffness to their movements. They seemed cumbersome, like the man who had attacked them in the park, George realised.

'Time we were going,' he said.

'A little too late for that,' Liz said. Her face was white as she pointed to where more of the men were already starting up the ladder towards the gantry.

'There must be another way down,' George said.

'There is.' Liz pointed further along the gantry.

But through the steaming yellow-tinged mist rising from the machines, George could see more workmen climbing that ladder too. 'They're coming at us from both sides,' he realised. 'We're trapped.'

Chapter 19

Sir William shook his head. 'There is one other way we can go.'

George and Liz both looked each way along the gantry. Men were now climbing on to it from the ladders, starting along the narrow metal walkway towards them.

'I don't see . . .' George started. Then he stopped, realising that Sir William was pointing to the ladder just ahead of them. It led upwards, towards the roof. 'You have to be joking,' George finished.

Sir William raised his eyebrows. 'If you have a better idea, young man, then I suggest you come out with it pretty sharpish.'

George looked at Liz. He looked at the men making their ponderous way along the gantry towards them He looked at the ground, twenty feet below, and imagined being shoved over the flimsy guard rail that ran along the gantry. Then he looked back at the ladder. 'I'll go last,' he said. 'In case they try to follow us.'

'And what do we do when we can't go any higher?' Liz demanded, following Sir William as quickly as she could up the ladder.

'Don't ask,' George hissed back at her.

Sir William's voice floated back to them through the thickening mist. 'We climb out of one of the skylights and down the roof, of course.' This time, George could tell he wasn't joking. The skylights were level with the next gantry, wide open and sucking the smoke out into the cold night beyond. He hurried up the ladder after Liz and Sir William.

This ladder was much the same as the one they had already climbed. But higher up, it was full in the path of the rising steam. The bolts holding the ladder to the walls of the foundry were rough with rust, flaking away as the ladder strained against them under the weight. George watched black showers of corroded ironwork drop away from the bolts, the rungs, the sides of the ladder as he climbed. Looking down, he saw the first of their pursuers starting up the ladder after them. The ironwork creaked and groaned in protest and he shouted for Sir William to hurry.

Sir William stepped out on to the upper gantry, just as the ladder pulled away from the wall. One of the upper bolts sheared, the extra strain immediately breaking the bolt on the other side with a screech of tearing metal. The top of the ladder lurched outwards.

Liz screamed, and Sir William had to lunge to make it to the upper gantry.

'Go on, quickly!' George shouted.

Sir William was reaching across for Liz. She grasped his hand, jumped. She slipped, her feet suddenly dangling over the edge, in space. George reached out desperately, managing to get his hand under one of her feet and push upwards just as Sir William heaved Liz towards him.

With a gasp of relief as Liz joined Sir William on the safety of the gantry, George hurried to follow. The ladder was pulling further and further away from the wall, away from the connection to the gantry. He would have to jump. Liz was beckoning for him, ready to try to catch him. He braced himself as he reached the top rung.

And a hand closed over his lower leg, gripping it tight. George gave a yelp of surprise. He kicked out with his other foot, holding on tight to the sides of the ladder with both hands. The grip loosened, and he managed to rip his leg free. He jumped at once.

Just in time. The ladder continued to break away. Several more bolts sheared off and fell heavily into space, clattering to the lower gantry thirty feet below one after another. The top of the ladder was swinging more rapidly now, pulled over by the weight of the men climbing up it. As George's stomach crashed into the gantry, as he struggled to hold on, as he hauled himself on to it, the ladder finally tore from the wall with a squeal of tortured metal. Liz helped him to his feet, and they both glanced down as the ladder crashed to the floor below.

Sir William was also looking down. But not at the falling ladder, or the men sliding angrily back down to the gantry below. He was looking out over the manufacturing floor. Liz joined him, breathing heavily. Standing behind them, George too saw the larger metal exoframes arranged behind the ones they had seen before. And beyond that, the shadowy outline of more ironwork being assembled from the most distant engines and furnaces. Silhouetted in the drifting smoke, George could see the vague shapes of struts and braces sticking up like broken teeth.

'Glad you could join us, young man,' Sir William said. 'But I think we should hurry.' He led them over to a skylight, fastened open to allow the smoke and steam to escape. It was easily large enough to climb through, and Sir William called back that there was a ladder down on the other side.

'Lucky,' Liz said.

'An informed guess,' Sir William called back. 'They need to get in from the outside for maintenance after all.'

George let Liz follow Sir William. 'They'll soon realise where we're going. We'd better get a move on or we'll find them waiting at the bottom of the ladder.' He pushed through the open section of roof after Liz. The steam and smoke swirled round him – wet and hot. Outside the London smog was cold and damp. For a moment, caught between the two, eyes stinging and unable to breathe, George imagined what hell must be like.

Eddie did not see the figures hiding close to the iron gates that led out of the park, even though he had been half expecting them. Only when they moved – detaching themselves from the shadows and stepping towards him – did he realise they were there.

With a cry of surprise, he turned to run. But more figures were appearing through the mist, closing in on him. He was trapped, and his only option was to stand and fight. He hefted the orange-shaped stone in his hand wondering whether to keep it as a weapon or to hurl it at the first man who came for him. He hoped it would be Blade.

It was not. It was a tall, spindly figure that Eddie recognised immediately as Lorimore. As the figure scuttled towards him, rubbing its bony hands together with satisfaction, Eddie saw that his features were as thin as his body. His nose was barely more than a line down his face, his eyes narrowed to slits.

'Well, well, well.' Lorimore's voice was as sharp and pinched as his features. 'What have we here? A young lad who would appear to be missing his coat, and on such a cold night too.' He paused several feet from Eddie, teeth visible between thin lips as he smiled malevolently. 'Do you perchance have a spare coat that might fit this young man, Mr Blade?'

Blade's voice came from behind Eddie, making him jump. 'I did, Mr Lorimore, sir. Only trouble is, it got all ripped to pieces.'

Lorimore shook his head slowly, and Eddie thought of a cobra he had once seen at Regent's Park Zoo. 'Such a pity. But I suppose the thing to do is to make sure that the lad matches his coat. Ripped to pieces, you say, Mr Blade?' His whole body seemed to shake with laughter at this – a high-pitched nasal whine like a pig in pain.

Blade too was laughing, great guffaws that almost doubled him up. If he was going to make a move, Eddie realised that this might be his only chance. He raised the stone, and ran straight at Lorimore, shouting with rage.

Lorimore stopped laughing at once. As Eddie grew closer, running now at full pelt, stone raised, he saw Lorimore's eyes suddenly open wide. A skeletal finger pointed at Eddie and Lorimore's mouth was open in what might be fear, or surprise, or . . .

Eddie launched himself at Lorimore, sending them both flying. Eddie fell on top of the man as they hit the ground, winding his opponent while guaranteeing a soft landing for himself. Eddie smacked the stone down as hard as he could.

Lorimore twisted, desperately reaching to grab Eddie's hand as it hammered down at him. He managed to deflect the blow and almost prised the stone from Eddie's grip. But then the blow hit home – glancing off Lorimore's shoulder. The man screamed out in pain. Eddie wrenched himself free, rolled to his feet, and still clutching the stone he bolted straight for the gates.

Lorimore's men were running to help their master, and only Blade gave chase. He was knocked sideways by one of the thugs running the other way. He spun away into the mist with a loud curse. Over and above Blade's shout, Eddie could hear Lorimore yelling at his henchmen to leave him, that he was all right, that they must get after the boy . . .

But Eddie was already out of the gates and running down the main road – sprinting after a cab that rattled past. He shouted for it to stop, managed to get level with it for a few seconds, and saw the driver's muffled face staring down at him in surprise.

Then a heavy arm made a grab for Eddie. He gave a screech of surprise and fear.

'Steady on,' the driver said in a gruff voice as he hauled Eddie up on to the seat beside him. 'You got any money for your fare, then?'

'We should have stayed with him,' George said again.

Liz held his hand. She knew how he felt – she felt the same. But as Sir William had pointed out, and as they both knew, to stay in the park would have meant certain capture.

'He had a good chance,' she said quietly. 'They can't have known he was hiding inside the statue.'

'Then why isn't he here? He should have got here well before us – he'd have come straight here.'

'He might have had to remain inside for hours. Who knows?'

'Or he might have been caught, trapped inside or grabbed as he tried to get out of the park. We were lucky enough to get away ourselves.' George pulled his hand free and turned away. 'We should have stayed.'

The three of them were sitting exhausted in Sir William Protheroe's office. They had checked and re-checked that the British Museum was no longer being watched. It seemed that all of Lorimore's men had been at the Crystal Palace. The Museum was deserted – eerily quiet and unlit. The first staff would not arrive for hours yet. Liz yawned, wondering if she was going to get any sleep at all tonight.

'How long do we wait for Eddie?' she wondered as George sulked silently and Sir William leafed through the paperwork on his desk. 'What if he's been here, found we weren't back yet and left again?'

'To go where? He will have waited, I'm sure. I really wouldn't worry,' Sir William went on without looking up. 'If any of us is capable of outsmarting Lorimore's employees and escaping his clutches, it is young Eddie. I imagine he's on his way back here now.'

'I wonder if he found anything,' George said quietly.

'I hope so,' Sir William replied. 'Otherwise I must confess I shall be at rather a loss as to what to do next, despite our brief visit to the foundry.'

'So we just wait,' Liz said.

They did not have to wait long. Eddie arrived a few minutes later. He was, Liz noticed, wearing a new jacket. At least, it was new to Eddie. To be honest it had seen better days, and it hung heavily to one side as if he had stuffed the pocket with weights.

'Where have you been?' she cried at once. 'We were so worried.'

'Had to walk back from Marylebone, didn't I?' He sat himself down on the desk, prompting Sir William into a rapid scramble to move papers and books before they disappeared under him.

'You got a train?' George asked in surprise.

'No, a cab,' Eddie replied, equally bemused. 'But I only had enough money to get to Marylebone I'm skint now, if anyone can sub me,' he added hopefully.

'I think,' Sir William said, 'that we should repair to the laboratory. There is room there for us all to sit down and compare notes as it were.'

While Liz had been to the British Museum several times before with her father, she had never found herself 'backstage' before. She was fascinated by the corridors and rooms hidden away out of public sight – the areas used for administration, for storage and for research.

Sir William's laboratory was just down the corridor from his office. It was a surprisingly large room, dominated by a central wooden workbench. Tall cupboards lined the wall opposite the door, and the other walls were covered with shelves and cabinets full of glassware, equipment and specimens of all shapes and sizes. Liz could see what looked like bones on one shelf, strangely carved statues on another. Leaning up against one of the cupboards was what looked like a plunger for unblocking drains, though it was attached to the end of a telescopic rod made of shining silver metal.

There was a bench along one wall of the laboratory, and George, Liz and Eddie sat here while Sir William paced up and down in front of them.

'We shall also,' he said, 'have less chance of being overheard down here. Now then, Eddie, tell us what you found.'

'Nothing,' Eddie said.

Sir William stopped mid-pace. 'Nothing? Nothing at all?'

'He was interrupted,' George said. 'He didn't have much time.'

'I had enough,' Eddie said. 'There was nothing in there. Well, nothing much.' He reached awkwardly into the pocket of his new jacket and dragged out the stone. 'Just this stone, which was really handy when I needed to get away I can tell you.'

Sir William frowned. 'Where did you get that jacket?' he asked. Immediately he shook his head and waved his hand dismissively. 'No, don't tell me. I've a feeling I don't want to know. Some washing line or laundry basket between here and Marylebone, no doubt.'

Eddie opened his mouth to reply. But Sir William shook his head again and lifted the stone from his hands. He turned it over several times, examining it closely. 'Curious,' he muttered. 'Very even shape, isn't it?'

Liz watched him closely, aware that George and Eddie were also leaning forward in anticipation and interest.

'Quite smooth too. Yet it hasn't been machined or worked so far as I can see. Hmmm.' Sir William weighed it in his hand, then put it down carefully on the workbench beside him.

'What is it?' Liz asked, with a mounting sense of excitement.

'What?' For a moment, he seemed not to realise what she was asking. Then he gave a short laugh. 'Oh it's probably just an old stone,' he said. 'Curious, but I imagine unremarkable. Though I should like to examine it properly when all this is over and done with and I finally have some time to myself.' He sighed. 'But just at the moment we have something of a problem. Either we were wrong about our evidence being inside the iguanodon, or we were too late and it has already been removed. Either way, the question is: what do we do now?'

He tapped his fingers on the workbench as he considered the problem. Liz glanced at Eddie and George, but neither of them seemed to have a clue what to do next either.

'We must have missed something. Something in the diaries,' Liz decided.

Sir William nodded thoughtfully. 'I agree. Let me see that scrap of paper from the diary again, would you?'

George retrieved it from his wallet. 'You have an idea?'

'Just a notion. Almost certainly nothing, but you never know . . .' Sir William took the small piece of paper and held it up to the light. 'Well, we shall soon see,' he murmured, and put it down beside Eddie's stone on the workbench while he busied himself on the other side of the room.

'What's he up to now?' Eddie wanted to know.

Liz shrugged. Sir William was hunting through a

collection of bottles and jars. All three of them – Liz, Eddie and George – were so intent on what Sir William was doing that they failed to notice the movement from the other side of the laboratory.

Liz was the first to realise they were not alone. A figure had emerged from one of the tall cupboards where he must have been listening to their deliberations. He ran to the workbench where the precious scrap of paper from Sir Henry Glick's diary lay. He was a young man, thin and gangly with slicked back dark hair.

Sir William turned at the sound of running feet and Liz's cry of warning.

'Berry? What are you doing, man?' he demanded.

But Berry did not answer. His eyes were fixed on the workbench, and his hand shot out towards the paper.

George was already there, knocking the young man's hand away and trying to grab hold of him. But Berry twisted out of George's grip and took flight. He was across the laboratory and out of the door in a moment. Eddie was after him at once.

'It's all right!' George shouted after Eddie. 'He didn't get it.'

But Eddie had already gone. George ran after them both, the door banging shut behind him.

'He's right,' Sir William said to Liz in the stillness that followed. 'We need to talk to Berry. Short of trying to see Lorimore himself, which I do not think would be a good idea, Berry may be the only lead we have left.'

George could see them both ahead of him as he ran. Berry glanced back frequently, the fear on his face easy to see. Eddie had his head down and was running for all he was worth. He was gaining on Berry, but not enough to catch him.

Berry slammed a door behind him and it crashed into Eddie, knocking him into the wall. But he was up again in an instant. George caught the door before it closed, and pelted after them.

They charged through the foyer, but Berry was already disappearing through the main doors. Eddie was close on his heels. George, out of breath, was still too far back. He tried to forget that he could hardly breathe, tried to ignore the blood drumming in his ears, and raced after them – out of the doors, down the steps.

The fog was swirling in the black night, thickening the darkness. A figure solidified out of the air in front of George, and he grabbed at it.

But it was Eddie.

'He's gone,' Eddie said. 'I lost him in the fog. He's got away.'

Chapter 20

After losing himself in the fog, Garfield Berry had no idea what to do next. He had no wish to find Mr Blade again, and he could not return to work at the Museum. People would be looking for him – Blade wanting details of what he had discovered. Or Protheroe. They would look for him at home, and while *he* wasn't there, his family was. Berry was not concerned about Sir William Protheroe confronting Lucy and the children. But Blade was a very different prospect. His men would be waiting for him.

He hurried home.

'What is it? What's wrong?' Lucy asked him in the little hallway as soon as he came in.

'Nothing,' he said quickly, the words coming out in a nervous rush. Are you all right? What are you doing up, I thought you'd be asleep. I told you I would be late. Very late. Has anyone been looking for me?' He took her by the shoulders, looking deep into her eyes and trying not to cry at how lovely she looked.

'There was a man,' she said slowly, pulling away confused. 'It's the middle of the night – I told him you were out on business. But he said you would be on your way back here. I didn't believe him.' She turned away. 'How did he know?' she asked quietly. 'Are you in trouble?'

'Did this man say that I was?'

She turned back, her cheeks damp. 'He didn't say anything. Only that you would soon be back and he would wait.'

'Wait? You mean he's still here?' Berry was unable to keep the fear out of his voice.

'Something *is* wrong, isn't it?' Lucy said quietly. She clasped her hands together in front of her. 'Oh why won't you tell me what it is?'

'I . . .' What could he say? What could he tell her? He was so ashamed of himself already, without the burden of confession. Without her condemnation as well. She had been so proud when he got the job at the Museum. How could he tell her he had betrayed the man who was so generous to him? And for what? Money – money they desperately needed to keep the bailiffs from the door. But it was just money. The same thing that had seduced Judas.

She could tell he would say nothing more. She wiped her hands on her apron and nodded towards the door to the tiny sitting room. 'He's in there. I'll be in the kitchen.' She walked briskly away without turning back.

He expected Sir William. Blade would have struck terror into Lucy merely by his appearance. In a way, Berry wished it was Blade – he would know where he stood, how to react. But what could he say to Sir William?

It was neither. Berry did not recognise the figure that stood by the fireplace, though he knew at once who it must be. The man was staring down into the glowing embers. He was tall and incredibly thin, his whole face and body apparently composed of sharp angles. He did not look up as Berry came in, and Berry gave a stammered account of what he had discovered at the Museum. He wasn't sure how he knew that this was Augustus Lorimore, but he was somehow certain of it.

'I believe you owe me rather more of an explanation than that,' Lorimore said quietly. 'You have provided information, told Mr Blade that they have what I want in the Museum with them. Yet you have been unable, or perhaps unwilling, to acquire it for me.' The man's voice was sharp and angular too. Still he did not look up from the fire. 'You know these coals burn inside as well as out. When the fire around them has gone, they still burn within. It happens underground sometimes – a whole coal seam can burn under the ground. All it needs is a little air to breathe. Until it has exhausted all the inner fuel and burns itself out.'

He turned and fixed Berry with a startlingly fierce gaze. His eyes were themselves pin-pricks of coal that burned deep inside. 'Has your inner fire gone out, I wonder,' he said quietly. 'Have you exhausted your usefulness, and declined to help me just when I need you most?'

He crossed the room in two rapid strides, spindly fingers suddenly clamped tight about Berry's throat, squeezing hard. 'Because if that is the case, then you won't need that little air to breathe any more, now will you?'

The room blurred, running red as Berry tried to focus, tried to drag the hands away from his neck. He could feel himself sagging, his strength ebbing away. His inner fire going out . . .

Then suddenly he was sprawling, gasping on the threadbare carpet.

The man's voice was deadened by the rush of blood in his ears and the rasping of his breath. 'Or could you perhaps summon the fire for one more simple task? Hmm?'

Berry's hands were rubbing at his throat, feeling the swelling and bruises. The man leaned down and pulled one of his hands away. Berry gave a hoarse cry of fright, but the man had pulled a plain white envelope from his inner jacket pocket, and he slapped it into Berry's palm.

'I could entrust this to the post, but it is urgent and I am a generous man. I shall give you one last chance to redeem yourself.'

'Thank you, Mr Lorimore,' Berry croaked.

'I would like this delivered into Sir William Protheroe's hand this morning. Coming from you, he is more likely to accept it, and he will be sure it is genuine. In return I will pay you what I promised for this month. After that, our obligations to each other are ended. Is that clear?'

Berry nodded, his throat still burning inside.

Lorimore paused in the open doorway and looked back pityingly at the figure still sprawled on the floor. 'It may be that Sir William wishes you to deliver a reply,' he said. 'If so, you will bring it promptly to Mr Blade who will be waiting outside the Museum. If not . . .' His mouth twisted and turned as he considered this eventuality. 'If not, then I suggest you tender your resignation and come straight home. No doubt your charming wife will be worried about you.'

The sound of a baby's crying came through the open door. Lorimore listened for a moment, then stepped out into the hall. His reedy voice floated back to Berry. 'I hope you are less of a disappointment to your family than you are to me. I shall see myself out. Good day to you.'

The front door banged shut. Berry crawled to an armchair and climbed into it, collapsing exhausted. He closed his eyes, and rubbed at his throat with one hand, gripping the envelope tightly with the other. When he opened his eyes, Lucy was standing in front of him. Little Davey was over her shoulder, quiet now as his mother patted his back.

'I have to go out,' Berry said, his voice a dry croak. 'I'll be back as soon as I can.'

Lucy said nothing. She watched him all the way to the door, followed him into the hallway.

'I love you,' he said. She did not reply.

To his undisguised irritation, Eddie had been volunteered again – this time to keep watch at the main doors of the Museum. Not that it was actually possible to see very much through the foggy night. He could hear the sound of cautiously approaching footsteps long before he could see anyone, and he prepared to run.

He was surprised to see that it was Berry, who seemed even more nervous than Eddie. He stammered out an explanation, showing Eddie the envelope he had brought for Sir William, and Eddie waved him past. The man didn't seem much of a threat, so Eddie stayed where he was. On guard. In case Berry had brought any friends with him.

After Sir William had sent Berry away, declining to reply to Lorimore's letter but accepting Berry's sheepish offer of resignation, Liz and George crowded round to see what the letter said.

There were just two lines written on the thick cartridge paper:

You know what I want. You have one hour from the receipt of this message.

It was unsigned.

'Why does he still want the page from Glick's diary?' George wondered. 'If Berry overheard us talking, then he can't learn any more from this.' He jabbed his finger at the slip of paper.

'Perhaps Lorimore does not know that,' Sir William suggested. 'Or perhaps he knows more than we do about it.'

'Or he knows we have the previous volumes of the diary and wants those,' Liz suggested.

'Whatever he wants,' George told them, 'he is demanding it from a position of strength. He knows where we are, so I doubt we'd be allowed to just leave. And we have nothing.'

Sir William raised his finger. 'Not true,' he insisted. 'We have one hour, or slightly less. But that in itself proves that you are right, young man. They are watching, they must be to know when this was delivered. Watching and waiting.'

'Which leaves us less than an hour, then,' Liz said.

'Well,' Sir William continued, 'we do have something he evidently wants very badly indeed. So the question is, does he want the slip of paper for himself, or does he want to prevent us having it?'

'But neither makes sense,' George said in frustration.

'On the face of it that would indeed seem to be the case. So I can only assume we are still missing something here. Something important. Something that this paper means or would convey to Lorimore which we have so far failed to discern.'

Liz nodded. 'And either he wants to know what that is, or he wants us to surrender the paper before we manage to work it out.'

'Or both,' George added. 'But what can it be?'

'I was about to run some tests on this paper.' Sir William was examining the scrap again, as he had done an hour earlier. 'It is possible that it was this that prompted Berry to reveal himself and try to steal it. Or, of course, it may be simply that he saw an opportunity.'

'What tests did you have in mind?' George wondered.

'It seemed rather tenuous and unlikely at the time, but I did wonder if Glick had perhaps written another version of events on the same diary pages, but in invisible ink.'

'Invisible ink, is that possible?' Liz asked in astonishment.

'My father showed me, when I was a boy,' George remembered, 'how to write using lemon juice instead of ink. It dried so you couldn't see it.'

Sir William nodded enthusiastically. 'Citric acid, a

very useful substance. It does as you say dry invisibly. Then the application of heat, from a smoothing iron or some such, will cause the writing to appear in a dark brown form.'

'We used to toast pages of invisible writing in front of the fire,' George said quietly. He had a dreamy expression as he stared back fondly into the past.

'I assume there are other forms that invisible ink can take,' Liz said.

'Oh indeed yes, my dear,' Sir William agreed.

'What's wrong with lemon juice?' George asked.

'Just that this paper has already been subjected to considerable heat,' Liz told him. 'And there is no evidence of hidden writing having appeared.'

'Oh,' George said, recalling the fire. 'Yes.'

'But we are agreed on the general principle, are we not?' Sir William said. 'In some manner, this paper is more than it seems. And because of that, either because Lorimore wishes to know its secrets or because he is desperate for us not to learn them, either way we must at all costs keep hold of it. Are we agreed?'

The others nodded. It did seem the only option.

'It does at least give us a position of some strength to bargain from,' Sir William added.

Liz agreed: 'Give up this paper, and we give up everything.'

'Splendid.' Sir William rubbed his hands together in

delight as if the whole matter was now completely sorted out. 'Well, I'll get on with testing this piece of paper in any and every way I can think of.'

Forty-five minutes later, George and Liz had tired of watching Sir William busying himself with the scrap of paper. Every few minutes they glanced at the clock. Now it was nearly time – the hour that Lorimore had given them was almost gone.

'I'd better go and get Eddie,' George said. He had warned the boy what Lorimore had said, and Eddie had agreed they would be best advised to stay put.

'We can defend ourselves here,' Sir William had told George. 'And soon, when morning comes and the staff begin to arrive, he'll have to call off his thugs or someone'll call the police.'

Liz went with George and together they joined Eddie on the steps outside the Museum, peering into the foggy night.

'I can't see more than about six feet in front of me,' she said.

'You hear things,' Eddie told her. 'Cabs, people shouting, and stuff.'

'We might as well go back to Sir William and look for somewhere to hide,' George said.

'I doubt he'll leave his precious collection,' Liz remarked.

But Eddie was waving at her to be quiet. 'Listen,' he hissed.

A moment later, George could hear it too. Carriages. Several of them, judging by the clop of so many horses' hooves and the rattle of the wheels over the cobbles. It was muffled by the fog, but the sound was clear enough.

'Inside!' George said quickly.

The fog seemed to have crept inside the building itself. It hung like smoke in the foyer, where Sir William now stood waiting. He was holding the slip of paper saved from Glick's burnt diary.

'Nothing,' he proclaimed, as soon as Eddie and the others were inside.

George slammed the door shut, sliding heavy bolts into place and turning a large key in the lock.

'I have tried everything I can think of. Nothing.' Sir William nodded towards the closed door. 'Is that really necessary?'

'Yes,' George said simply.

'Lorimore is here,' Liz explained.

'And it sounds like he's bringing Blade and his mates,' Eddie added.

Sir William raised an eyebrow but seemed otherwise unimpressed. He glanced down at the paper in his hand. 'Perhaps I have missed something then.'

There was a loud crack from the door behind them. The wood shifted visibly in the frame, creaking as something large and heavy collided with it. A moment's pause, then another, louder crack.

'I don't think that's going to hold for terribly long, you know,' Sir William observed just before the third crack of splintering wood. 'Let's get back to the laboratory.' He turned and led the way briskly across the foyer and out into the Great Court.

'Will we be safe there?' Liz asked. 'Shouldn't we get out the back door or something?'

'As safe as anywhere, my dear. Lorimore is likely to have all the exits watched. At least we know the territory. Come on.'

Behind them the door was already splintering apart.

They worked hurriedly to barricade the laboratory. Together they managed to drag the heavy workbench across the door. Eddie retrieved his smooth stone from the work top and stuffed it into his pocket.

'You realise that there's no other way out of here,' George said. 'If they find us, we're trapped.'

'We'll be trapped soon enough wherever we go,' Sir William said. 'Our only chance is to bargain. And in here we can bargain, I hope, from a position of strength. We have the paper from the diary, and we have the means to analyse it – and to destroy it if need be. And now, thanks to our visit to his foundry and the time I have had to ponder this in the last hour, we have a good idea of what Lorimore is up to. More or less.'

'And what is he up to. More or less?' Liz asked.

Sir William was filling glass flasks and beakers from a tap over a small sink at the back of the room. 'Help me stopper these up, will you. I'd like an impressive collection ready for when the time comes.' He had taken off his jacket and rolled up the sleeves of his shirt. Satisfied that Eddie and George were able to put the rubber stoppers into the flasks and cover the beakers with glass lids, he turned to Liz.

'Lorimore has coupled his fascination with modern technology with his love of fossils and dinosaur discoveries. His plan, it would seem, is to create a dinosaur for the modern age. A work animal that has the strength and power of the dinosaurs, the reliability and stamina of British steam technology, and the intelligence and intuition of humans. Although I think he has some way of regulating the brains of his subjects . . .' Sir William paused, then corrected himself. 'Or rather, his victims. I believe from Albert Wilkes's behaviour that so far complete control of the individual has eluded him. He can either leave the reasoning faculties intact, along with their free will, or he can assume control – as he does with that monster   but at the cost of any individual thought and initiative.'

'But why is he doing it at all?' George asked as he arranged the last of the flasks on a small table.

'I would guess, from what I know of his character

and ambition, that his ultimate aim is to ensure that the British Empire endures for a thousand or more years. And that he, Augustus Lorimore, plays a prominent role in its governance.' Sir William smiled thinly. 'It may sound a trifle melodramatic, and I doubt if he has thought of it in entirely these terms, but I believe that Lorimore wants to rule the world.' He surveyed the collection of flasks and beakers. 'Yes, I think that will do for now.'

'It's just water,' Eddie said.

'You and I know that,' Sir William said. 'But don't tell anyone else, will you?' He looked up sharply as the handle of the door rattled.

A moment later, something crashed into it, shattering the lock. The door moved barely an inch, stopped by the heavy workbench. The bench shifted slightly, with a scraping sound, pushed backwards by whatever was on the other side of the door.

'His ultimate goal,' Sir William went on, apparently unperturbed, 'must be to somehow recreate the animal and achieve a true marriage of living dinosaur and technology. But to do that he would need more than dead bones and corpse's brains. He will need some living tissue, some animal material that has survived down the millennia and could still be viable.'

'Viable?' George echoed. 'For what?'

'Why, to breed from. To grow and harvest cells that can be transplanted on to his mechanical frames and driven by his engines. He doesn't want to spend forever working with the bodies of the dead. No, no, no. He wants to create life.' The workbench slid back another inch. 'You know, I don't think he wants to stop at ruling the Empire,' Sir William said thoughtfully. 'He also wants to be God.'

The workbench shivered, then shifted again. Slowly but inexorably, a gap was appearing. An arm – huge and bulging with muscles – poked through the gap, an enormous hand feeling round.

'And these employees of his,' Liz said, anxiously watching the hand as it fumbled over the door frame, 'you implied they were somehow enhanced in this way.'

'The strength of a dinosaur in the body of a man,' Sir William said quietly. 'Demonstrably the case, wouldn't you say? Now all he needs is the ability to breed rather than manufacture. So much more efficient.'

The workbench was still slipping slowly back. The door was opening further. Something was heaving itself through the gap, the top of the door bending as it forced its way through. A head appeared, huge and bony. Eyes glittered with malevolent triumph as the man – if he was a man – stared at Sir William and the others.

'Now I wouldn't stand there too long, if I were you,' Sir William said. He had picked up one of the flasks and was holding it up so the man could see it clearly. He agitated it, letting the clear liquid inside slosh about. 'Do you know what this is?'

'It's water, innit?' The man's voice was a deep gravel-rasp.

'Certainly it looks like it. But as you will discover if you come through that door and force me to throw this at you, it is nothing so benign.'

The man was frowning, unsure what Sir William was telling him.

'I suggest you tell whoever is in charge out there that we are willing to listen to any reasonable request or offer. But if any of you so much as set a foot through that door again, then he will get a face-full of concentrated sulphuric acid. Now perhaps you don't know what that would do to you. How it would blister and burn and destroy your face before eating into your brain, or what Lorimore has left you of it. But I suspect your employer will. So you might want to check with him before we close up the breach with your steaming dead.'

The man stared at them for several seconds. Eddie was holding his breath. If he forced his way into the room, he would soon discover that the flasks and beakers held only water. What then?

Sir William sighed, raised the flask. 'Very well,' he said sadly, and drew his arm back ready to hurl the flask.

But the man was gone.

'Now what?' Liz asked.

'Now, I hope, Lorimore will be forced to offer us some sort of deal. Something which may give a further clue as to what he is after. Remember, we still have something he wants.'

'But,' George said slowly, 'how badly does he want it?'

The answer came barely a minute later. A clanking, hissing, thumping from the corridor outside. Mechanical and rhythmic, like the mechanism of a gigantic clock. But organic too – breathing, sighing, a sore-throat scraping like someone trying to speak through unbearable pain.

'It can't be that monster,' Eddie said. 'It would never get down the passage.'

'Our mistake was perhaps in assuming he had just the one monster,' Sir William admitted quietly.

The door was flung fully open. The workbench was shoved backwards by the impact. Steam blew through the doorway and hung warm and oily in the air. Through the smog, a shape slowly solidified as it approached. Every step was measured, deliberate, accompanied by a breath of steam and a whirr of gears.

It was something that George had seen before, albeit in its component pieces – at Lorimore's foundry. Waiting to be assembled into exoskeleton frames like this. But what confronted them now was not merely the metal frame that had been assembled at the foundry.

'Two lines of experimentation,' Sir William said, nodding sadly. 'Replacing the bones internally, or this – an exoskeleton to strengthen the existing body even as it rots away.' He shook his head, more sad than afraid. 'Grotesque,' he murmured. 'Devilish.'

The exoskeleton, as Sir William called it, was like an enlarged human figure. It was crude and distorted, like a child's drawing outlining the figure held inside, keeping it rigid and upright. Its limbs were bulky and long, iron bolts and supports erupting from the pale bone and connecting them to the metal frame. When the man moved, so the heavy metal frame around him also moved. Or perhaps it was the other way round. Steam hissed out from the joints – from the elbows, knees, shoulders . . .

Worst of all was the face. A deathly white face, drawn and emaciated. The cheekbones all but poking through the parchment-thin translucent skin. The remains of a tangle of white hair flopped uncertainly to one side, away from the scars and stitches across the scalp.

Pale, watery eyes fixed on George. Was there a flicker of recognition, somewhere deep behind the irises? Or was it just a trick of the light? Whatever it was, George was unable to take his own eyes off the face. The face of what had once been a man.

Had once been a man he knew.

'Albert?' George said, the word sticking in his dry throat. 'Albert Wilkes?'

Chapter 21

The grotesque figure inside the metal frame swung round, surveying the room. Moist, unblinking eyes were fixed on Eddie. Long arms stretched out, metal braces holding them rigid as they reached for the boy.

Eddie scrambled backwards. 'What do you want?' His voice was shaking.

'Just keep out of its way.' George had to shout to make himself heard above the steam and the pistons and the gears. There was something else too – the groaning and whimpering of Albert Wilkes as he made his tortuous way across the room towards Eddie.

'God help us,' Eddie was murmuring. 'Don't let it get me.' He was at the back of the room now. He grabbed an empty glass beaker off a shelf and hurled it at the Wilkes-creature. The glass shattered across the metal frame, fragments lodging in the man's face. But he did not so much as blink, not so much as slow down as he advanced on the cowering Eddie.

'Leave the boy,' Sir William yelled. 'It's not him you

want, is it? It's this!' He was holding up the slip of paper from Glick's diary – the only thing they had left to bargain with. 'Here – take it!'

The creature paused to look at Sir William through rheumy eyes. But only for a moment, then it turned away again, back towards Eddie.

George could not just stand by and let the thing – the thing that had been his friend – attack Eddie. He ran across and grabbed the enormous arms, the metal cold, biting into him as he tried to force the arms back, tried to push the thing away. George's face was close to Albert's, and he could taste the oil hanging in the air around him. The bloodless lips were moving.

'George?' Wilkes murmured. His eyes were unfocussed. 'George is that you?' The voice was barely more than a whisper, a plea. 'Help me. Please, help me. I tried to contact you before . . . Heard your call . . .' George could hear tears in the voice, tears that had not been allowed to reach the eyes. 'I'm sorry . . . I can't . . .'

Then George felt himself being pushed away. Gently at first, then as if another gear had kicked in, he was flung across the room, smashing into the shelves on the wall, falling to the floor bringing wooden shelves, glassware, specimens crashing down on top of him.

He shook his head to clear his vision, just in time to see Liz snatch the slip of paper from Sir William's hands and run towards the advancing figure of Wilkes. She was waving the paper, shouting at the creature:

'Here – this is what you want. Take it!'

She thrust the paper into Wilkes's face. But he ignored it. As if he was swatting at an annoying fly, one of Wilkes's metal-framed arms lashed out. It caught Liz across the shoulder and sent her flying backwards. George cried out as she cartwheeled, and spun across the workbench. Even above the clanking of the engines and the hiss of the steam, George heard the sickening crack as Liz's head hit the floor. She struggled to sit up – seemed all right.

But then her eyes flickered, and she slumped backwards.

'No!' George cried, scrambling across the floor, ignoring the broken glass cutting into his hands. He struggled to get to Liz, praying she was all right.

As he cradled her unconscious head, George became aware of movement in the doorway. Two of Lorimore's thugs were standing inside the room. Framed between them was Lorimore himself. His lean face distorted by a mixture of anger and triumph, he stared at George for a moment before dismissing him and turning to watch his ghastly creation close in on Eddie.

Sir William was pleading and arguing with the creature that had once been Albert Wilkes. 'Listen to me – if there is any reasoning part of your mind still there, please listen. There must be something. Lorimore is using the motor centres of your brain to operate this *thing*. He's revived you using electrical stimulation or some such technique. Fight against it – try to think for yourself. I know you are dead, but there must be *something* left . . .'

But it did no good. Sir William too was finally pushed aside.

There was only Eddie left – defiant now against the wall. He was looking at George and the unconscious Liz, his face white with fury. With a sudden shock, George realised that Eddie too had recognised Albert Wilkes – perhaps he blamed himself for not saving the old man from this fate. Whatever the reason, he was no longer scared, he was seething.

He put one hand in his jacket pocket. He pointed at Lorimore with the other. 'It's you that's the monster,' Eddie yelled. 'You're inhuman, you are.'

Lorimore just laughed. A dry cackle that was all but lost in the noise of his creation.

This infuriated Eddie still further. He charged, shouldering the metal-framed creature aside, and forcing it back several paces. It recovered at once, metal joints springing, reaching out for Eddie and grabbing at him as he passed. Knife-like metal fingers snapped shut on his jacket.

But Eddie ignored this. He was still yelling at Lorimore though his words were lost in a cloud of angry steam. Then he had his hand out of his pocket, and brandishing his treasured stone like a weapon, he hurled it with all his strength.

Lorimore ducked, surprised. The stone thumped into the splintered woodwork which was all that remained of the door.

From Lorimore's scream, George assumed the stone had hit him. He dropped to his knees by the door and scooped up the stone from where it had fallen. He cradled it in his hands, as if afraid it might have been damaged by the impact. His eyes were wide, shining as if lit from within as he backed slowly out of the room, holding the stone reverently in his cupped hands.

'What's going on?' George exclaimed, but his words were drowned out by the metallic clanking of Albert Wilkes as he strode mechanically past.

In the doorway, Blade was shouting for Wilkes to hurry up. Eddie looked both relieved and perplexed. Sir William's expression was unreadable.

'At last,' Lorimore's words floated shrilly back to where George still cradled the unconscious Liz. 'At last, I have it. The final link in the great chain of life. Now, I can finally bring my dreams to life.' Then even his voice was gone. As if he had already forgotten about George and the others, or dismissed them as irrelevant.

'What was he talking about?' George demanded.

'It's just an old stone,' Eddie was saying.

Sir William was rubbing his forehead. 'No. No it's not.' He wiped his hand away from his face, looking much older now than he had even moments before. 'Don't you see? That's what he was after all the time. That's what he wanted. Not the page from Glick's diary – he just needed that to lead him to that fossil. If only I had realised sooner. "I know which came first," was a clue sure enough. And we missed its meaning completely.' He shook his head in regret. 'He must have known we had it, Berry told him we'd found it – that we'd followed Glick's clue and saved him the trouble of solving it himself. And now . . .' He sighed, coming to a decision. 'We have to get it back.'

'But why?' Eddie wanted to know.

George was beginning to realise. 'So, it's not just an old stone. It's a fossil.'

'So what?'

'So what?' Sir William countered. 'You want to live in a world where people are turned into the sort of creature we just witnessed? Where even the dead are not permitted to rest in peace? Where abominations like what poor Albert has become populate the factories, the foundries, even the army?'

'Foundries,' George repeated as he realised what Sir William was saying. 'Those frames we saw being made. There were dozens of them.'

'Exactly,' Sir William replied gravely. He gave Liz a brief, sympathetic look before walking quickly and purposefully across the shattered laboratory. 'We have to get Eddie's stone back.'

George gently let Liz's head rest on the floor. He pulled off his jacket, folding it into a pillow and pushing it carefully under her fair hair. She murmured, but did not wake. She would be all right, George was sure. 'I'll be back in a minute,' he whispered. 'Or I'll find someone, send them to look after you.'

'What's so important about a lump of rock. Even if it *is* a fossil?' Eddie was shouting after Sir William. He ran back and grabbed George by the arm. 'Come on, we've got to stop him!'

Reluctantly, George allowed Eddie to pull him to his feet. He glanced back at Liz, apparently sleeping peacefully now, then together they ran after the old man.

Sir William did not wait for them. He called back over his shoulder. 'Don't you see? You found it inside the statue. It is Glick's proof – what he was going to produce during his speech. He knew which came first, like in the riddle. He realised how dinosaurs reproduce and he found the evidence to prove it.' Now Sir William did pause. He looked at them. 'We have to get it back before Lorimore can somehow reactivate the living matter fossilised inside that stone. However he brought Wilkes back to some semblance of life, that's how he'll do it. Don't you see?' he said. 'It's a dinosaur *egg*.'

Then he turned, and hastened down the passageway, after Lorimore.

Eddie and George exchanged looks, then hurried after him.

'Wait!' George yelled. His voice echoed off the panelling. 'Wait for us!'

They reached the end of the passage, passing the open door to Sir William's office, and raced into the foyer. The main door was hanging off its hinges. A heavy mist of mingling steam and fog still lingered in the air. George could see the shape of Sir William through the mist as he hurried out of the door and down the steps.

George and Eddie sprinted after him. But a huge figure stepped out in front of them. One of Lorimore's thugs, arms stretched out ready to stop them. They pulled up sharply, and ducked back out of reach.

Through the doorway, over the man's shoulder, George could see Sir William. He could see the men closing in on him as he hefted his broken cane and prepared to meet them. He could see the skeletal shape of what had once been Albert Wilkes step down behind Sir William, arms raised and ready to strike.

Then the enormous bulk of the man filled the doorway. George and Eddie had no choice but to back away, into the Museum. From outside they could hear a muffled cry, the sound of a scuffle. The clanking of a steam-driven mechanism. They heard Blade shouting, and the man stepped away. The fog rolled in, covering everything in a grey shroud and blotting out the moon.

When the air cleared and the moonlight again struggled through, the courtyard was dark and empty. Somewhere in the distance a carriage clattered over cobbles. The metallic scrape of inhuman feet faded into the smog. Thunder rumbled.

'They've taken him,' Eddie said into the silence.

'Insurance,' George said. 'To make sure we don't interfere with Lorimore's plans. Or perhaps he thinks he might need Sir William's help. But whichever it is, he has the dinosaur egg, and now he has Sir William. Let's get back to Liz.'

'At least things can't get any worse,' Eddie grumbled as they hurriedly made their way back to the laboratory.

But he was wrong.

George's jacket was lying where he had placed it, carefully folded, the depression made by Liz's head still visible. But Liz herself was no longer there.

Chapter 22

Light smeared painfully over Liz's eyelids and she blinked. The first thing she saw was the scar. A single image, stamped across her retina – the scar running down Blade's face directly in front of her.

'She's awake, Mr Lorimore.' Blade grinned at Liz before moving away.

The second thing she saw, as her eyes refocused, was Sir William Protheroe sitting in the chair beside her, one of Lorimore's thugs close behind him.

'I trust you slept well,' Lorimore said in his shrill almost birdlike voice. 'At least you were spared the indignity of being brought here kicking and screaming like Sir William.'

Liz's head felt as if it was about to split open, and when she blinked residual images of lightning flashed behind her eyes. But slowly she was able to look round and observe her surroundings.

She and Sir William were sitting on upright chairs at the back of a large laboratory. The three outside walls were dominated by large windows, and Liz could see the fog pressing in from the outside, and the hint of stars. The moon was just visible within the fog as it shone down through a vast, domed glass ceiling. Behind her, when she turned to look, Liz found another of Lorimore's henchmen standing guard. Clearly Lorimore was taking no chances this time. Beyond her guard, Liz could see double doors that gave into the main drawing room of the house.

But this laboratory was clearly where Lorimore conducted his grotesque work. A large wooden workbench, similar to the one Sir William had used, dominated the space in front of them. Spread across it was all manner of equipment and specimens. Bones, fossils, large jars of murky liquid that contained things that Liz would rather not look at.

Lorimore was at the workbench, Blade assisting him as he pieced together more apparatus. Wires and cables were joined into a metal bowl. In the other direction they trailed across the workbench, down to the floor, to a huge iron tank standing at the side of the room.

Sir William was also watching with interest. He glanced at Liz, and saw where she was looking. 'A battery, I believe,' he said quietly. 'A means of attaching electrical power to that metal bowl, in which I imagine he intends eventually to place the egg.' He clicked his tongue as if about to admonish a dim student on his slow progress, and quickly explained the significance of Eddie's stone. 'How are you feeling, by the way?' he asked when he had finished.

'Apart from a headache, not too bad,' she said, making light of how she really felt. 'What about you?'

'I feel rather stupid to have got myself – and you – into this,' he said. 'Otherwise I have no complaints.'

'I should think not,' Lorimore said from the other side of the workbench. As he spoke, heavy clouds drifted across the moon, throwing his face into sudden shadow. 'I am hoping that we are in for a storm,' Lorimore went on, looking up. Somewhere in the distance was a rumble of thunder. Or possibly the roar of the monster Liz guessed was roaming the grounds outside to keep out any locals who slipped past the guard at the gate.

Whichever it was, it pleased Lorimore. 'Excellent.' He turned to Blade. 'Exactly as forecast. Which will save us worrying whether the battery power is sufficient for reanimation. Put up the lightning conductors, will you? I think we can afford to wait a little while for the storm to break.'

'Of course, sir.' Blade spared Liz and Sir William a scowl as he strode past them and into the house.

'You propose to reanimate the egg?' Sir William said. 'With electrical energy, is that correct?'

'Absolutely correct.' Lorimore paused in his work and walked round the workbench, coming over to them.

'You are a very clever man, Sir William. Such a shame your intelligence has been so wasted up until now. But at least you will be a witness to this historic moment.'

Sir William snorted with apparent amusement. 'You really think this mad scheme of yours will work then?'

The change in Lorimore was abrupt and frightening. His face paled, even in the dim light, and his eyes flared with anger. 'Of course it will work. I have calculated everything down to the last detail. My foundries are already hard at work. You can't stop me now. No one can stop me now. All I needed was Glick's discovery. Now I have that – I have the power to create life. And I intend to exercise that power.'

Liz had no doubt that Lorimore believed he could do it. 'How long?' she asked, her voice shaking. 'How long before this happens?'

'Once Blade has put out the lightning conductors, and I have completed the circuitry. An hour perhaps.'

'And what if there is no storm, no lightning?'

Lorimore smiled again, anticipating the moment. 'Then we shall manage without. The battery will be sufficient, though it may take longer to build to a useful level. A sudden jolt of high power would be a far more effective and rapid way to reverse the process of fossilisation and infuse life into the egg.'

'And then what?' Sir William demanded. 'Once you have a living egg, what will you do?'

Lorimore strode back to the workbench. 'Why, let it hatch of course,' he told them. 'And use the creature that emerges. No need for the intricate, time-consuming surgical replacement then. With the techniques I have pioneered on our friend Albert Wilkes, I can adapt it, control it, be its god. And unlike Wilkes, it will not rot and decay. It will be *alive* – the first of a new race that will combine animal and mechanical. Dinosaur and steam power. The start of a new world.'

Liz turned slowly towards Sir William, conscious of the two men standing silently behind them. 'He's mad, isn't he?' she said.

Sir William's answer was matter-of-fact, as if he was discussing some trivial matter of politics in his club. 'Oh yes, my dear. Utterly mad. And very dangerous.'

They worked for what seemed like hours. George's first thought had been to go to the police. But Eddie had persuaded him that this would not be the best course of action.

'They'll think we're barmy' he said. 'They won't believe a word of it. They might listen to Sir William, but he ain't here.'

'I suppose you're right,' George admitted. After all, he himself scarcely believed the events of the last few days, and he knew them to be true. Setting their improbable story against the reputation of an establishment figure like Augustus Lorimore, and Eddie was right – the police would be no help.

Which meant they were on their own. 'What can we do?' George wondered out loud. He looked round the laboratory – the floor strewn with debris, the workbench lying on its side, the door a tangled, splintered mess. He did not think they wanted to be there when the first Museum staff began to arrive in a few hours.

'We've got to rescue Liz and Sir William,' Eddie told him.

'That won't be easy. And we also have to get back your stone.'

'The dinosaur egg. And we have to stop Lorimore.' Eddie was picking through some of the broken apparatus lying on the floor. 'There must be something here that can help. Something we can use to fool Lorimore, or distract him or something.'

George could see nothing. He thrust his hand into his jacket pocket and sighed. Then he smiled, feeling the cold hard metal in his pocket. The glimmerings of a plan were beginning to shine deep inside his mind. 'There may be something,' he said. 'Something we can adapt. But not here, come with me.'

'Where are we going?' Eddie wanted to know as he hurried after George down the passageway, and up the main stairs.

'I'm going to show you where I work,' George said.

Blade had returned from deploying the lightning conductors and was now up a ladder, connecting cables to metal brackets set into the ceiling of the laboratory.

Sir William had earlier got to his feet, smiled affably at the man standing guard over him, and tried to stretch some life back into his tired limbs.

Lorimore glanced up from his intense work. 'I do apologise for the delay,' he said. 'But everything must be exact, as I am sure you of all people will appreciate. By all means feel free to look round. I have some fascinating automata and specimens in my collection. You may go into the drawing room, but no further.' He paused, before adding for the benefit of the two guards: 'Miss Oldfield may go with him. If either of them touch anything or attempt to escape, kill them both.'

It was said in such a straightforward tone of voice that it took a moment for Liz to register what he had said. She swallowed, her throat dry with fear.

'Shall we?' Sir William suggested.

'I suppose we might as well.'

They left Blade up his ladder, reaching for the glass roof and the metal sockets set into the supporting braces. Cables trailed down to the metal bowl on the workbench below.

'We have to do something. Escape or anything,' Liz whispered to Sir William once they were in the drawing room. The two guards with them could probably hear her, but she didn't care. Without specific instructions she hoped they would do nothing.

But Sir William ignored her too. He was peering in fascination at one of the automata – a train that was fixed to a loop of track running under a mountain. 'I imagine that once wound, the train runs round the track, and the mountain is somehow made to smoke in sympathy. Like a small volcano.' He smiled at Liz. 'It really is very clever and intricate.'

Liz sighed, not at all interested. 'But what are we going to do?'

Sir William shrugged. 'As things stand at the moment, my dear, I don't think there is anything very much that we can do. Except wait.'

'For what?' she demanded in exasperation.

'For help. Though I must confess I have no idea whether it will come, or if it does what form it will take.'

From out in the hallway came the sound of a bell ringing insistently. It seemed somehow out of place in the still of the house.

'Who can that be at this hour?' Lorimore's voice demanded from the laboratory behind them. 'It's not yet six in the morning. Blade, see who it is.'

'Sir.'

Blade barely glanced at them as he strode past on his way to answer the door.

'Help?' Liz suggested quietly. She hardly dared hope.

'Who knows?' Sir William whispered back.

They did not have to wait long to find out. Blade returned within a minute, carrying a wooden box the size of a small suitcase. Liz and Sir William exchanged glances and followed the man back into the laboratory, where he set the box down on the workbench in front of Lorimore.

'What is it?'

'I'm afraid I don't know sir. The boy said he had strict instructions to deliver it here as soon as possible. That he had been told Mr Lorimore would want to see it straight away.'

'Boy? What boy?' Lorimore asked suspiciously.

'Just a delivery boy. Barely more than an urchin by the look of him. He didn't wait – in a hurry to get home.'

Lorimore considered this. 'I wonder.' He glanced at Liz and Sir William. 'But what can they do?' he murmured. His fingers tapped against the top of the workbench like the legs of a spider. 'And we can do nothing either, not until the power builds to a precipitate level. So, open it, Blade,' he ordered, nodding at the box. 'But, be careful.'

Liz and Sir William watched curiously from the back of the room as Blade took out his knife and levered the lid off the wooden box. Nails squealed in protest as the lid tore free. Blade pushed his hand under it and ripped it away, dropping it to the floor. Frowning, he reached inside the box and carefully lifted out the contents.

Lorimore had come round the workbench to see what it was, blocking Liz's view. Whatever Blade was holding was obviously large and heavy. Lorimore swept the empty box off the workbench and gestured for Blade to set down the object.

'No packing slip, sir,' Blade said. 'Nothing to say who sent it.'

'There will no doubt be a letter in the first post this morning, Blade. But let us be cautious, just in case . . .' Lorimore's voice was hushed with awe, his suspicion diluted as he examined the object on the workbench. 'Look at this. The workmanship, the skill that must have gone into it. Look!'

As he spoke, he stepped aside so that now Liz was afforded a clear view of the object on the table. She heard Sir William's sharp intake of breath as he too saw it.

It was a model ship, exquisitely made from wood and metal and about a foot long. Without realising it, Liz had walked with Sir William across the laboratory and joined Lorimore and Blade as they stared down at the impressive craftsmanship.

'Magnificent,' Sir William said.

Lorimore looked up at him, with the trace of a

smile. 'Indeed.' His eyes were shining with enthusiasm as he gently turned the ship round. 'And see, here, on this side – it is a clock.'

There was, Liz could now see, a clock dial set into the side of the ship. It was showing the right time so far as she could tell – several minutes to six. She could see the intricately fashioned figures of the captain and his crew going about their business on deck and in the rigging – ticking through the everyday motions as the second hand clicked round. But this was not what surprised and interested her most. Her eyes were fixed on something else and she stared at it as hard as she could, willing Sir William to see what she could see.

Set into the deck was a silver plate where one might expect to see a hatchway down into the hold. The middle of the plate was indented, gently sloping inwards to form a shallow bowl. It was a plate she was sure she had seen before – in the hands of George Archer. But now, resting in the centre of the plate was a small wooden barrel – a powder keg. A tiny fuse was sticking out of one end of it, and a sailor stood beside it, his hands outstretched towards the fuse.

'I have seen something like this before,' she said quietly to Sir William, hoping that Lorimore would not pick up on her meaning.

Lorimore ignored her. But Sir William met Liz's gaze. He was smiling, and nodding. 'So have I, my dear,' he replied in the ghost of a whisper, so quiet that only Liz could hear him. 'So have I.'

Before he could explain further, Sir William gasped. Lorimore looked up at him sharply, but the gasp had become a cough, and Sir William whipped out a large handkerchief and blew his nose noisily.

Lorimore frowned. 'Yes,' he said slowly. 'Perhaps we should leave our examination of this exquisite but unexpected gift until after we have completed our more pressing tasks.' He tapped a long finger on his chin. 'It may be from Lord Chesterton. He sent me Thierry's monkey only last week . . .' He shook his head. 'No matter. Mr Blade.'

Blade nodded and returned to his work, connecting up the final cables. This done, he moved the ladder to the side of the room, out of the way of the trailing wires. Then he attached the other ends of the wires to a set of three heavy levers attached to the end of the workbench, close to the metal bowl.

But Liz barely noticed. She had glanced at where Sir William had been looking – at one of the enormous windows looking out on to the grounds of the house. Liz could see the fog pushing in against the glass, blurring the lawn beyond as the first light of dawn struggled to illuminate it. And, pressed up close to the window, looking in, were two faces. George Archer and Eddie Hopkins, watching Lorimore as he returned to his business, Blade as he completed his work, and Liz and Sir

William as they stood next to the model ship on the workbench.

Liz looked quickly away again. She struggled to make no sound that might betray what she had seen. Lorimore glanced back at her as he worked, and smiled thinly. The slightest reaction from Liz could betray her friends.

But it was hard not to react, not to shout and point and try to warn them as a huge reptilian shape of metal and bone solidified out of the foggy air behind them. An angry roar split the calm of the morning, like an express train speeding past. Steam and oil sprayed across the window, blotting out Eddie and George as they turned in surprise and alarm.

'Ah my friend,' Lorimore said without turning. 'Not long now. When the power builds and I throw these levers to channel it into the egg. To create life itself . . .'

The glass cleared, and Liz stared at the window, desperately trying to see what was happening outside. But there was only the grey of the fog, the snarl of the creature outside, and her own pale frightened face reflecting back at her.

Chapter 23

Augustus Lorimore lifted the fossilised egg carefully, reverently, and carried it across to the metal bowl. The wires jutted out from the bowl like the legs of a silver spider. They spilled across the workbench, fed into junction boxes, looped round and over before going either to the tank-like battery at the end of the room or up towards the ceiling where they joined the metal brackets that were attached to the lightning conductors outside.

Liz could not help looking up, following the wires with her eyes. The first splashes of rain were streaking across the glass roof. A distant rumble, unmistakably thunder now, mingled with the noise of the creature outside. Splashes joined, droplets linked, and a tiny river of rainwater ran unevenly down the sloping glass. Liz watched it, trying not to think about what was happening outside in the murky first light of the day.

From behind her came another sound. Liz and Sir William turned towards it. The creature that had once been Albert Wilkes lurched in from the drawing room and stood at the back of the laboratory. The metal frame around him was like some medieval cage built to prevent the prisoner inside from even moving. Except that this cage moved with its prisoner. The dead eyes were a uniform milky white, watching Lorimore as he placed the stone dinosaur egg inside the metal bowl and stepped back, rubbing his thin hands together in delight.

'Now we can begin,' Lorimore proclaimed triumphantly and waved impatiently at Blade. 'Start the battery, man. Make the final connections.'

Blade hurried to obey. Beside Liz, Sir William leaned forward slightly, checking the time on the dial set into the hull of the ship.

'It's almost six o'clock,' he said.

Lorimore threw him a glance. 'Noting the time for posterity, Sir William?'

'If you think it is important,' Sir William agreed. 'Here, see for yourself.' He stepped forward and gently turned the clock-ship so that the dial was facing across the workbench at Lorimore.

Lorimore gave a grunt of annoyance. 'I have no time for trivialities,' he declared. 'Any moment now, I shall create life. And you trouble me with trinkets.' He pushed forward the first of the three levers to which Blade had attached the wires. Immediately, the room throbbed with the increased power. Like a heartbeat.

'Hardly a trinket, sir.' There was an edge to Sir William's voice. 'Whatever insane experiment you are engaged upon, and I have no doubt whatsoever that it will fail, here in front of you, if you will only take the time to look at it, is as exquisite a piece of engineering as you will ever see. I thought you were an expert in such mechanisms. It seems I was misinformed.' He turned angrily and pointed at the former Albert Wilkes, held rigid in his metal frame. '"What a piece of work is a man",' he quoted. 'Not any more apparently. You have reduced Man himself to a simple mechanism, so why not spare the time for a mechanism infinitely more complex and intricate than you could ever hope to manufacture. Compared to whoever made this, you are a third rate hack, a butcher. Inept.'

Lorimore's eyes were blazing with fury. 'How dare you?' he shouted. He stalked across the room towards Sir William, the intensity of his gaze making Liz take an involuntary step backwards. 'I create life itself and you dare to impugn my scientific genius?'

'Six o'clock,' Sir William declared, and stepped smartly aside.

The second hand of the clock in the side of the ship completed its circuit. The minute hand swung on to the twelve. With a metallic click, a mechanism inside whirred into life. The bell at the back of the ship chimed out a short tune.

Lorimore paused, intrigued by the clock in spite of

himself. He leaned across the workbench to see it more closely. Three small hatches opened in the side of the ship facing him, mirrored by another three on the side facing Liz and Sir William. Inside each hatch, Liz could see a small cannon, and beside it a sailor leaning forward to touch a model match to the fuse. In that moment she realised why Sir William had moved. She saw that the hatches on her side were pointing squarely at the large man who had been standing behind Sir William.

Blade too saw what was happening. With a cry of warning he launched himself across the workbench. Not at the clock, but at Lorimore, knocking him backwards.

The cannon fired. Six pin-prick shots, one after another in rapid succession.

The guard who had been behind Sir William cried out, clutching at his chest. His eyes rolled upwards as he collapsed slowly to the floor, his shirt stained three patches of red. In the same moment, Liz turned and stamped as hard as she could on the foot of the man behind her. He cried out too, staggering back.

Lorimore was unharmed. Two of the shots went over his head as he fell back. One of these cracked into a supporting post between panes of glass. The second went clean into one of the huge panes. The glass exploded outwards with a crash.

The third shot caught Blade in the head. For a split-second Liz could see the ball bearing embedded in Blade's cheek. Then he too was falling backwards, eyes staring. If he cried out, the sound was lost in the crashing glass behind him.

Through the shattered window, Liz could hear the rumble of the gathering storm. Lorimore was struggling to his feet. The man whose foot Liz had stamped on was recovering, grabbing at Sir William. Wilkes was moving stiffly across the room, joints hissing and steaming.

And on the deck of the ship, a sailor clapped his hands together. Hands that were flints. Hands that tried again and again to ignite the smallest of sparks. The plate beneath the powder keg moved so slightly that if Liz had not been looking straight at it she would have seen nothing.

At the edge of her vision, Liz saw a hand raised in anger, ready to strike. Lorimore's arm swept across the workbench towards the ship, about to dash it to the floor. Liz had to stop him.

She suddenly felt calm. She fixed her gaze on the shattered window and gave a huge sigh of relief.

'George, thank goodness. I knew you'd come.'

Lorimore's hand paused in the air. He turned, looking where Liz was looking. Saw nothing.

'Quick, hide before he sees you!'

Lorimore looked around in confusion, convinced that George was there in the laboratory. He stepped back from the workbench, wary, eyes narrow. 'Where is he?' he demanded of the man holding Sir William. 'Did you see him?' His voice was heavy with menace.

The guard merely grunted. Lorimore glared. 'You're useless,' he spat. 'And you,' he said advancing on Liz, 'are very clever.'

His voice froze with his body as he caught sight of the slight movement – the hands clapping together. His mouth dropped open – surprise and anger mixed with sudden fear.

A spark flew. The end of the fuse flared, burned. The weight of the miniature keg delicately balanced on the metal plate lightened as the fuse burned away. Lorimore reached out, but too late. The plate sprang upwards, pivoting at one end, flinging the tiny wooden barrel high into the air towards the outside walls.

The keg turned end over end. The fuse burned to nothing. Close to the main laboratory window, at the height of its trajectory, the little powder keg exploded.

The wide expanse of glass that made up the end wall shattered under the blast. Liz and Sir William threw up their hands to protect themselves from the sharp splinters and flung themselves to the floor. The man who had been holding Sir William wasn't quick enough. A blast of broken glass knocked him off his feet and tore through his flesh as the glass ceiling rained in, sweeping him bloodied to the floor.

Lorimore was screaming with rage. A percussive

thump as the thunder roared above them. Rain poured through the broken windows and shattered roof as the storm finally broke. Lightning arced down. The battery fizzed and spat. Power hummed along the wires.

And Eddie and George leapt into the laboratory, racing to help their friends.

Sir William pulled Liz to her feet. He had blood on his face, from a small cut below one eye – a line of red, dripping. One of the men on the floor groaned and shifted. But he did not get up. Lorimore was looking about him in furious amazement, shouting at the remains of Albert Wilkes. A slice of glass had embedded itself in Wilkes's arm and stuck out like a blade. But he seemed not to notice or care. More, smaller pieces of glass peppered his face. But there was no blood. Wilkes lurched forwards, arms out. Lightning flashed off the facets of the glass as he lumbered towards Liz and Sir William. Then a figure swept past them as George flung himself at Wilkes, driving him back.

'Hold him!' Lorimore screamed at Wilkes. Liz heard the hiss of pistons, saw the metallic claws that had been grafted to the end of Wilkes's hands snap shut on George's arms, holding him vice-like. George struggled and kicked, but to no effect.

Lorimore seemed to have recovered. He was standing beside the workbench, the trace of a smile on his face despite the loss of his henchmen and Blade and the chaos all around him. He looked as if he was once again in total control. He was standing beside the bank of levers, and he was holding a gun. He pointed it directly at Liz.

'I advise you not to try anything,' he said to Sir William, standing beside Liz. 'I can kill you both in less time than it would take you to call out.' He raised his reedy voice slightly to add: 'And that goes for you too, Mr Archer. And your urchin friend, whatever may have happened to him.' The gun remained steady, fixed on Liz as Lorimore's eyes swept the room. 'Where are you boy? Come out wherever you are.'

When George had hurled himself at Wilkes, Eddie had dived across the end of the workbench and ripped the fossilised egg – his lucky stone – from its metal mount. With the egg, they still had a chance. Now he emerged sheepishly from underneath the workbench. He was holding the stone defiantly, but he knew it was over. Lightning stabbed into the room, flashing off the broken glass. Thunder roared as Lorimore stretched out his hand and Eddie reluctantly, hesitantly, placed the stone in his bony palm.

'I apologise for the slight delay,' Lorimore said, though it was not at all clear whom he was addressing. Keeping the gun aimed with his right hand, he reached across with his left and replaced the stone in the metal bowl. Then he stepped back and pushed home the second of the three levers on the workbench. The hum of power was rising. Lightning again split the retreating night. Acid steam flowed over the top of the battery tank like a waterfall of fog.

'Remember me, Albert,' George pleaded to his inhuman captor. 'You must remember me. I'm George – George Archer, remember? And you were – are – Albert Wilkes. You knew me before, at the Museum. Please remember!'

The creature that had been Wilkes made no reply. Made no movement that might show it understood. Held him firm as Lorimore laughed and stretched out his arm triumphant.

'Now we have the power. Now it happens!'

The howl from outside might have been his monstrous creation agreeing with him.

'Now what happens?' Sir William shouted above the roar. 'What lunacy? What madness?'

Lorimore did not answer. Sparks showered down from the wires above, fizzing in the rain. The metal bowl was glowing white hot, the stone itself a dull red.

'Now!' Lorimore shouted. He threw the final lever.

Chapter 24

When the monster had lunged out of the foggy dawn, bearing down on George and Eddie, they were ready for it.

There had been a guard patrolling just inside the main gates of the house, but George had quickly dealt with him. Even as the man fell to the ground, stunned unconscious, Eddie heard the baleful cry of the creature further off in the grounds.

'Sounds like we still have company,' George said. He checked that he had done no lasting harm to the man at his feet, then straightened up. 'Now that I've had a good look at it, or as good as we can hope for without being bitten in half, I have an idea of what we can do.'

They crept through the thinning fog towards the house. Eddie guessed that Lorimore intended to work on his fossilised dinosaur egg. But before they went searching for that, Eddie had a job of his own to do. He was carrying a wooden crate, awkward but not heavy. He held it carefully, not wanting to unbalance or damage the delicate apparatus inside. The clock that he and George had spent several hours discussing, designing and adapting.

'How do I look?' he asked George as they approached the front door.

George nodded. 'Fine,' he decided, pulling down Eddie's cap so the peak obscured his face almost completely. 'Keep your head down. In every sense.'

Afterwards, they crept warily round the house, keeping to the grass to avoid making a noise on the gravel driveway, making for the large room at the back. The light was on, and that seemed to be where Lorimore and Blade had come from when they went to tend their monster. George had explained what he wanted Eddie to do when the creature found them, as they were both sure it would. Strangely, George seemed to be looking forward to the moment. Eddie was less keen.

For a while they watched through the laboratory window. They saw Lorimore and Blade examine the ship. They saw Liz and Sir William join them, and hoped their friends could guess what George's modifications had done. Sir William had seen the clock before, and Liz had seen the mechanism George had built to hurl a ball bearing across the room, if only briefly, at the theatre. Eddie recalled how she had done little more than glance at it, but he said nothing.

Then the monster came at them. Bathed in the full moonlight, for the first time they could clearly see the enormous creature that roared up above them. They could see the metal jaws lined with fossilised teeth; the machined claws that slashed down towards them; the steam from the engine snorting out through exhaust pipes set into its head. The creak of hydraulics and the clanking of machinery as the huge creature – part automaton, part prehistoric recreation; part metal, part bone – lumbered towards them.

The ground shook. Greasy vapour swirled round the creature's monstrous head. Machine oil dripped from its jaws and the roar of its engines shattered the night. Razor-sharp metal claws split the air as an arm of overlapping steel plates hurtled mercilessly towards Eddie and steam enveloped him in a fog of terror.

He shouted and waved, trying to draw the creature's attention. It had seen him before, had been given his scent. He hoped it could be drawn again.

As the monstrous beast lunged down at Eddie, George disappeared into the fog behind it. Eddie pictured him climbing on to the thing's tail. Making his way up the slippery metallic scales of its back. Reaching for the pipes and connections and joints.

The steam burned on Eddie's cheeks as the creature closed in again. He rolled desperately to one side. But this time the beast anticipated him. Its metal jaws opened wider than Eddie could have believed was possible. The head slammed down, teeth thudding into the ground either side of Eddie's head.

Then – nothing.

The creature seemed to sigh. The steam drifted away, as if dispelled by the shafts of dawn light that were breaking through the fog above the dew-drenched lawn.

'Are you all right in there?' George called from the other side of the creature's head. Now it was just a mass of metal and bone, like an exhibit in the British Museum, or one of Lorimore's dead display animals. 'Shan't be long,' George called. 'Just a few adjustments, though I confess I don't understand the half of how this works, how it is controlled. It must have some reasoning ability of its own and we know it can see and smell. But there are a few things I can do. Then it needs to get up steam again, which will take a few minutes. I had to open the safety valve and relieve the pressure.' He was shouting to be heard above the rumble of thunder. The first rain was starting to fall.

Eddie ignored him, concentrating on crawling and clawing his way out from the monster's mouth and into the pallid light. He sat shivering in the mist.

'There, that should do it.' George sounded pleased with himself, wiping his hands on his coat as he jumped down to join Eddie. 'Ideally I'd have scuppered it completely, but all I can do now is vent the steam. Once the pressure builds up it'll be off again.

Albeit with some adjustments, a few re-routed pipes and doctored valves.'

Eddie's voice was trembling almost as much as his body was. 'It'll have to do,' he assured George.

Just as the shots rang out, and one of the smaller panes of glass in the laboratory shattered and fell.

'Any moment now, I reckon,' Eddie said.

George nodded. He glanced back at the creature. 'My modifications took longer than I had hoped. Are you ready?' His face was grave. 'I think we'll have to do this without the help of our mechanical friend.'

Things had started so well. Eddie had grabbed the egg from within Lorimore's apparatus. George could already imagine Liz's grateful smile. Maybe even a thankful hug.

But then the clanking metal nightmare that housed the mortal remains of his old friend Albert Wilkes had grabbed George and held him tight. Held him so he could see Lorimore with his revolver pointed at Liz, and Eddie forced to hand over the smooth, oval-shaped stone.

All the while George pleaded with Albert. Begged him to remember who he had once been, that George was his friend, that Lorimore had done terrible things to him.

'I know you can hear me, Albert,' he said urgently. 'I

know there's something left. You contacted us – at the séance. Remember? Somehow you were able to move the upturned glass. You knew we were trying to help. Knew, and did something about it. Somewhere, somehow, on some level you still have a soul – a conscience. Use it! Help us!'

But it seemed to have no effect. There was nothing left, George realised. It was simply a machine, with enough remaining intelligence to obey Lorimore's orders, but no more than that. The blank white eyes stared back at George, unblinking. No flicker. No recognition. Nothing.

George finally shouted at Wilkes in frustration: 'Let me go!'

'Now!' Lorimore shouted in victory as he pushed home the last of the three levers in front of him.

And the metal claws that were eating into George's upper arms suddenly relaxed their grip, and he realised he was free. Was the thing that had been Albert Wilkes confused? Did it think – in whatever way it could think – that its master had ordered it to let George go? Or had George's pleas finally hit home? Was there somewhere deep inside the rotting cadaver a vestige of memory of who he had once been?

The stone glowed red hot in the metal equipment, almost too bright to look at. Across the room, George could feel the heat from it. It even warmed the rain as it splashed across his face.

A shower of sparks joined the rain, pouring down from the fractured roof and spilling on to the workbench. A cable broke free and snaked down, the broken end of it spouting flames that guttered and died as it fell.

Lorimore's gun wavered, but it was still pointing at Liz. His face was a mask of fury and confusion. The egg faded from red back to the pale colour of stone. Nothing happened.

'What's wrong?' Lorimore demanded. He looked round, as if accusing Sir William and Liz of interfering. 'What have you done?'

'You know we have done nothing,' Sir William replied. 'How could we?'

'What's the problem?' Eddie asked. He was grinning, and George could guess why.

'It hasn't worked,' Lorimore said frantically. 'Why hasn't it worked? The egg should have been reanimated. It should have hastened the process of life. This egg should be *hatching*!' he yelled, reaching out for it.

His hand stopped short, feeling the heat, and he snatched it back. Instead he held the gun in both hands thrusting it towards Sir William.

But it was Eddie who spoke. 'It's just an old stone,' he said. 'That's all.'

'It is *not* a stone,' Lorimore hissed. 'It is life itself. The earliest life. Fossilised and preserved, and waiting for me to reawaken it.'

'It's just an old stone,' Eddie repeated. 'I should know. I found it.'

'Where Glick left it, inside the iguanodon statue,' Lorimore insisted.

'No,' Eddie told him.

'What?'

'I didn't find *that* stone inside any statue,' Eddie said. 'I found it out in your garden. Near the gates. Took me a while, though.' He pulled something from his pocket and held it up – a stone all but identical to the smooth pebble he had returned to Lorimore. '*This* is the one I found in the statue. I took it out of your contraption just a minute ago.'

Lorimore's face was as red as the stone had been. 'Give it to me!'

Eddie laughed at that. 'No chance.'

'Give it to me, or I will shoot your friends.'

Eddie did not reply. Instead he tossed the egg across the workbench. Lorimore lunged forwards, arm out, desperate to catch it. The gun fell from his hand and clattered to the wet floor falling amongst the broken glass.

The egg lazily spun in the air, falling into the outstretched hand of Liz.

Lorimore was climbing rapidly across the workbench towards her. A glass tank filled with murky liquid slid away from him and crashed to the floor. Something flopped out as the viscous liquid spilled from the shattered glassware. George stepped forward quickly, aware of the hiss of gears and pistons as Wilkes followed him.

Just as Lorimore reached for her, Liz quickly tossed the egg to George. He caught it easily. Lorimore was already scrambling towards him as George pushed the metal plate on the top of the ship back into place. He put the egg on it, and stepped back.

With a cry of relief, Lorimore leapt down from the workbench and reached for the ship.

At that moment, the internal mechanism clicked. The metal plate again flew upwards. The fossil was hurled up into the air. With an anguished cry, Lorimore watched it fly high above him.

He only had a moment, but George was already diving to the floor, sliding through the broken glass and reaching for the gun. Eddie was there ahead of him, his hands cut and bleeding from the razor-sharp shards, his hair plastered to his head with rain.

The egg was falling again. George grabbed the gun from Eddie and spun round to see. Lorimore was standing under the egg, waiting. But another figure thrust him aside, and caught the stone as it fell.

Albert Wilkes.

George raised the gun.

The thunder sounded as if it was there inside the laboratory with them. And it was. The huge dinosaur-like creature stamped in through the broken wall, ripping apart what was left of the fabric, sending more glass and masonry flying. Its claws lashed out, uncontrolled. Its head was swinging desperately back and forth as steam poured out of its joints.

A massive foot crashed down heavily next to George. Steam exploded from it, burning George's hand. He dropped the gun with a cry, and it rolled away under the belly of the creature.

Lorimore stared up at his creation, smiling thinly. He reached out towards the grotesque automaton that had been Albert Wilkes.

'Give me the egg, my friend.' He sounded calm, almost soothing.

Wilkes held up the fossilised egg in a trembling metal fist.

When he spoke, Albert's voice was a husky, tortured rasp. 'I know who I am,' the fragile voice said. 'And what you are.' A jet of steam blew out from between the metal fingers as they gripped the egg more tightly. Gears and pistons whirred and strained. Lorimore's face was etched stone as he watched, realising what was happening. His mouth was a silent 'no'.

The egg shattered under the pressure. Fragments of stone exploded outwards. One of them whipped by George's cheek. Liz and Sir William reeled back, away from the blasting shards. Eddie dived under the workbench.

Lorimore caught several pieces of sharp stone in his face. He dropped to his knees, looking up at Wilkes's dead face, shaking his head in numbed disbelief. Then he seemed to notice the huge metallicised leg of the dinosaur creature beside him.

'Kill them!' Lorimore screamed in fury. 'Kill them all!'

The monstrous creature towering above George hissed and wheezed into uncertain life. In an effort to obey its master one last time, hydraulics strained and steam pressure built up. But George had rerouted the pipes, he had stripped the gears and moved the cables, so it was barely able to control itself. George and Eddie had planned to send the creature into the laboratory when the powder keg exploded – to let it run riot and out of control while they rescued Liz and Sir William. But the pressure had not built up again sufficiently after George vented it.

Now it had.

Unable to control itself, but knowing that its master – its creator – needed it, the enormous creature tried to move. Claws flailed, feet stamped, steam spat through the air. The creature's desperate roars echoed off the broken glass.

George hauled himself to his feet, trying to avoid the creature as it spun and thrashed. A scaly arm lashed out towards him – about to connect, to knock him lifeless across the room.

But with a frantic hiss of steaming motion, Albert Wilkes moved to intercept the blow. The metallic dinosaur's claws raked across the metal exoframe, sending Wilkes crashing across the room. He slammed into the workbench. Metal struts detached, fell away, clattered to the floor. Liz screamed. George dived out of the way as the dinosaur continued its stampede.

Equipment and cables were shattered and ripped apart. Slivers of glass were stamped to dust. George ran to Wilkes, but a glance was enough to tell him the man was completely dead. Again. Perhaps there was a faint smile on his face, or perhaps it was the way the morning light cut across him. Perhaps his lips moved and he tried to say farewell one last time to his friend, or perhaps it was just an illusion caused by the moisture George blinked from his eyes.

Behind him Lorimore was shouting and screaming at his creation – begging it to stop as it ripped apart his life's work. He stood before it, arms outstretched in supplication, paying homage to the life he had created, worshipping his own achievement. As the creature's heavy claws slashed uncontrollably through the steaming air. As the feet slammed down. As Lorimore screamed for the last time and his bones joined the powdered glass strewn across the floor.

The metal brute stared down at the broken figure through mechanical eyes. Steam poured from its face, its neck, its every joint. An irregular clanking came from somewhere deep inside. Then with a final eruption of steam and a grinding of the broken mechanisms, the creature's head fell heavily forwards on its neck. It stood there dejected and defeated for a moment, wreathed with the fading steam. Then its legs buckled under its own weight and the creature crashed down on top of its creator. A broken lifeless mass of metal and bone.

There was a trace of mist in the chilly air. The cold of first light was refreshing after the oily steam of the laboratory. Eddie shuddered as they walked slowly down the driveway, shuddered at the memory of the cold dead eyes watching him from the display cases in the hallway. What sort of person, he wondered, collected dead things? What sort of person wanted to create life where there was none?

He frowned, wondering where the fascination he had himself felt in helping bring a clock to mechanical life strayed into the unacceptable dream that Lorimore had pursued.

In front of him, George was walking with Liz, carrying the intricate ship that they had spent so long adapting to rescue them.

'Well,' Sir William said to Eddie as they followed their friends, 'it's been quite a night.'

'I'll say.' Eddie turned to look back at the house behind them. It looked so normal in the morning light – a large house set in its own grounds. The only unusual thing was that it was hidden away in the heart of London, cordoned off from the city by a high wall. The smoke rising from the back of the house might be the last of the morning mist burning off as the sun gained strength.

When he turned back, he saw that Liz was helping a man to his feet, relieving him of the shotgun that had been slung over his shoulder. 'I don't think you'll be needing that,' she told him.

'I should go for the police, if I were you,' Sir William told the startled guard. 'And you'll probably need to find alternative employment.'

The man stared at them, but said nothing. Then, abruptly, he turned and ran ahead of them to the gates.

'I dunno what the peelers will do when they find that lot,' Eddie said.

'Oh, I imagine they'll do what they always do when they find something so strange and bizarre that it defies explanation,' Sir William replied. His eyes were twinkling in the cold light.

'And what's that?' Eddie stuck his tongue out at the lizard watching from the top of the gatepost as he stepped out into the street. George and Liz were waiting for them a few paces ahead. They were holding hands again.

Sir William gave a short laugh. 'They will send for me, of course,' he said. Then he clapped his hands together, rubbing enthusiastic warmth into them. 'And for my new assistant, Mr Archer. We shall have some work to do – both here and at Lorimore's foundries, I imagine.'

'So, what will you tell them?' Liz asked, looking from George to Sir William. 'What will I tell my father?' she added quietly. 'If he even notices I've been gone.'

'Yes,' George said, 'what will we say to the police?'

Sir William frowned. 'I don't know about you,' he said, 'but I shall tell them . . .' His voice tailed off as he considered. 'Yes, most definitely,' he decided. 'I shall tell them that I need breakfast.' Then he clapped Eddie on the back, laughing with him and leading the way down the road. 'Let me treat you, my friends,' he declared. 'I think you deserve it.'

'Oh no,' Eddie told him, running to catch up. 'Let me treat you.' He pulled a leather wallet from his pocket and opened it to show them the bundle of notes inside.

'Where did you get that?' Liz demanded.

'Lorimore's pocket,' Eddie said. 'I reckon he owes us breakfast. And,' he added, 'I don't reckon he needs this no more. Just one thing . . .'

'And what is that?' Sir William asked.

'Bacon and stuff is fine,' Eddie said. 'But no more eggs. All right?'

Read on for a sneak preview of
Justin Richard's new novel!

THE CHAOS
CODE

Out in hardback on 5 April 2007

Chapter 1

As Matt watched the rain through the window, the rain watched him back.

He wasn't looking for a face, but it was there. If he had run his finger over the grimy window of the train, tracing the paths of the drips and rivulets and pausing where the water hung in bubbles, then he might have made out the rough features. Mouth, nose, eyes . . .

But he was more interested in watching the way that the tiny drops joined into streams that became unpredictable rivers that ran down the other side of the glass. The steady rhythm of the train had soothed Matt into a state somewhere between waking and sleeping. Just watching the rain.

By the time the train got to London he was fully awake. Matt was the first at the door, clutching a plastic bag with the packed lunch he hadn't eaten and the book he hadn't enjoyed, with his rucksack over one shoulder and his suitcase tilted back on its little wheels. A fifteen-year-old boy eager to get home from boarding school, dark hair in need of a wash, a cut and a brush. Coat grubby and creased where he'd been sitting on it.

As the train passed under a final bridge, Matt's reflection stared back at him, broken by the spattering rain. Then into the grey cloudy daylight again and the reflection was gone. The train shuddered to a halt, jolting Matt sideways. The doors slid open and he joined the unpredictable stream of passengers hurrying to the exit barriers, tickets clutched, jostling and pushing.

Mum was waiting the other side of the barrier, checking her watch. 'Nine minutes late,' she announced. 'Not bad, I suppose. These days.' Then she smiled, as if suddenly remembering this was pleasure rather than business. She pulled an immaculate small white handkerchief from the pocket of her immaculate jacket, licked the corner of it and dabbed at Matt's face. 'Chocolate,' she accused as he brushed her hand away, embarrassed. 'And have you been using that spot cream I got for you?'

'Yes, Mum. I can't wait to get home,' Matt said. 'Thanks for meeting me.' Usually she was working and he got a taxi.

'Let's just grab a coffee while we're here, Matthew,' Mrs Stribling said.

From the fact she said it, and the way she called him 'Matthew', Matt knew he wasn't going home.

There was a Starbucks in the station, and Matt had orange juice. His mouth was dry after the long journey from his school in Havensham. He was quiet, sulking – he'd been looking forward to spending the holidays at Mum's flat in London. It didn't look like that was going to happen now, and he could guess what the alternative was. He wanted to tell her that it was knowing he'd come home for the summer that had made boarding school bearable.

Mum had a latte, and Matt thought she'd probably only got that because she thought it wouldn't be so hot and she could drink it quicker. Sure enough, as soon as they were seated: 'I have to go in thirteen minutes,' Mum told him.

That was typical of her. So precise. Matt liked to be precise too. He preferred his digital watch that told the exact right time to the second rather than one with a face and hands that you had to look at and work out where everything was to tell the time. But Mum took it to extremes. Thirteen minutes – why not 'quarter of an hour', or 'soon'? She had to be so exact. Probably because of her job.

She used to work for a large computer company, but left when it was bought out by an even larger rival. Now she had her own company, though the only employee was herself. She did 'computer consultancy', which as far as Matt could tell meant she got other companies to pay her to do what she had always done. She was into network balancing, and requirements prioritization, and systems analysis. Matt didn't really understand the business terms or that side of it. But he had picked up enough about computers from spending time with Mum and messing about with the equipment she kept. Matt knew all about computers and how they worked.

That was one of the attractions of coming home. Mum's flat was full of computer hardware and the latest digital kit. Cameras and digital recorders and webcams and DVD-rippers and PCs and Macs and mainframes and even games machines.

'Why the rush?' he asked. 'Where are we going?' He stressed the 'we' to let her know he wasn't just accepting it.

Mum sighed and put down her coffee. There was a faint pale line along her top lip from the milk, but Matt didn't tell her. She reached across the table to take his hand. He let her.

'I'm not going to Dad's,' he said.

She took her hand away. 'It won't be for long,' she promised.

'That's what you said at Christmas.'

'It wasn't for long then.'

'Two weeks. That's long enough. I'm staying with you.'

'You can't,' she said flatly. 'I'm sorry. I shan't be here. I've got a job.'

'I can look after myself during the day. I've done it before.'

'The job isn't in London, Matt. It's not even in this country. It's a marvellous opportunity and the money's good.'

'Great.' At least he was 'Matt' again. He tried to sound interested: 'So who's it for?'

'I . . . I can't tell you,' she said, looking round as if she expected someone she knew to be sitting nearby. 'Client confidentiality.' She turned back and laughed to show it was all so silly. 'I'm sorry but he – er, they – insist.'

'Mum – you're my mum. What if I need to talk to you?'

'My mobile will work.' She frowned as she said it. 'At least, I think it will. Anyway, I know where you will be.'

'So do I,' Matt muttered. 'Either in the spare bedroom or up to my knees in mud. It's just awful, Mum. I mean, Dad's all right, when you can make him listen to anything you say. But at Christmas my bed was covered in books and papers, there was no food. I mean, at *Christmas*. The village shop was shut for a week and the freezer was full of ice samples from some Antarctic survey.'

Mum smiled. 'That sounds about right,' she admitted. She checked her watch. 'I do know what it's like to live with your father,' she said gently.

'Yeah,' Matt told her. 'And you gave up doing it.'

She ignored this. 'I've got you a ticket. You'll have to get a taxi from Branscombe, I'm afraid. But your father can pay for that.'

'Give me some money anyway,' Matt said. 'He won't have been to the bank.'

'He knows you're coming,' she said. But she sorted out a couple of notes from her purse anyway. More than enough.

Matt took the money and the ticket, realizing that at some point he had just accepted that he was going. 'He doesn't know I'm coming,' he corrected her. 'You've told him I'm coming, that's different. He won't remember. He'll be planning some dig, or going through some ancient papers, or writing some lecture about pre-whatever pottery fragments found in an old cellar in Nottingham. Or something.'

Mum drained the last of her coffee and Matt realized he had hardly touched his juice. He made one last appeal: 'Can't I at least stay with you till you have to leave? Even if it's only a day, I can get some shopping done, go to the museums . . .'

'You hate museums,' she told him. 'And shops. Look, if I'm to make my flight I really need to leave now. And your train goes in seventeen minutes.'

'Can't you even stay and see me off?'

'I have to pack and then catch a plane.' She stood up, expecting him to do the same. Matt stood awkwardly in front of her, knowing what was coming next. Mum gave him a quick hug and pecked him on the cheek. 'You'll manage. You're a big boy now.'

He watched her hurry out of the station, checking her watch on the way. 'So treat me like one,' he said.

☩

Struggling with his luggage, Matt went to look for a book in the newsagent's. But he could barely get along the aisle between the bookshelves, and people glared at him as if having a suitcase and bags in a railway station was completely thoughtless and unnecessary. One woman tutted audibly as she was forced to move slightly to let Matt past. So he made sure he drove the case over her foot.

'Oh, I'm sorry.' He smiled apologetically, hoping she realized he didn't mean it.

But when she mumbled, 'Yes, well, that's all right, young man,' Matt felt instantly bad about it and turned quickly away.

There was nothing really that he fancied reading. But he chose a book anyway – something about a kid who turned into a werewolf and fell in love with a werewolf girl. He paid for it out of the money Mum had given him. There was still more than enough for a taxi.

As it was, he dozed off almost as soon as the train pulled out of the station. He was jolted awake an hour later, surprised to see how far they had already got as the train pulled out of yet another tiny village station. Better not fall asleep again, he thought, or he'd miss his stop.

Another hour and the train finally drew into the little station at Branscombe Underhill. Sure enough, just as Matt had expected, there was no sign of Dad. It was an hour's brisk walk from here to the even smaller village where Dad lived. But with his luggage there was no way that Matt was going to attempt it, even though the rain had stopped.

In the waiting room there was a phone that connected directly to a local taxi firm. Matt knew from experience that he'd probably have to wait half an hour for them to bother to send a car.

'Oh, what bad timing,' a cheerful lady at the taxi company said when Matt told her where he was. 'Charlie's just left there.'

'Then tell him to turn round and come back,' Matt thought. 'Never mind,' he actually said. 'I guess I'll have to wait, then.'

'Be about ten minutes,' the lady told him.

Matt hung up the phone. 'No, it won't,' he said. And sure enough, it wasn't.

Half an hour later, the summer afternoon was clouding over into an autumnal twilight. The taxi driver insisted on talking non-stop about nothing in particular. Matt sat in the back and made the occasional half-hearted comment or reply. It seemed to suffice.

'Don't know why anyone wants to live out here,' the driver said as he turned into the narrow lane that was the only road through Woldham. 'Not even a pub.'

'There's a shop,' Matt said. But he had no real enthusiasm for defending the place. The driver was right – it was tiny, it was in the middle of nowhere, there wasn't a pub and the library came to call once a month in a van. If it remembered.

'So dark, too.' The driver wiped at his misty wind-screen with the back of his hand.

'No street lights,' Matt pointed out.

'And the wind's kicking up something rotten.'

Matt wasn't sure you could really blame the village for that, but he said nothing.

'So where shall I drop you?' He made it sound as if right here would be best for him.

'Just up on the left, before the war memorial. There's a turning.'

The turning was into an even narrower lane that ran past just four houses. They were all the same, though built at slightly different angles. Modern, boxy and boring. Not the sort of house where Matt would ever have expected his dad to live. There were fields behind, leading down to a river. Maybe he'd chosen the place for the view rather than its character.

Matt paid the driver, and tipped him just enough to avoid being glared at. The driver didn't get out to open the boot, but pressed a button on the dashboard and let Matt unload his own luggage. You get what you pay for, Matt decided. He watched the headlights cutting through the gloomy evening as the taxi turned in the little close and then drove back down the lane. They were somehow too bright and clear and clean for the village. The whole place seemed happier once the taxi was gone and the gathering darkness began to close in once more.

The driver had been right, it was windy. Leaves were swirling like water going down a plughole. Skeletal trees dripped and swung. Clouds skidded across the darkening grey sky and somewhere an owl hooted forlornly. But there was a light on in the house, shining softly through and around the drawn curtains of a side window. Dad's study. Dad was working – probably hadn't noticed the time.

But at least he was here. Matt gathered up his bags and, for the first time since he met Mum, he felt as if things were not so bad after all.

✟

The feeling did not last. He rang the bell and waited. And then he waited some more, before sighing heavily and putting down his suitcase. Dad was probably too engrossed in some old, dusty text to hear the bell. Fortunately, Matt had a key. Somewhere.

He fumbled in his pocket and finally managed to extricate his set of keys – school locker, suitcase,

Mum's flat and Dad's house. It was difficult to see where the hole in the lock was, so Matt pushed the key at the rough area and moved it round, waiting for it to slide into the keyhole.

But instead the door moved. It wasn't locked. It wasn't even shut properly – the latch hadn't quite caught. The hall was in darkness. Matt pushed the door fully open and hefted his suitcase and rucksack inside.

'Dad – it's me!' he called.

No answer. He found the light switch and the hall was bathed in sudden white light. It was a mess. Muddy footprints criss-crossed the bare wooden floor. Unopened post lay beneath the letter box. What looked like a shroud was lying at the bottom of the stairs, and there was a pile of papers by the study door. It had top-pled over, leaving pages scattered across the doorway.

Matt dragged his case into the living room and dumped it by the sofa. Not that you could see much of the sofa under the books and papers that were strewn across it.

'He's getting worse,' Matt muttered. 'Dad!' he shouted again. 'I'll put the kettle on. If I can find it.' Dad lived on coffee, and Matt held out little hope that he'd find Coke or lemonade in the fridge. There was a door from the living room through a tiny dining room to the kitchen. The dining table, and most of the chairs round it, were also piled with papers and jour-nals. So, no surprise there.

The kitchen looked like the scene of a major disaster. Matt switched on the light to be greeted by the sight of dirty dishes and cooking utensils. Pots and pans were everywhere – even on the floor. There were dirty mugs on every available surface. Bits of broken plates lay scattered across the worktops and on the floor, and the fridge door was open. Matt didn't dare look inside, just pushed the door shut. The fridge was humming loudly in protest as it tried to keep cool.

'Keep cool,' Matt said out loud. 'What's happened here?' This was worse than usual – worse than it should be. Even without the broken plates, he was beginning to sense that something was wrong. 'Dad?' he called again, but he wasn't calling so loudly now – a plea rather than a shout for attention.

More anxious with every passing moment, Matt went back to the hall. He hesitated outside the study. Should he knock on the door? But what if there was a problem. What if Dad was ill, or . . . Or what? Only one way to find out.

He pushed open the door.

It was difficult to tell if the study was in more of a mess than usual. The light was on and the curtains over the side window were drawn. But the French windows behind Dad's desk were standing open. The wind was blowing papers off the desk and across the floor. The desk light was on, but angled upwards, towards the ceiling, where shadows danced and fought frantically.

The floor was a mess – as if someone had emptied the desk drawers and every filing cabinet across it. Books had been pulled from the shelves and lay bent and twisted. Matt looked round in open-mouthed amazement.

And a hand clamped over his open mouth, cutting off his cry of surprise. Rough, sharp, like sandpaper, he felt the palm of the hand biting into his face as he was dragged backwards. Someone had been standing behind the door, waiting for him. Matt struggled to break free, his only view of his attacker a huge shapeless shadow entwined with his own across the floor. But now the hand was over his nose as well – cutting off the air. He was gasping and wheezing, trying desperately to breathe.

The room turned and swam. Papers blew off the desk and spiralled down. The shadows darkened and the carpet seemed to be hurtling towards Matt's face.

Then everything was dark.

✝

The wind had dropped, though the French windows were still open. It was completely dark outside now. Matt's head was throbbing and he had to blink to get rid of the spots of light in front of his eyes.

He picked himself up from the floor and stumbled over to close the French windows. What had happened? It all seemed hazy now, like a bad dream. Matt leapt to his feet, turning quickly – suddenly afraid there was someone behind him, ready to attack again. But the room was empty. There was no one there. Had they gone? He walked quickly and cautiously to the windows and pulled them shut. Then he locked them. A burglary? But then where was Dad?

Maybe, Matt thought, Dad had gone to the station and missed him. Maybe he was there, waiting for Matt to arrive on the next train. Still wary and disorientated, he wandered back to the living room, his heart racing with every shadow he passed. He almost expected them to solidify and reach out at him with grey, shapeless hands. He took a deep breath and told himself not to be so stupid. Whoever had been there was gone now. The only sound was Matt's own anxious breathing.

Clearing a space on the sofa, Matt flopped down. He rubbed his eyes with the heels of his hands and began to feel a bit better. Looking up, he saw the telly and DVD player were still sitting in the corner of the room. In fact, there didn't seem to be anything missing – just untidy. So maybe not a burglary. Easy to check, he realized.

In the kitchen there was an old brown teapot on a shelf above the worktop. The spout was chipped on the side facing away, so you couldn't see. Inside, Dad kept spare cash – odd notes to pay the milkman and provide funds when he'd forgotten to go to the bank. If the teapot was empty . . .

Well, actually that wouldn't prove anything, Matt realized, as he went back to the kitchen. Except maybe

Dad had not been to the bank for a while and the milk and papers needed paying for.

But the teapot was lying broken on the counter top. The spout had been knocked off and the handle was cracked. The lid was lying close by and several ten-pound notes were sticking out of the debris. So, not a robbery. Not for money, at any rate. Had he really been attacked – grabbed and thrown to the floor? Or had he fallen somehow? The more he thought about it now, the less certain he was of what he really remembered. It didn't make sense. He must have fallen, or fainted. It had been a long day. Long, and stressful, and he was hot and bothered, and probably dehydrated, after the journey.

Matt got himself a drink of water, rinsing the mug well first. He had been putting it off, he realized, but he should really check the rest of the house. Maybe Dad was asleep in bed. Maybe he'd taken a sleeping pill or been up all the previous night working, or . . . Matt wanted to believe it, wanted to open the bedroom door and see his father staring blearily back at him and asking what time it was. What *day* it was, even.

But the house was empty. Every room was a mess, almost every floor covered with papers and books and journals. Even the bathroom. But there was no one – no Dad and no intruder. Matt was sure of that. He was alone in the house.

Without really thinking about it, he went back to Dad's study. He rubbed at his face where it was sore –

from the rough hand that had grabbed him? He couldn't be sure.

He picked up the papers that had blown across the floor and plonked them on the desk. Dad could sort them out when he got back. Though Matt was beginning to wonder if Dad was coming back. He checked his watch and was astonished to see that several hours had passed since he had arrived at the house. It must have been some bump on the head. He should check the answerphone, he decided. Look to see if there was a scrawled note by the phone, telling him Dad was out and not to worry and he'd be back soon. And if not . . . What? Should he call the police? It seemed sensible, except – what would they say? What would *he* say?

He mentally went through the conversation he might have. Was there any sign of a break-in? Well, no, not really. Had Matt's father ever just gone off before without leaving any message or any indication of where he might be? Actually yes, all the time. Did Matt see who attacked him? No. Was he sure he had actually been attacked? Yes – well, *almost* sure. Any signs of the intruder? No, Matt thought. It could all be just his imagination. He was sure it wasn't, but there was no way he could convince anyone else of that. No real evidence at all. Except . . .

There were *footprints*. Matt saw them as he turned to go. A trail of pale, sandy marks led past the desk to the French windows. He had not noticed them before.

But then he had not been looking, and his vision had still been blurred and speckled from the blow. Or fall. Curious, Matt followed them, opened the windows and stepped out on to the patio outside.

The moon had struggled through the clouds and, combined with the light from inside the study, Matt could see that the footprints continued across the paving slabs and to the lawn.

He stood at the edge of the patio, trying to make out if there were marks on the grass – indented foot marks, or more sand . . . Where had the sand come from? Where did it lead? He shuddered as he wondered why anyone would walk out across the back garden, where there were just fields and the river, rather than round to the front of the house and the lane. Unless it was Dad . . .

Matt stared into the night, out over the garden. For a moment, he thought he saw a dark shadowy figure standing at the fence, in front of the field. A cloud covered the moon for an instant and the wind picked up, whipping the trees into a frenzy of thrashing branches. Matt stepped back, out of the light, afraid he might be seen – that someone might be watching him.

When the moon returned, a moment later, the figure was gone. The sandy footprints had also disappeared, blown away by the breeze and scattered across the garden. Matt stepped back inside. He shivered, and not just from the cold of the night.